# The Haunted House Symphony

*Sue Latham*

Lonely Swan Books

"A delightful combination of intrigue and mystery with just enough logic and humor to please any reader."

—Rita Dear, author of the *Eutopian Destiny* series

The Haunted House Symphony

Copyright 2011 © Sue Latham

ISBN 13: 978-0-9835843-0-8
ISBN 10: 983584303

Published by Lonely Swan Books
3883 Turtle Creek Boulevard Suite 1202
Dallas, Texas 75219

Cover design Brian White

# Contents

# Bettina - 1827

*Bettina clutched* her father's hand tightly. He seemed to be in such a hurry and she almost had to run to keep up with him. She longed to stop and look around, to take it all in. She'd never been to this part of Vienna before. The noise was deafening, the sights and smells overwhelming. It was the most exciting thing to happen to her in all her six years. But Papa said they didn't have much time, and she tried her best to be good. Maybe if she behaved herself, he would bring her here again.

A carriage waiting at the curb caught her attention. A footman was helping a lady step into the carriage. Bettina had never seen such a lovely woman; her dress was so beautiful Bettina could hardly take her eyes off it.

Bettina's father jerked her arm roughly as a cart clattered by only a few inches from her nose, the horse's hooves clopping rhythmically on the cobblestones. "Please, child, pay attention."

"Yes, papa," she answered meekly. Bettina soon forgot her brush with catastrophe and they continued briskly on. They passed a bakery. Bettina longed to stop and gaze at the display window, which was full of delightful cakes and pastries. It made her hungry, even though she'd had a huge breakfast not an hour ago.

They approached an imposing building. A small crowd of people were standing in front of it in clusters of two or three, speaking quietly. Occasionally one of them would gesture sadly toward a window on the second floor.

"What's going on here, Papa? Why are all these people standing here?"

"Hush, child. They're waiting."

"Waiting for what, Papa?"

Papa sighed. "Bettina, must you ask so many questions? There is no time to explain now. We mustn't be late." He steered her past the anxious people and down a passageway. "Now remember—not a word of this to Mama."

In a small courtyard behind the house, a woman was waiting for them in a doorway. Her long, dark dress was clean but faded and fraying around the hem. A few tendrils of steel-gray hair peeked out from her white ruffled cap and framed her bony face. She clutched a thin knitted shawl around her bony shoulders.

"Herr Doktor Prantl." She bowed slightly.

"Please, dear lady, no one must know that I'm here," answered Bettina's father. He glanced around nervously, but they were alone in the courtyard, which was as quiet as a cemetery. For a fleeting moment, Bettina wondered why no sounds of life filtered from behind the many closed doors and windows that overlooked the courtyard. But the woman spoke again and Bettina turned her attention to her.

"Please, Herr Doktor. Take pity on a poor old woman. He won't live out the week. And what's to become of me?"

"Frau Sali, have you no family? No one to turn to?"

The old woman closed her eyes and shook her head wearily. "I have no one, thanks to that mad Frenchman who wanted to conquer Europe. My poor boy."

"My sympathies, Frau Sali."

She sighed and hunched her shoulders against the cold. "It was a long time ago." She was silent for a moment, lost in her memories.

Finally Papa said, "If you please, madame. The sooner we conclude this business, the better for all concerned. May I see it?"

"Certainly," she said, with a small curtsey and disappeared into the dark interior of the house. She returned a moment later carrying a flat parcel wrapped in paper.

"Please, Herr Doktor. It's only a matter of days," she said, handing the parcel to Bettina's papa. Bettina was astonished to see that her father's hands were shaking as he opened the package and examined its contents.

To no one in particular the old woman said, "I can't bear the thought of what will happen to it once he is gone. That one that calls himself a friend—he's no friend. He's a...a vulture, that's what he is."

"Frau Sali, surely you don't mean Herr Schindler?" asked Papa, obviously astonished.

"That's exactly who I mean, Herr Doktor," she replied bitterly, and pursed her lips tightly.

Bettina watched, alarmed now, as Papa wiped tears from his eyes with his handkerchief. The only time she'd ever seen her father cry before was when her baby brother died. Bettina couldn't imagine what could possibly be in a bunch of papers that would make her father cry.

"My dear lady," he said at last, his voice shaking, "do you know what you have here?"

"Yes, Herr Doktor. I do know. And I also know that if you value it as I do, you will take it. For otherwise he won't be cold in his grave before it vanishes. By that time I will be out on the street and it will be too late to do anything to save it."

Bettina's father returned the papers carefully to the package and dropped some coins into the woman's hand.

"Bless you, Herr Doktor." She curtseyed and disappeared inside without another word.

Papa took Bettina's hand. "Come along, Bettina. Your mother will be worried."

"Papa, who is Herr Schindler and why doesn't Frau Sali like him?"

"Hush, child. I wish you had not overheard that."

"But Papa, what was..."

"Shhh—quiet, Bettina. We mustn't talk about this here." He tucked the package inside his heavy overcoat. Then he bent down and looked into the girl's eyes. "Bettina, I need your solemn promise that you will obey me."

"Yes, Papa, of course."

"That's a good girl. What I have here is something very special indeed, something priceless. It belongs not to you or to me, or to Frau Sali. This is a treasure that rightfully belongs to all civilized people. And eventually, we will share it with the whole world. But the time is not right just now and we mustn't talk about it. Not even to Mama. When the time comes, I will explain it all to her. But in the meantime, you must not talk about what happened here today—to anyone."

"I promise, Papa."

"Very good. I promise some day this will all make sense." He smiled for the first time since they'd started out that morning. "Now come along." Together they walked back through the passageway and out to the street. The crowds of people were still there. No one paid any attention to the man and the little girl.

Two weeks later, as the first spring flowers were beginning to push up through the cold earth, a fever raged through Vienna, claiming many hundreds of victims. Bettina bravely wiped away her tears as she watched her father's coffin being lowered into the grave. But she remembered her promise to him, and vowed that she would do whatever was necessary to keep his treasure safe.

# Margo Monroe, Ghost Hunter

*I have* quite possibly the coolest job in the world. Officially, I call myself a "research specialist." I chose this job title because it sounds innocuous enough and doesn't raise many eyebrows. But what I really am is a paranormal investigator—a ghost hunter. I work with a top-notch team. We rely strictly on scientific evidence and use the latest in twenty-first century ghost hunting equipment.

By way of introduction, my name is Margo Monroe. You probably haven't heard of me, even though you've no doubt read about some of my cases in the news. You may recall, for example, the elderly widow who suddenly became convinced her house was haunted by demonic entities. The "demonic entities" turned out to be her nephew, who was just smart enough to realize that the lot his aunt's house was on would soon be worth a fortune thanks to a planned rezoning. Luckily for her, word got back to us. The nephew won't be trying to scare any more little old ladies.

I live in a quiet little town called Indian Springs that some might describe as quaint. My exact age I will leave to your imagination. Let's just say I'm old enough to remember life before cell phones, computers and the Internet. But just barely, mind you.

I like to consider myself "between boyfriends." My

former significant other—at my request—recently removed his power tools from my garage and his shaving stuff from my bathroom. I don't miss him. I have many good friends and a job that I love. Who could ask for more?

On the day we got the first frantic phone call from Marsha Darnell, I was looking forward to a little bit of down time. We had spent most of the night before in a tavern inhabited by a particularly rambunctious poltergeist, and I had taken a thunk on the head from a flying beer bottle.

It was an obscenely early hour for the phone to be ringing, considering that I'd only gotten home just as the sun was coming up. I was tempted to let it roll to voice mail until I saw it was my research assistant. Sandy only calls for business, so I decided I had better answer it. I fumbled with the phone, and Sandy's face filled the palm-sized screen.

"What's up?" I asked, perhaps a trifle rudely.

"I just got a call from a lady named Marsha Darnell, who insists that we come to her house right away. She's on the verge of hysteria. I had a hard time calming her down enough so that she could explain what the problem was." When I didn't comment he continued. "She's been having some fairly typical phenomena, unexplained footsteps, cold spots, and creepy feelings—the usual stuff. The activity only started a few weeks ago."

"There's an elephant tap-dancing on my head and you woke me up for footsteps and cold spots?" Apologies to Sandy. I'm not at my best in the morning.

"It gets better. She's seen what to me sounds like a full-bodied apparition. And—here's the good part—she's convinced it's trying to tell her something."

This got my attention. "Sounds promising. Where does she live?"

"She's over in Lone Oak, in one of those old Victorians. Says it started when she started remodeling." Lone Oak was one of the older neighborhoods in Indian Springs, just off the town square. A few years ago that area had become a tad seedy, then it was discovered by empty nesters and refugees from the 'burbs. Now it was the trendy place to live for those who could afford it. The neighborhood was full of quirky bungalows and imposing Victorians in various stages of decay and rebirth. Honestly, I'd be surprised to find a house there that didn't have a ghost.

"OK, Sandy, thanks. It sounds like a big job. I'll call Elaine and see if she can help out. Have you talked to Ernie about it?"

"No, he's not in yet, but I'll tell him as soon as he gets here. I'll tell him to call you."

We hung up and I managed to drag myself out of bed. There's nothing like a good haunting to get the old neurons firing.

# A Textbook Haunting

*I was* in the kitchen in my fuzzy bathrobe, trying to decide whether I would rather have coffee and a doughnut or tea and a banana for breakfast when the phone rang again. This time it was Ernie.

"How's your head?" he asked, referring to the encounter with the poltergeist the night before.

"I'll survive, but I've felt better. Have you talked to Sandy?"

"A few minutes ago. It sounds like a textbook case, but he told me he promised the client someone would come over right away. Can you meet me at her house in an hour?"

He gave me the address and suggested I put some ice on my throbbing head.

I never would have imagined in a million years that Ernie and I would some day work together. He was one of my best friends in high school, which has been more years ago than I care to think about. He's a mysterious sort. I used to wonder if maybe he was really gay and just wasn't admitting it to himself. Then he confessed he was hopelessly in love with Elaine, with whom he has about as much of a chance as a snowball in hell. But Ernie is the most rational person I know (except for his crush on Elaine), and he has found a perfectly natural cause for a good many supposedly paranormal happenings. His inventions have saved us hours of tedious work and helped us spot subtle evidence we might otherwise have missed.

I dragged myself into the bathroom and turned on the light. As I do on most mornings, I silently cursed the decorator who came up with the brilliant idea of putting mirrors on every wall of a room. The theory was that it would make a small room seem bigger. That may be, but my just-out-of-bed self is not really what I want to see from all angles this early in the morning. Even without my glasses, I could see well enough to make out that the bump on my temple was already turning an obnoxious shade of purple. I would have to artfully arrange my hair to hide it and hoped I had enough styling gel. My auburn hair is wavy and flatters my complexion, but it has a mind of its own and has to be beaten into submission with the hairdryer most days.

The bump was starting to throb as I climbed into the shower. I soon felt marginally better and spent way too much time letting the hot water pound my head and shoulders. It was with great reluctance that I finally stepped out and dried off. Armed with the hair dryer I wrestled with my hair, but quickly decided the struggle was useless and gave up. No artful styling was going to hide the bump; I would have to think up an entertaining story to tell people if they asked. I could tell people I got whacked in the head by a poltergeist, but who'd believe me? I tried covering it with makeup, but that was painful and only made it look like I had a bump on my head that I was trying to cover with makeup.

Back in the kitchen a few minutes later, the tea and banana won the breakfast battle, accompanied by a handful of aspirins.

My kitchen, I'm the first to admit, needs work. The previous owners of my house had more money than taste. When I moved in, everything—including the sink—was avocado green. The death of the old green fridge shortly after I moved in was a joyous occasion; I was more than happy to fork over the cash for a shiny new stainless steel one. I spend a lot of my spare time painting walls. I actually enjoy working around the house, but it's taken me the better part of five years to get rid of the peach and mint-green color scheme. Don't let anybody tell you that a house is not a time- and money-pit. I spend so much time at the hardware store downtown I'm surprised they haven't started charging me rent.

I made some tea then went into the bedroom to get dressed. I stared at my closet trying to decide what to wear and hoping for a flash of inspiration. The day was shaping up to be plenty warm, not unusual for summer in this part of the country.

One of the advantages of my job is that I don't have to follow anybody else's sartorial rules. Happy was the day when I donated my conservative suits and tasteful blouses to charity. Still, Lone Oak hardly seemed like the place to make a fashion statement, so I opted for black pants and a leopard-print blouse. Nothing too flashy, but it would have landed me in trouble at my old job.

I poured my tea into a to-go cup and navigated the path through the garage to my car, squeezing past a row of shelves packed with ghost hunting equipment and old cans of paint. Juggling the tea, I backed my aging station wagon out of the driveway.

The drive from my house to the center of town is like traveling backwards in time. The houses get older, bigger and more expensive the closer you get to the town square. My house is a mid-century ranch-style a little too far from the center of things to be fashionable. I drove down my street and past several blocks of post-war houses that had once been identical to mine.

In my job, it helps to understand the history of the buildings we investigate. People usually think that only old buildings are ever haunted. But we have found unexplained phenomena in all kinds of places. A local library, for example, housed in a new but spectacularly ugly building on the outskirts of town, finally had to close. Books had a tendency to fly off the shelves, sometimes only narrowly missing a patron. A succession of librarians quit without notice after arriving at work to find every single book on the floor and the shelves bare. This investigation was unfortunately one of our less successful ones. Whoever or whatever it was refused to come out and play while we were there. We tried running video cameras all night, but never caught a single flying book on film. The library finally moved to another building a few blocks away and they haven't had a single incident since. My route this morning took me past the original building. Not surprisingly, it's still vacant.

After a few blocks I turned onto a street of compact bungalows. Many of them are unique, even eccentric, in their design. Most of them have seen better days, but even the fixer-uppers are out of my price range. I took a detour past a house that I've had my eye on for years, in case by some miracle it's for sale. Its pointed gables and stained glass windows remind me of an illustration in a book of fairy tales I had when I was a kid. It is my dream house, and I am sure it must be home to at least one ghost. But no "For Sale" sign was in the yard today. In fact, the owners appear to be getting ready to do some landscaping.

The caffeine and aspirins were starting to kick in by the time I turned down a street full of sprawling villas. No cozy bungalows here. This street has a distinct Frank Lloyd Wrightishness about it. A few of these houses have been designated local landmarks; here and there I saw an official-looking plaque near the front door. I wondered, as I always do, what these people do for a living. I'm guessing they don't hunt ghosts.

Unfortunately, my caffeine buzz didn't last long. I made a wrong turn and found myself driving down a wide parkway lined with trees and flanked on either side by imposing residences. My house would have fit nicely in most of the garages with room to spare. Idly wondering which of them might have a resident ghost, I spotted a familiar car out of the corner of my eye. I told myself that I had to be mistaken, so I decided to drive around the block just to be sure. I wasn't mistaken. It was my ex-boyfriend's car all right, and it was parked in front of a Spanish-style villa that looked like a movie set. Nevertheless, it was one of the smaller houses—in this neighborhood it would be considered a mere starter mansion. I guessed it was at least twice as big as my house.

Just as I slowed down the front door opened. An expensively-dressed young woman navigated the steps carefully on alarmingly high heels. She looked to be about 25. When a masculine form appeared in the doorway, I didn't stick around long enough to confirm that it was Roger.

This was an unexpected blow to my ego. Not only had Roger apparently recovered from his recent broken heart, he seemed to have moved not just on but also up, judging from the neighborhood. I was in a nasty mood by the time I found the client's house.

I parked in front of a turn-of-the-century Victorian

and double-checked to be sure I was at the right
address. It certainly looked like a haunted house. It
had a mansard roof and a wide front porch complete
with ornate wooden scrollwork sporting a fresh coat of
paint.

Ernie arrived a minute or two later, looking decidedly
smug as he got out of his battered 1967 Austin Mini.
Almost twenty years later, Ernie doesn't look all that
different than he did in high school. He's always been
annoyingly skinny and still has most of his hair, which
he still wears a little on the long side. It suits him. But
his big brown eyes and long, thick lashes are the first
thing you notice about him, and he hates it. A few
years ago he started wearing glasses with thick black
frames. I didn't have the heart to tell him that the
glasses only enhance the puppy-dog effect. He's cute
and sweet, if a little on the nerdy side. Women fall all
over him, but Ernie has eyes only for Elaine.

"You're about to be forever in my debt," he said.

No doubt, my face bore a skeptical expression.

"No really. My new invention will save us hours
analyzing evidence." It's true that examining the
evidence after an investigation takes hours and is
boring beyond description. "I've perfected a data
compression method that can isolate anomalies in
digital video footage. It analyzes the contents of each
frame and tosses out all the frames that are identical to
each other. So all you're left with is anything that

shows movement or change."

"Well, it sound like you've really outdone yourself this time," I said. "I can't wait to try it out."

"Do you think Elaine will be impressed?"

"Well, if she isn't, I am. Come on, let's go meet Ms. Darnell."

Marsha Darnell answered the door almost before the bell stopped ringing. We introduced ourselves and I gave her my card.

"Thank goodness you're here," she said, ushering us inside nervously. She was forty-something and dressed to impress. Almost every article of clothing, jewelry, and accessory displayed a prominent designer logo. Her perfectly highlighted hair and dragon-lady nails probably cost more than my mortgage payment. She had presumably sized us up in turn. I'm guessing she found us both lacking.

"It happened again last night," she sniffed through tears that sounded rather theatrical. "It all started when I started remodeling this moldy old mausoleum. Please, I need to do something about this right away."

"Probably the best place to start is for you to give us a detailed account of what's been happening and show us around," I said.

"Well, as I said on the phone, I'm remodeling. I wanted to bulldoze the damn thing but the town council wouldn't let me," she sniffed indignantly. "I can't touch the outside—can't even change the color of the paint on the trim, can you believe that?"

Yes, I could believe it. This neighborhood was known in this neck of the woods for the quality and integrity of its architecture. Apparently Marsha wasn't from around here. I wondered why she didn't check into this before she bought the house.

She continued, "So I'm going to gut the interior and turn this crumbling heap into the showcase of the neighborhood. Then I'm going to flip it. It should bring me a nice profit."

People like Marsha utterly confound me. Did she not understand that this was one of the most exclusive addresses in Indian Springs—precisely because of the historic nature of its houses? No wonder her ghosts were upset.

"Do you know anything about the history of the house?" I asked.

She stared at me blankly. I might as well have been speaking Romanian. "We're looking for anything that could be helpful for our investigation," I added helpfully. "For example, did the town council give you any information when they denied your request to tear it down?"

She shook her head, obviously finding my questions pointless. "Look, it's just an old house. I could bring some class to this backwater if they'd let me." The more she spoke, the less I liked her.

I stole a glance at Ernie. He smirked back at me. "Why don't you show us the areas where you've had the most activity," he said.

She led us through a couple of rooms in various states of disarray, to a wide staircase with carved wooden bannisters. "Twice I've heard footsteps going up these stairs." I jotted a note in the little notebook I always carry. We followed her up the stairs to the landing. A stained-glass window at either end provided the only light. Although it was shaping up to be a warm, sunny day, the hall was gloomy. The air seemed clammy for such a warm day and I could smell something musty. I shivered slightly and hoped our client didn't notice. She didn't.

"Then, last week, I saw what looked like a woman dressed in a long white dress going down this hall. She looked right at me, then disappeared into this door here. Just...disappeared!"

Ernie cast a sideways glance at me. "Did she seem aware of your presence?" he asked. He had a valid reason for asking. There are different kinds of manifestations. Sometimes we encounter what appears to be a repeated reenactment of a specific event, like a moment frozen in time. The entities do not seem aware of their surroundings. They're harmless and relatively common, but can certainly be unsettling.

However, if an entity is unaware of our presence, we don't have much chance of making contact with it, which is, after all, the whole point of what we're doing.

Ernie repeated, "Did she seem aware of your presence?" Marsha just nodded mutely.

"Can you elaborate?" I asked gently.

She seemed almost reluctant to continue. "The thing is, she pointed and then motioned to me, kind of like this." The gesture she made was unmistakeable: "follow me".

"So what's behind this door?" I asked.

"Oh, just a bedroom. It's next to be redone."

"Mind if we take a look?" asked Ernie.

"No, no, of course not."

I opened the door to the room, which was in an advanced stage of mayhem. A few rolls of old carpeting stood lined up along the wall. Part of one wall had been knocked out, and the carpet had been ripped up to reveal an old wood floor that had seen better days.

"Any voices, bumping noises?" I asked.

She nodded mutely. Maybe her arrogance was masking genuine fear. For a minute, I almost felt sorry for her. "I'll show you the rest of the house." We strolled through several rooms, some incongruously modern, others still unmistakably Victorian. I made notes of where she'd experienced creepy feelings and unexplained cold spots.

"Well, all right. It sounds like an emergency, so I suggest we come back tonight. We can set up..."

"Night?" she interrupted. "I can't have strangers in my house at night!"

"Ms. Darnell," said Ernie patiently, "paranormal investigations are conducted at night with good reason. Have any of the events you've described happened in the daytime?"

"Well no, but...," she said. "Oh, all right."

"Don't worry," I said. "We'll disturb you as little as possible."

We said our goodbyes and agreed on a time to return with our equipment.

Ernie didn't say much as we walked to our cars, but I could tell by the look on his face that the gears were spinning madly in his head. He paused by the Mini with his hand on the door handle. "Lots of activity here. You think we could use a third person?" he asked.

"I'll be sure Elaine joins us. Even if it means we have to kidnap her."

&

I hoped I wouldn't have to make good on my promise to kidnap Elaine. Ernie and I could probably have handled this investigation ourselves, but it never hurts to have an extra person. Besides, I was hoping she would have time to talk. I badly needed to rant about my ex. Ernie was not the person to talk to about this, no matter how sympathetic he was. Ever the realist, he would only point out that I was the one who had kicked Roger out. That wasn't the point, and it wasn't what I needed to hear right now.

Elaine and I used to work at the same company. She transferred to Indian Springs a few years ago when she was between husbands. I was around when she met the second Mr. Wrong and helped her through many a crisis a few years later when that relationship came to an end.

In some ways, Elaine and I are polar opposites. She's insect-thin and always devastatingly elegant. Most days, she looks like she just stepped off the cover of Vogue. I wish I had her flair for style; she can get away with outlandish outfits that would look like a Halloween costume on anybody else. I am insanely jealous of her long, black hair, which is straight and shiny and has a white streak down one side that's entirely natural.

I touched a few buttons on my phone and Elaine's face appeared on the tiny screen. She adjusted something on her computer and the image shifted slightly.

"Can you talk?" I asked when she answered.

"I have a meeting in a few minutes. What's up?"

"Sandy called this morning with a case. I just came from the client's with Ernie. We promised to investigate tonight, and we could use a third person."

"Just a second." I waited while she tapped around on her computer. "Sure, I'd be happy to. I won't be able to leave here before seven—at the earliest." She said to someone unseen, "I'll be with you in just a moment. Look," she said, returning to me, "I'll have to call you back."

"Okay, I'll call you later...," but she'd already disconnected.

Driving home, I tried to analyze the phenomena our client said she'd experienced. Could the sightings Marsha described be just the inventions of an attention-seeking drama queen? It happens. But I didn't think that was the case here. I can usually spot a fraud a mile away. A drama queen she might be, but I doubted that she was that talented an actress. She was genuinely upset. I considered the possibility that someone could be trying to scare her.

I drove home, taking a different route. I admit that I just couldn't face seeing Roger's car in someone else's driveway. I'd like to be able to say I'd forgotten all about it by the time I pulled into my driveway, but it was not to be. I hoped tonight's investigation would give me something more pleasant to obsess over.

# On Becoming a Ghost Hunter

*I'm often* asked how I happened into my line of work. It wasn't my idea. It all started when Elaine was convinced that her cat Nacho, recently deceased, was trying to communicate with her. So we read a few books on ghost hunting, bought some cheap equipment, and set out one dark and stormy night to make contact with the former feline.

However, Nacho had never been a particularly amiable cat when he was alive, so I frankly didn't see why he should change now that he was dead. Much to Elaine's disappointment, I was right. As it turned out, it wasn't Nacho who was trying to get Elaine's attention after all. There was, however, someone—or something—else. Nothing could have prepared me for the first time we played back a recording and heard the disembodied voice of someone unknown. Elaine was a tad creeped out to realize she wasn't alone in her own home until I explained that it's just a person like anybody else. They just happen to be dead.

Forgive me for sounding ghoulish, but there's nothing quite like the thrill that comes from making contact with the other side. It's downright addictive. So Elaine and I, and sometimes Ernie, started looking for any place that might have a ghost or two. We started with the usual places: cemeteries, old hotels, that sort of thing. We even went to a haunted wax museum once. Talk about creepy.

Disembodied voices have told us to get out; others implored us to help them. Some entities just seem happy to have someone show some interest in them. Others don't seem to even know we're there. In a town the size of Indian Springs, it's hard to keep secrets. Word got out quickly and before long, we were getting calls from worried homeowners and local tourist attractions.

During the week, I endured my boring office job and waited impatiently for the weekend. We used to joke that it would be nice if we could somehow reverse the work/ghost hunting ratio. Then one day I got a call from Ernie, who said he needed to see me as soon as possible. So I conjured up a dentist appointment and quietly disappeared from the office.

Ernie works at the local college, which is in Throckmorton, the next town over. What he did for a living had been something of a mystery to me, though I've known him since high school. He tells people he's in IT, which I now know to be true...sort of. I always thought he was a network administrator or did technical support, or something like that. On this point I was *way* off base.

The college is in Throckmorton, about ten minutes down the main highway. It's a pleasant enough little place and rather trendy compared to Indian Springs, although I suspect none of the hip little shops along Main Street would stay in business very long without traffic from the students.

The college campus is a jarring mix of ornate old buildings and hypermodern glass and concrete boxes. Not knowing my way around, I had to rely on Ernie's dictated directions, which I had scribbled down hastily and without benefit of corrective eyewear. I was now having a hard time deciphering my own handwriting, which is bad enough under the best of circumstances. When I parked in front of a small brick building in a remote corner of the campus, I was certain I was in the wrong place. It looked more like a garden center than any high-tech facility I'd ever seen. My suspicions increased when I saw engraved over the door "Horticulture Pavilion 1857". Then I saw Ernie coming down the steps toward me.

"This is where you work? I thought you were in IT."

Ernie looked a little bit sheepish. "Well, yes, I am. But it's...different."

"Define 'different'."

"No time right now," he said, propelling me by the arm up the stairs and into the building. Inside, it looked just like...a horticulture pavilion. A glass roof supported by painted iron struts let in plenty of light for hundreds of plants neatly arranged on shelves. Each plant was carefully labeled. The air was stifling.

Beads of humidity dripped down the walls and thick iron pillars that supported the roof. A hygrometer showed the humidity to be close to 95 percent.

"Careful," he said, steering me around a puddle.

"Ernie, is this some kind of a joke?"

"I assure you it's not. It'll all make perfect sense in a minute. Right through here." I followed him through a door and into a corridor. We walked past a couple of open doors; inside I saw nothing more interesting than desks littered with papers and a file cabinet or two. At the end of the hall, he unlocked a door and ushered me into...a janitor's closet.

"Ernie, what the—?"

"Don't worry. I know it's weird, but you have to trust me. It'll all make sense shortly."

To one side of a rusty utility sink was another door, hidden in the shadows. Beside it, looking very much out of place, was a device of some sort that I'd never seen before. Ernie touched his fingertips to it and the door clicked softly. "After you," he said, opening the door for me gallantly.

A welcome blast of cool air hit me in the face. Gone were the plants; we were in a corridor with vinyl floors and fluorescent lights that could have been in any office building anywhere. On one wall was a monitor showing a view of the hall with the janitor's closet we had just come through. He led me into a small room and invited me to sit down. "I'll be right back."

He returned in a few minutes with a gray-haired man wearing a threadbare tweed jacket and rumpled jeans. Shaking my hand, he introduced himself as Dr. Ben Holmes, department head. It didn't occur to me to ask which department.

"Ms. Monroe, I'll be frank. I don't know where to start, so I'll just jump right in. This school—much to everyone's surprise—has recently received a large grant for the express purpose of conducting controlled scientific research on paranormal phenomena. Our mission is to gain a complete understanding of what ghosts or spirits really are, and how such an entity is able to make itself known to the living. Our ultimate goal is to learn how to communicate with the dead."

As I was rendered momentarily speechless, Dr. Holmes continued. "The benefactor's identity is a closely guarded secret and the terms of the grant are very clear. We are required to hire a full-time, experienced paranormal investigator who conducts investigations into claims of paranormal activity. We need to find someone ASAP. Your friend here recommended you.

"We can match your current salary; in fact, we can probably even do a little better. We realize, of course, that this is not an eight-to-five job, so you'd have, we hope, more than enough personal freedom to conduct your research as you see fit."

After we spent a few minutes discussing salary and working conditions, I was tempted to ask him if he'd pinch me so I could be sure I was awake. However, I decided that might be a little melodramatic and said finally, "Frankly, it all sounds a little too good to be true."

He nodded. "There is one other thing to consider." I knew it. When is there ever not a catch? He continued, "How are you with plants?"

In my mind's eye appeared a vision of the small, rather ragged collection of potted plants on my kitchen windowsill. "Well, it isn't my primary hobby."

Professor Holmes nodded and said, "You'll need to ... ahem... enroll as a student of Horticulture. As a graduate student, naturally. The department will see to it that you're accepted, of course, and that your tuition and books are covered."

By now I was utterly confused. I wondered if Ernie was playing an elaborate practical joke on me. But one glance at their faces convinced me otherwise.

"Um...okay. But don't you think I'm a little old for school? I mean, I'd be a good fifteen years older than most of my classmates."

"Not necessarily," he said. "Currently the oldest student here is 72. You won't actually have to attend lectures. The students and most of the staff believe this is nothing more than a greenhouse. The deception, unfortunately, is necessary because we need to keep a low profile with this project. Some of the more conservative alumni, upon whose financial backing the school depends, might object to having something so controversial going on here. Ms. Monroe, I've discussed your ghost hunting adventures with Mr. Stapleton here. I'm convinced you're uniquely qualified."

"Oh, of course." The job apparently was mine if I wanted it. I'm guessing they don't get too many applicants for such a position. "Maybe I could have the weekend to think about it?"

"Of course!" He beamed at me, the first smile I'd seen from him. He shoved a packet of papers at me and smiled apologetically. "Your application for admission. Then I can expect to hear from you early next week?"

"Yes, I'll let you know my decision first thing Monday." Smiling broadly, Dr. Holmes stuck out his hand and we shook

After Dr. Holmes left, Ernie showed me around. It was then that I learned what he really does for a living. He took me into a room that I first assumed was storage for dead computer hardware. Several tables were covered with computers and gadgets in various stages of dismantlement, and along one wall were more computers.

"So let me get this straight," I said to him. "An eccentric zillionaire wants to talk to dead people, so he or she is willing to pay someone like me to hunt ghosts for a living?"

Ernie shrugged. "Why not? Rich people have to spend their money on something."

Who can argue with logic like that? "So show me what you do, then."

He led me over to a table covered with various disemboweled gadgets. "Well, for example, this thing—if I can get it to work—will stream temperature data wirelessly to a computer that continually checks for temperature anomalies and sends out an alert if it finds something." We walked over to a computer and touched the screen. The display came to life, showing a multi-colored series of zig-zag waveforms. "This program maps out a 3-D representation of the electromagnetic radiation in a room."

"Sounds interesting. How does it work?"

"With standard electromagnetic field detectors. I added wireless capability to these EMF detectors so that they stream data to a computer. The computer builds an image of the electromagnetic hot spots. My theory is that it will help us differentiate between background radiation and genuine anomalies."

"And? Does it work?"

"Well, yes, but so far the largest space I've been able to test it on successfully is that closet over there," he admitted.

We moved to the other end of the table. "Here is something I've just started working on. These things here," he said, pointing to some otherwise unidentifiable gadgets, "are various sensors capable of recording all kinds of measurements. For example, this one started out as a seismometer. When I'm finished with it, it will be able to record a petal falling off a flower. Here is a sensor that registers minute changes in the barometric pressure. It's attached to this device, which streams the data to a computer, where it can be monitored in real-time, or recorded and examined later. The goal is to detect the slightest changes in a room."

"And they pay you to do this?"

"They pay me to do this."

In retrospect, I'm not sure why I had my reservations about it. At the time, it seemed like a risky prospect. Who ever heard of a professional paranormal investigator anyway? When people asked me what I did for a living, what was I supposed to tell them?

Ernie ushered me back the way we came—checking the monitor first to be sure no one was around—through the closet and into the greenhouse. It was like walking into a warm, humid wall. "Look, it wouldn't be that different from what you do now, except that you'd get paid for it. It's not the ghost hunting you'd have to keep quiet about, it's the fact that the school is backing you."

"So I get paid to hunt ghosts and we get money for equipment and whatever else we need, as long as nobody finds out about it?"

"Something like that. You've already established your reputation, and now you'll have all the equipment you need, and the time and resources to analyze your findings. We keep up the appearance that it's a garden center, and people for the most part leave us alone. I mean, the whole point is to establish paranormal research as a legitimate scientific pursuit. Hopefully some day we won't have to hide anymore. In the meantime, people ignore us until they want to know how often to water their zinnias. Actually, I'm starting to rather enjoy myself."

I followed him over to a shelf lined with plants. "These are some ordinary hothouse tomatoes I crossed with an heirloom variety. They're hardier than the heirloom plants, which are quite fragile, but taste tons better than the ones you get at the store. Here, this one's ripe." He plucked a misshapen, purplish orb from the plant and and handed it to me. "Try it in some guacamole. You'll see."

I stared at the strange-looking thing. It didn't look like any tomato I'd ever seen.

"You know, Ernie, I have a mortgage to think about."

"Yeah, and so what? How many people get to do what they do for fun and get paid to do it."

He was right, you know. But it all still seemed so risky. Paranormal research—who'd ever heard of such a thing? What if we weren't successful? What if the rich guy changed his mind and decided to pull the plug? Then where would I be? In a town the size of Indian Springs, good jobs were few and far between.

I argued with myself about it all the way home. For dinner, I made guacamole. Ernie was right, the tomato was like nothing I'd ever tasted before. I made up my mind about the job, then changed it, at least four times before I finally fell into bed, exhausted, and still at a loss for what to do.

But in the meantime, in an incredible stroke of good luck, my boss had somehow gotten wind of my extracurricular activities. A particularly odious man named Noel Hill, he proudly sports a cheesy handlebar mustache of a type that was last in style when I was a toddler. When he called me into his office bright and early that Monday morning, my bad angel followed me.

Noel informed me that my activities were not appropriate conduct for a representative of the company. He issued me an ultimatum: choose between ghost hunting and my job. When I smiled sweetly and asked him if he had any idea how many unknown life forms were making their home in his mustache, he did me the greatest favor he ever could have done—he fired me. So I did what any normal person would do under the circumstances. I became a professional ghost hunter.

When I got home that afternoon—several hours earlier than anticipated and lugging a cardboard box full of my personal belongings—I immediately called Ernie.

"So it looks like we're going to be working together after all." I filled him in on the day's events.

"You didn't really say that to Noel, did you?"

"You should know me better than that."

"Holmes will be happy. He'll want you to start right away. We have a backlog of cases. "

So I didn't even get the luxury of taking a few days off.

Here's something you might not want to hear: unseen entities are all around us. Do you think that just because your house is brand new those noises you're hearing could not possibly be caused by a ghost? Think again. You don't know what was on your property a hundred years ago.

We once investigated a house that still smelled like

fresh paint. The very first night in their new home, the proud owners were awakened in the middle of the night by sobbing and whispers emanating from the bedroom of their sixteen-year old daughter. At first, the parents assumed that their daughter was homesick for the old neighborhood, but the sounds continued. Meanwhile, the daughter, a sound sleeper, was oblivious. When the sounds continued night after night the parents began to suspect something was terribly wrong. Things reached a crisis when, to the absolute befuddlement of the daughter, they announced they were taking her to a psychotherapist. Luckily, the parents were smart enough to believe their daughter when she told them she'd been sleeping like a rock every night.

The whole family stayed awake one night, camped out in the daughter's bedroom. Image her surprise when heart-wrenching sobs suddenly started emanating from the very walls. Not surprisingly, she refused to spend another night in the room. That's when they called me.

We found the first clue to this mystery when Sandy found out that the entire subdivision was built on the site of a defunct shopping mall. The mall had been plagued by one disaster after another since it was built in the 1950s near what was then the edge of town. Fire gutted the interior several times and mall security guards regularly reported seeing people in the corridors late at night, long after closing hours. When a rifle-toting former employee of the security company went on a rampage and held three movie theater employees hostage for several hours, the mall's days were numbered. It finally burned to the ground one Christmas Eve and the police naturally suspected arson. They never found a single shred of evidence, however, and the case remained officially unsolved.

We, on the other hand, were more enterprising. Sandy, Ernie and I spent a morning at the library going over old maps. It didn't take us long to find out that the mall was built on a forgotten cemetery in which were interred mostly children who had perished in a cholera epidemic in the 1890s. We couldn't find any evidence that the graves had been moved. You might think this kind of thing only happens in the movies. I can personally assure you that it happens all the time.

This case didn't have a particularly happy ending. The family eventually sold the house and moved away. Once the neighborhood residents began comparing stories, word got out and sales screeched to a halt. The property developer soon went bankrupt. Many of the original residents tried in a panic to sell but couldn't find a buyer. Although a few stalwarts stayed behind, claiming that they rather liked the idea of living in a haunted house, many simply walked away, leaving the derelict houses to decay along with their neighbors' property values.

Oddly enough, some of my clients want their property to be haunted. They get downright irritated when we tell them it's just the plumbing making those spooky noises. One of them even told me, in all sincerity, that having a presence in the house adds to the resale value.

I pondered these mysteries as I got ready for this investigation. We have only a few hard and fast rules about dressing for an investigation. Rule number one is no hard-soled shoes. Ghostly footsteps are a common phenomenon, so we want to be sure we're not throwing our own into the mix. Ditto bling. Clothing or jewelry that sparkles or shines is never a good idea on an investigation. The last thing we want to do is to tell a client something is an anomaly when it's just the reflection off of someone's sequins. Perfume is also out; very often entities try to communicate through smell. And I personally always try to remember to bring a jacket with me, even if it's a hundred degrees out. A sudden drop in temperature might or might not be something paranormal, but it can get mighty uncomfortable in a hurry. Normally I wear jeans on investigations but it was supposed to be quite warm tonight, so I decided on shorts.

I was still looking for my sneakers when Ernie arrived. He was followed shortly by Elaine. Although impeccably attired as usual, she looked a bit frazzled after her tough day at work. She climbed out of her car carrying a large sequined tote bag. "You sure you're up for this?" I asked.

She waved a hand, making the stack of bracelets on

her wrist jangle softly. "No worries. This is just what I need after a day like today. Just let me get changed."

She darted into the house and returned a few minutes later wearing designer jeans and the latest high-tech running shoes. "You know that guy you thought was so sexy?" she asked, removing the bracelets and shoving them into the tote bag.

"What, the one who worked in Accounting?"

She nodded. "He got laid off today. I saw Security walking him out the door."

"Always a great way to start off your weekend."

Ever notice how most firings take place on a Friday afternoon? I'm sure there's a logical reason for this, but I never figured it out. Do the people in Personnel think you're so dumb that by Monday morning you will have forgotten that there used to be somebody sitting in that empty cubicle next to you?

"It sounded like you were having a busy day when I called. You sure you're up for this?" I asked.

"What? Are you kidding? This is just what I need!" She shoved a laptop case into the back of the car. "Did we forget anything? There's actually still some space here."

I glanced over the equipment checklist. We were missing a camera tripod, which at that very moment Ernie was carrying out my front door. "Looks like we're all set."

"Who's riding with me?" asked Ernie cheerfully. But to his consternation, Elaine was already climbing into the front seat of my station wagon.

Elaine snapped the seatbelt and turned suddenly to me before I'd even had a chance to start the car. "Is something wrong?"

"What do you mean?"

"You're awfully quiet," she said. "I get the feeling you're upset about something."

"I didn't know you were psychic," I grumbled irritably. "Yeah, on the way to the client's this morning I took a wrong turn and found myself in that neighborhood just before you get to Lone Oak. You know, those *really* nice houses. Well, I saw Roger's car. It was parked in the driveway of one of them. A mansion, and not a starter mansion. You can't find a garden shed in that neighborhood that sells for less than a million. This was early in the morning, so, you know—it was probably there all night."

"I thought you were over him long before you kicked him out of the house!"

"Well, I am. But he's already found someone new. Now I'll think about it every time I'm home alone on a Saturday night."

"You mean you'll brood about it. Look, relationships are not a competition. That's what got the two of you into trouble in the first place, isn't it?"

I had to admit it was. She continued, "So what's the big deal? He's probably picking up every floozy that gives him the time of day, just to get back at you. If you let it spoil your day, he wins. Anyway, remember what a hard time he gave you over the whole ghost hunting thing? Would you really ever want to go back to your old job?"

She's right, you know. Roger was the Boyfriend from Hell. What did I care whose house his car was parked at? But Indian Springs is a small town, and I could count the dates I'd had since we broke up on the fingers of one hand.

Elaine doesn't have the same problem. I've seen guys trip over each other for the chance to talk to her. Poor Ernie. He's just one in a crowd. It's hard to pinpoint exactly when I began to suspect Ernie was falling for Elaine.

Not long after I started working with Ernie, we were called to investigate an old theater in Deerfield, a town about the size of Indian Springs on the other side of Throckmorton. The theater was a little bit too big for just two people, so I enlisted Elaine's help. We didn't find much in the theater except for some cold spots and a few EMF spikes, but we did have a bit of a scare when an old shelf holding some stage props collapsed. No one was hurt, but an old-fashioned cast-iron skillet missed Elaine's head by inches. She shrugged it off; but it dawned on me later that Ernie was more rattled by the incident than she was.

My suspicions were confirmed the next day when the three of us met over lunch to discuss the investigation. Ernie is always polite and attentive. Women love this about him. (Single guys, take note.) But I noticed he was more solicitous than unusual as they compared their bruises. Elaine was in a hurry as usual and didn't have time to linger with us over lunch that day. I couldn't help noticing how Ernie watched her through the window until she got in her car and drove away.

He finally realized he was being watched. "Looks like the cat's out of the bag," he said sheepishly. "I've never met anyone like her."

"Your secret is safe with me. But you know, Ernie, she's gone through two painful divorces. I don't think she's looking for a relationship right now."

"I know. But I can dream, can't I?"

I always wondered why Ernie recommended me and not Elaine for the ghost hunting job, so finally one day I asked him.

"Look, I think you're a first-rate investigator, and you're serious about it," he said. "Plus, I've known you for a long time and I knew we'd be able to work together. Anyway, Elaine really loves her job. She may complain about it, but they'd have to drag her out of there kicking and screaming."

"Thanks, bud." I know Ernie well enough to know a sincere compliment when I get one. His feelings for Elaine haven't been an issue so far on the cases where she's worked with us. I was worried about it at first, but he's strictly professional.

The one thing I haven't figured out is whether Elaine is aware of Ernie's feelings for her. I figure it's none of my business, so I've never discussed it with her. If the two of them ever do connect, I very much fear it would be the end of Elaine's participation in our investigations. Having a dating couple on your team is a sure-fire recipe for disaster. Still, Ernie deserves to find a nice girl. He's fun to be around, doesn't take himself too seriously, and he's not bad looking.

I wanted to ask her more about the guy from Accounting, but we were already at the client's house. I parked behind Ernie, and the three of us went to the door together.

When she greeted us at the door, Marsha seemed a trifle friendlier than she had earlier. While I introduced her to Elaine, Ernie started setting up the tripods for the video cameras. I was expecting some complaints, but Marsha had apparently mellowed since this afternoon. "Put your things wherever you need to," she said. "I'll be in here if you need me," and disappeared into another room.

The first thing we do is position some wireless night-vision cameras with a view of all possible entrances.

It's an easy and efficient way to make sure that no uninvited guests have crashed the party. We position a few with a view of halls and doorways inside as well so we can verify where everybody is and what was going on around them at any time. Unfortunately we discovered such precautions are necessary when a client once thought it would be fun to play a little trick on us. Luckily, we discovered the intruder before wasting much time on the investigation. Things like this don't happen often. Most of our clients want a professional scientific investigation as much as we do.

Next we go through the house to check the level of electromagnetic fields. There's nothing paranormal about this. All electrically charged objects produce electromagnetic radiation. But sometimes so do paranormal entities. A lot of cases turn out to be nothing more than old wires. So one of the first things we do is check the house with electronic temperature gauges and EMF meters, a small device that measures changes in electromagnetic fields, so we know what's normal for a particular location. An old house like Marsha's is just about guaranteed to have some unshielded wires and drafty spots.

While Ernie worked on setting up the various cameras, Elaine and I walked around with our gadgets. My EMF meter didn't register anything unusual until I held it near the floor, when it beeped madly and registered a huge spike. Elaine got the same reaction with hers. "Maybe we should see what's in the basement," she said, heading off in the direction of the basement stairs.

"So what else do you know about the guy in Accounting?" I asked as we crept down the stairs into the typically dank and creepy basement.

"Not much, except that he's not married and doesn't have any kids. I tried to discretely pump Stephanie in HR for more information, but she swears she doesn't know anything."

"She's probably sworn to secrecy anyway," I said.

My meter was going off like crazy. Not surprisingly, a tangle of antique wires was tacked to the basement ceiling. They ran the length of the house and branched off in various directions.

Elaine poked at a bundle of wires, dislodging a cluster of dust bunnies. "Mystery solved. She really ought to re-wire while she's remodeling. It doesn't make much sense not to. Actually, what worries me at work is that I'm noticing more and more empty cubicles lately. Nobody will tell me whether he got fired or laid off."

"By the way," she continued, "did you get any evidence in that poltergeist investigation? Other than that bump on your head, I mean."

"We caught a few objects moving on video—including the bottle that got me." I touched my forehead gingerly. "I don't think it's an intelligent entity. The best thing to do is put them in touch with someone who specializes in poltergeists."

Poltergeists are not well understood. In this type of phenomenon, inanimate objects move, apparently by themselves, and sometimes quite violently. Some researchers think they're not paranormal at all, but psychokinetic energy resulting from some kind of emotional disturbance. Very often there's a teenager or pre-teen involved. An image of the tavern owner's stepson sprang to mind. A surly young man clad head to toe in black, he had removed the headphone from one ear only long enough to grunt something I presumed was a greeting. We're supposed to be researching ghosts, so I had no problem passing this case along to someone better equipped to deal with it.

We went back upstairs. Elaine was unusually quiet. I could sympathize with her—the company she worked for was noted more for looking after its bottom line than its employees.

The rest of the house didn't turn up anything out of the ordinary except one of those old fashioned fuse boxes. "Talk about an accident waiting to happen," remarked Elaine.

We recorded our findings on one of the touch pads, then went upstairs to see how Ernie was doing. He had decided to set up the video cameras at the foot of the stairs and in the upstairs hall where our client had seen the ghostly lady in white. We found him adjusting the angle of the upstairs camera and checking the video stream on a computer.

"Can we help?" I asked.

"Hmm, no. Almost finished here," he answered absently. "Unless you want to look for a place to set up the rest of that stuff over there." He waved toward a pile of gadgets.

I went to investigate and found a barometer and Ernie's modified seismometer along with an assortment of unidentifiable odds and ends. Because the hall was where the client saw the apparition, it seemed like a good place to put the barometer and seismometer. Unfortunately, they both needed electrical power and there wasn't a single outlet in the hall. So I grabbed a power strip and an extension cord and set out to look for someplace to plug in. The best bet seemed to be the nearest bedroom, the one into which Ms. Darnell's apparition had disappeared. I opened the door cautiously and glanced around in the rapidly failing light.

Like many old houses, this one didn't have a surplus of electrical outlets. Crawling around looking for a place to plug something in is one of the less glamorous tasks that befalls the dedicated paranormal investigator. In this case, we had the additional complications of rotten floorboards and construction debris. Trying to remember when I'd last had a tetanus shot (third grade?), I traversed a veritable mine-field of spongy floorboards and rusty nails looking for a place to plug in the extension cord, only to find one of those old-fashioned outlets that doesn't take grounded plugs. Fortunately, we always keep a bag of assorted cables and adaptors on hand. I rooted around in it until I found an adaptor and made a note to look for a two-prong extension cord next time I was at the hardware store. I wondered if they still made such a thing.

Ernie and Elaine joined me as I was checking the feed from the two devices. Both seemed to be working.

"Everything's all set," Ernie announced.

"Then I guess it's time to get to work." We turned off the few lights that were on and turned on our various meters and gauges. Ernie disappeared down the stairs. Elaine set out a couple of voice recorders and switched them on.

As the last of the light faded from the stained glass windows, I pondered the possibility that we may have already completed the most interesting part of the night's activities. If I may be perfectly honest, ghost hunting involves a lot of tedium. It's not like in the movies where ghosts start zooming past levitating furniture the minute you bring a camera in. In real life, ghost hunters must rely on the subtlest of clues—a whispered voice, an unexplained smell, or a sudden, unexplainable temperature fluctuation. We spend hours and hours sifting through video footage and voice recordings after every investigation. More often than not, we get absolutely nothing. When we do find something, nine times out of ten it has a perfectly logical, normal explanation. Frankly, I wasn't expecting much from this investigation. Some people wouldn't believe in ghosts if they got a personal visitation from Abraham Lincoln. Others see a ghost in the headlights from every passing car. Marsha struck me as belonging to the latter category. I would be proven wrong before long.

We had been walking around the hall with the electronic temperature gauge for only a few minutes when I heard footsteps coming up the stairs. I couldn't see anything, but something that felt like a puff of cold wind swept right past me.

"Did you feel that?" I asked.

"Yeah, my temperature gauge is showing a 15-degree drop in temperature. It's moving this way," said Elaine, charging past me and ducking into one of the bedrooms.

The thermal camera would have come in handy at this point. Unfortunately, the only one we possess was downstairs with Ernie. I followed Elaine into the bedroom, switching on my iPod, which doubles as a voice recorder. Elaine was sweeping the room with the temperature gauge. "Well, I'm not picking up anything here," she said. "I can't tell if it was moving into this room or the room next door. I'm going downstairs to get the thermal camera." She turned and ran smack into Ernie, who had been monitoring the video camera downstairs when the footsteps started.

"Did you hear those footsteps? The video was on—I think we caught something on film," he said.

"We got a cold spot. Elaine followed it in here."

Making ourselves as comfortable as possible in the unfurnished room, we perched an EMF meter and the voice recorder/iPod on a roll of carpet and invited any entities present to communicate with us. We stayed a few minutes waiting for a response, then decided to move on to the next room. I always explain to whoever or whatever might be present that I might not be able to hear them but might be able to record their voice. I also explain how to make the device work. I mean, it doesn't seem logical to assume someone who lived before iPods and EMF detectors were invented will know what they are.

Ernie hung around, snapping a few photos. Being the gadget-hound that he is, Ernie is, not surprisingly, something of a photography buff. He usually brings a Polaroid camera on investigations in addition to the digital cameras that we keep on hand. He's convinced that there is something about Polaroid film that makes it better for paranormal research than a digital camera. That may be, but Polaroid film is wickedly expensive and hard to find. I will stick with my digital.

I went into the next room. The second bedroom was

the one with the rotten floorboard obstacle course that I'd gone in earlier as we were setting up. I was beginning to wonder where Elaine was with that thermal camera when I heard a snap and a screech behind me, neither of which was caused by anything ghostly. A floorboard had crumbled when Elaine stepped on it, sending her and the thermal camera tumbling across the floor. At that moment, Ernie charged into the room and almost tripped over Elaine in the darkness.

Elaine extricated herself from the floorboard and Ernie and turned on a flashlight. That she hadn't noticed the rip in her favorite designer jeans or the blood seeping from what would later turn out to be a nasty gash on her ankle meant either that Elaine was in shock or that she had found something really interesting. Luckily it was the latter and I crawled on all fours to see what she and Ernie were looking at.

One floorboard had snapped almost in two. We removed it carefully and crowded around, shining the flashlight into the space beneath. Carefully concealed in the space between the floor joists was a metal box. "Hey, there's something here!" Elaine exclaimed, fishing it out of its hiding place.

It was about the size of a thick paperback book, without any markings or ornamentation. A small latch held the lid closed. "Somebody went to a lot of trouble to hide this. Who knows how long that's been under there! Maybe it's shares in some stock and it's worth millions now! " She tried to pry open the latch, but it refused to budge. "Here, you try," she said, handing the box to Ernie.

Ernie took the box eagerly and tried the latch. The latch snapped in half. "Sorry," he said, prying the stub of the latch open. "At least we can open it now." But the box stubbornly refused to reveal its contents; the lid was stuck fast. Ernie wrestled gently with the box for a few minutes until, finally, the lid yielded slightly, opening just enough for him to look inside with the flashlight.

"So? The family jewels? Stock in Standard Oil?" I asked.

"Not even," he said, disappointed. "As far as I can tell it's just a bunch of old newspaper clippings."

"Well, they obviously meant something to somebody a long time ago, or they wouldn't have gone to all the trouble to fix up this hiding place for them."

"Boring," said Ernie. "So what do we do with them?"

"Well, I suppose we should at least look at them. What if they have some bearing on the case?" I answered.

"I doubt it. Anyway, it's all yours. I doubt if I'll be much use now," said Elaine ruefully, hobbling to her feet.

"All right. I'll see if I can open it and have a look at

what's inside. I may find something here that the Historical Society would be interested in."

Elaine insisted we stay and continue the investigation. She propped the injured leg up on a roll of carpet and spent some time trying to make contact using one of Ernie's inventions, a modified voice recorder with headphones and a super-sensitive microphone. She put on a brave face but the cut on her leg was painful and took a long time to stop bleeding. We couldn't find the first aid kit, so we didn't even have a bandage to put on it.

Ernie and I ran through the remaining rooms on the floor with our equipment, but we had lost our momentum. I admitted reluctantly that we wouldn't be able to do much else tonight. We were just getting started! I wasn't sure exactly what I would tell our client. I was certain she would be furious about the damage. I had a quick debate with my conscience over whether or not I should tell her about the box. It was Marsha's property, of course, and my conscience won. I hoped she would at least allow me to borrow it long enough to find out what was in it.

As Ernie went around turning on lights and packing up equipment, I went downstairs and knocked on the door where Marsha had disappeared earlier. She was on the sofa. The TV was flickering in the corner. How interesting. I wouldn't have pegged her as a *Bonanza* fan. She didn't stir when I opened the door; I couldn't tell if she was asleep.

"Marsha? It's me, Margo."

She sat up and punched the remote hastily, seeming slightly embarrassed. Hoss and Little Joe vanished with a soft click. "I'm sorry, Ms. Darnell, but we're having to pack up early tonight. One of our people had a minor accident."

"Accident?" Marsha lunged for the light switch, now wide awake.

"Well, you see, a floorboard upstairs collapsed and—well, there wasn't much damage, but...," I said, now stammering like a school kid.

"Damage?" She was staring at me with a wild expression in her eyes.

"One of our people has been injured, you see, and ..." This wasn't going well at all.

"INJURED?" She was starting to sound like a parrot.

"One of the investigators, Elaine, stepped on a bad floorboard..." She charged out of the room before I could finish my sentence.

Marsha thundered past me and up the stairs. At the top of the stairs, Elaine was dabbing at her ankle with a tissue and ruefully assessing the damage to her jeans.

"Are you okay?" asked Ms. Darnell.

"It could be worse, I suppose." Elaine picked a splinter out of her sock and held it up.

"Show me what happened."

"It's right in here." I led Ms. Darnell to the room where it happened. She stormed into the room. "Wait!" I yelled. I turned on the flashlight just in time to keep her from stepping into the hole. She froze as a loud "CRACK!" sounded from underneath her feet.

"Maybe it would be better if we discuss it out here in the hall."

Marsha crept backward, slowly, on tippy-toes. As if that would help if the floor gave way.

Ernie had appeared and was gently helping Elaine down the stairs and enjoying every second of it. "I don't think Elaine is seriously hurt, but it appears you have a rather serious problem here that has nothing to do with ghosts." I said.

She nodded mutely.

"We did have a few experiences, but we won't know if we were able to catch anything verifiable until we've had a chance to sift through the audio and video we took tonight. There is something else I want to talk to you about, though."

"Look, if she has any medical expenses, just have her send the bill to me."

That's when it dawned on me that she was worried about being sued. My bad angel (the same one that got me fired) whispered in my ear that perhaps I could use this to my advantage. "I'll let you two work that out among yourselves. We found this under the broken floorboard." I handed her the box, but she barely glanced at it and handed it right back to me.

"What's in it?"

"Just a bunch of old papers, we think. It's a long shot, but we thought it might possibly contain clues to your, um, strange happenings."

"You can keep it. I don't want it." She shuddered, as if she'd touched something disgusting.

Well, that was easy. "Then I guess we'll finish up here and be back in touch with you in a few days." She looked alarmed. Maybe it was the prospect of seeing us again. "To let you know if we found any physical evidence of a haunting."

"Of course."

I couldn't resist a last jab. "You should be careful about that floor. You wouldn't want any of the workmen to get injured and sue you," I said archly.

We finished carrying the equipment to the car did a last check around for any stray items that might have been left behind. Marsha saw us out, relieved, I suspect, to be rid of us.

Elaine insisted on helping us load the car, but she mostly just got in our way. I knew Ernie was just dying to offer her a ride back to my house but I guess he was afraid of pushing his luck. After we had everything loaded, Elaine climbed carefully into my car.

There was little traffic this time of night as we made our way back across town. "Strange client," remarked Elaine.

"Yes, but we've had worse. Remember that lady at the library in Throckmorton?" That investigation hadn't turned up anything spookier than a prehistoric furnace and some unshielded wires that must have been there since the Hoover administration. The librarian was miffed that we didn't find anything paranormal. She had informed us indignantly that we didn't have the "gift." We were still laughing about it as I turned into my driveway and opened the garage.

"We didn't have time to gather much evidence," said Ernie regretfully as he and I unloaded the boxes.

"Well, look on the bright side," I said. "It won't take long to review everything."

"True. It probably wouldn't even be worth going to the lab. You girls want to come over to my place?" We normally use our secret space at the Horticulture Pavilion to examine the evidence we've collected, but have been known on occasion to use Ernie's apartment as a remote lab. He owns more computers than NASA, and it doesn't hurt that he lives right around the corner from the best pizza place in the county.

"Works for me," I said. "Don't forget to call Sandy."

"So I guess I will see you both tomorrow," he said, sounding, I thought, rather wistful.

"I want to go by the clinic first thing in the morning," said Elaine. "I'll come over there as soon as I can."

"Call first," I told her. "If Ernie's new software works like he thinks it will, we might finish early. Put something on that when you get home. Are you sure you'll be okay to drive?"

She rolled her eyes and wedged herself carefully into her car. "It's just a scratch."

Ernie watched her drive away. "Well, I guess I'll go now. See you tomorrow," he said without taking his eyes off her car as she drove away.

After Ernie left I went back in the garage and rummaged around for some of that smelly stuff that you spray on things to loosen them up. I found a can lurking behind of a box of obsolete computer gadgets and made a mental note to myself that it was time to clean off these shelves. I sprayed the box's hinges with the goo and took it inside.

Sitting on the kitchen counter, it didn't look like much. But I was dying to get a closer look at what was inside. With a little careful jiggling, the lid finally loosened and I was able to pry it open just enough to get my hand in.

Exercising all my self-restraint, I put the box down and made myself a cup of tea. Then I took everything into the bedroom and put my jammies on. Thoroughly enjoying the unexpected time to myself, I settled in to read. The first paper I pulled out was a clipping from the Indian Springs *Herald* dated February 2, 1868.

"Mr. and Mrs. Ellsworth Taylor were proud to announce the engagement of their daughter Amanda to Mr. Fargo Jones of Myrtle Springs. The wedding will be held on March 13 at the First Methodist Church. After the wedding the couple will reside in..."

The only other writing was beginnings or ends of sentences. Puzzled, I turned the small, yellowing piece of paper over. The other side was an advertisement for Henry Grayson, Importer of Fine Teas and Spices. The ad included a drawing of the building and the address, which I recognized as one of the old buildings downtown. The drawing looked vaguely familiar. I made a note of the address and placed the clipping back in its place in the box.

The next piece of paper was thicker but brittle and turning brown around the edges. When I opened it, it cracked slightly at the fold. It appeared to be a bill of sale for something from Krompholz Musikwaren on Rathgeberstrasse in Vienna. The letterhead was printed in black ink and relatively unfaded. It looked authentic enough; the typeface was ornate and next to impossible to decipher. I recognized it as Fraktur, a category of fonts in common use in German-speaking countries before World War II. The specifics of the sale were hand-written, and the ink was faded almost to nothing. Intrigued, I held it up to the light next to my bed, but couldn't make out the date, amount or what the purchase had been. I could only guess that it was probably a musical instrument of some kind.

I was already starting to get sleepy but I couldn't resist looking at one more thing. I pulled out a carefully folded piece of paper that might have once been a pale lilac color. The years had yellowed it to a murky mauve, but the ink had faded only slightly.

"L,

I have it from a reliable source that Roland plans to ask you to the dance. I'm green with envy! Love, Clara."

In the corner, in a different hand with different ink and enclosed in a heart, was written "LG loves RH".

Oh, to be a teenager again with nothing more important to worry about than having a date for Saturday night!

This seemed like a good stopping point, so I turned out the light. I don't know what I had expected to find in the box, but as I drifted off to sleep, I wondered why anyone would go to so much trouble to hide a box that contained nothing more valuable than a teenager's notes.

# Carlson's Untimely Departure

*When I* woke up the next morning, my light was still on. I opened an eye and peeked at the clock, which bore the bad news that I would need to get up and get myself in gear—pronto. I had an appointment to meet Sandy at a potential client's house to discuss noises in her attic, then had some errands to run before going to Ernie's to sift through last night's evidence. Reluctantly, I dragged myself out of bed.

I showered and got dressed quickly; reviewing evidence can be tedious work and comfort is more important than style. I did what I could with my hair and slapped on a little mascara. The bump on my head was by now just a bruise, but it was turning a rather florescent shade of purple that clashed with my hair. "Let's hope I don't run into anyone I know," I said to my reflection.

I slipped into a T-shirt and my favorite grubby jeans and went into the kitchen to take inventory. A quick glance in the fridge and kitchen cabinets confirmed that the food situation was pretty dismal. I hate grocery shopping and had been putting it off. But it was now shop or starve. Indian Springs is not noted for its fancy cuisine, although it does have a handful of decent restaurants. So I have learned to cook, and usually enjoy it. It's the grocery shopping that I hate.

I still had a little while before I was scheduled to meet Sandy, so I scribbled my list and jumped in the car. Until recently, the epicurean choices in my vicinity were fairly bleak. Shopping for food typically meant driving to the outskirts of town to one of those enormous stores with a parking lot the size of Rhode Island. This morning my destination was a small neighborhood grocery store, recently opened, along my route to the client's house. It's one of those places that sells locally-grown produce and organic milk from happy cows. Stuff costs a little more, but the atmosphere is generally a little less manic.

I parked—right in front!—and commandeered a small shopping cart on my way to the bakery counter near the front of the store, where a selection of tasty-looking pastries beckoned. I bought a blueberry scone and ate it as I wheeled the cart up and down the aisles. The snack took some of the chore out of shopping. I was approaching the fruits and vegetables when a toddler squirmed out of her mother's grasp and darted past me, heading straight for a pyramid of shiny red apples.

The little girl reached for an apple near the bottom of the pile and laughed with glee as the carefully constructed mound crumbled to the floor. Dodging the bouncing apples with my shopping cart, I stopped just in time to avoid running smack-dab into a guy pushing his own cart.

"Hey, don't I know you?" he asked. Well, wouldn't you know. It was the cute guy from Accounting. "I'm Neil. I used to work at ..."

"Oh yes. You're in the Accounting department, on the third floor. Hey, did you just say you used to work there?" I asked, feigning innocence.

He proceeded to tell me his woes. I made the expected declarations of surprise and sympathy while taking the opportunity to size him up without seeming to. This was the first time I'd gotten a close look at him. In his shorts and faded polo shirt he somehow seemed shorter than I remembered. His light brown hair was beginning to recede and he was wearing glasses. I'd never seen him in glasses at work, but they didn't detract from his looks—much. Unfortunately, the fact that he hadn't shaved in a couple of days did. But who was I to judge? I'd flown out of the house with a minimum of preparation myself.

"So. What kind of cat do you have?" he asked, gesturing at my shopping cart, which at the moment contained only a couple of loaves of cheap white bread and a bag of dry cat food.

"Cat? Oh, you mean that. Um, it's for the ducks in the park, actually."

"You feed cat food to ducks?"

"Yeah, they totally love it."

"I see. Any particular brand?"

"No, just whatever happens to be on sale." So much for trying to be cool. His eyes wandered to the bruise on my forehead, but he tactfully didn't mention it.

"Well, hey. What about you? What are you up to these days?"

"Oh, I..um...do some research. That is, I'm studying horticulture."

"Horticulture?"

"You know, plants." This is the point at which I start worrying that people will ask me questions I can't answer. I fumbled around in my purse and handed him a card with my phone number and email address. "Here's my contact info. It was nice to talk to you."

From the look on his face, I suspected he was about to ask me for advice on his azaleas. It was time to make my exit. His shopping cart was almost empty and I hate running into people again after I've already said 'hello' and 'goodbye' to them, so I beat a hasty retreat to the checkout lanes. I hope the stupid ducks appreciate this, I thought to myself. They were the only ones that were going to be eating this week.

It's not often I get to go through the express checkout. "Do you need any help out with this?"

"Huh? No thanks, I can handle it." I guess they have to ask. My meager selections safely stashed in the back of my car, I climbed in and rummaged in the side console for the scrap of paper upon which I had written the client's address and some directions. I wasn't familiar with the street, but glancing at the dashboard clock I realized I had just enough time to get there. As I pulled out of my parking space, I saw Neil in the rearview mirror, a solitary figure carrying his lone grocery sack to his car.

A few minutes later, I pulled up in front of a tidy beige house. Sandy's bicycle was already propped against a hedge. Sandy doesn't own a car. If I tried to bicycle the five miles from Throckmorton, you'd probably have to put me in the hospital, but it was just a short hop to him.

Sandy is a handsome, strapping art student who couldn't be less interested in what we do. Our research lab doubles as his art studio. As long as he can work on his projects, he is happy to take calls, screen cases, and do some research for us. Sandy is drop-dead gorgeous in a blond, surfer dude sort of way. He looks for all the world like he should be dashing off to catch the next wave, but the closest beach is a five-hour drive from here. He's the perfect assistant, except for one tiny detail—he's positively terrified of ghosts.

I stuck a pen and small notepad in the pocket of my jacket and was climbing out of the car when the owner of the bicycle appeared on the front porch, followed by a petite elderly woman who barely reached his shoulder. Sandy bounded down the steps, looking rather like a human golden retriever.

"This is Fran," he said unceremoniously. "Fran, Margo."

Fran picked her way carefully down the steps. "Pleased to make your acquaintance," she said primly, extending a dainty manicured hand. She was neatly dressed in slacks and a navy cardigan. A pair of glasses perched atop her neatly coiffed head. Everything about her gave the impression of neatness.

"Likewise. So, what kind of problems are you having?"

"Please, won't you come in?" she said, motioning toward the front door. We followed her up the steps and into a cozy living room that, like its inhabitant, was exquisitely tidy. "You see," she continued, "ever since Carlson—my husband—passed away, I've been hearing the strangest noises at night."

We followed her down a hall into a tidy bedroom. On a nightstand next to the bed was a framed photograph of a younger (but still tidy) version or herself and a pleasant-looking man, presumably the late Carlson. "The sounds are coming from right up there," she said pointing to the ceiling. "It's Carlson, I just know it is. You see, he didn't say goodbye, and that's...well, it's just not like him."

Sandy was already on his hands and knees, examining

the baseboards. "Can you describe the noises?" he asked, without looking up.

"Shuffling, scratching...not very loud. And only at night."

I took out my pen and notepad. "Anything else? Any voices? Shadows, objects being moved?"

She shook her head, a little sadly, it seemed. "I called you because I want him to know it's okay."

"That what's okay?"

"That I'm not angry with him for leaving so suddenly."

Sandy and I exchanged looks over her head. It wouldn't be the first time we'd had to deal with a bereaved relative who hoped we could pass on a message to their dearly departed. "Fran," I said, "I have to be perfectly honest with you. First, only the tiniest fraction of the cases we investigate can actually be attributed to anything even remotely paranormal. The very first thing we do is look for a perfectly normal physical cause for these noises. Second, please understand that even if we are able to determine that the noises are caused by something paranormal, we might never know exactly who or what is causing them. And third, even if we could prove that it's Mr. Friedman, there's no guarantee that we will be able to communicate with him. We've only just begun our research in this area. We have a long way to go yet."

"Don't worry, dear," she said, patting my arm. "I have faith in you. How did you get that bump on your head?"

"Oh...I, bumped into something. I was, um...cleaning out my garage." I didn't think it would be a good idea to go into the details of the poltergeist haunting the Pig and Whistle. The owner wasn't too keen on word getting out.

"Well, it looks painful, dear. Try putting some arnica on it. Come, let me show you the rest of the house."

Sandy was out in the hall nosing around. "Can I have a look in the attic?" he asked.

"Certainly, dear. It's right there." A cord hung from a rectangle in the hall ceiling. Sandy pulled it to reveal a set of rickety folding stairs. He tugged on a rung and the ladder unfolded with a metallic creak. A puff of hot air filled the hall.

"Do be careful; it's only partially floored."

"I just want to take a quick look." He climbed up and glanced quickly around. "Thanks," he said, backing slowly down. He folded the stairs back up into the ceiling.

Fran showed us the rest of the house, so spotless it reminded me of a museum. Making our way to the front door, we paused in front of a table and Fran stopped to pick up a photograph in an ornate frame. It was her wedding photo. An inconceivably young Fran and Carlson beamed at me from half a century ago. I studied the photo for a moment, then handed it back to her without comment. "We were high school sweethearts," she said as she gently placed the frame back in its spot.

"Do you have any children?" I looked at her but she was looking at something behind me. I turned around and noticed a photograph on the wall of a teenage boy.

"Just one," she said, nodding toward the photograph. "Mike. He was killed in a car wreck his junior year in high school." I moved closer to the photograph for a better look. Mike had a cloud of unruly golden hair and a sunny smile encased in metal braces. He looked like half the guys I went to school with. Poor Fran. Why does bad stuff always happen to nice people?

She seemed so sad. "I'm really sorry, Fran. It sounds like you miss them both a lot. How long have you lived here?"

"We bought the place new, in 1972. Mike was just a toddler when we moved in."

I made a few notes while she spoke. Fran seemed perfectly rational and not overly inclined to paranoid fantasies. "Okay, I think we have everything we need. How about if we come back tomorrow night?"

She opened the door and we all went out on to the front porch. "That would be lovely, dear. Will it be just the two of you?"

"I'll be here, but I'll have a different investigator with me."

Fran looked disappointed. She seemed to have taken a liking to Sandy, which was altogether understandable.

"Sandy mostly handles our, um, administrative stuff." I figure the less said about a paranormal investigator with a morbid fear of ghosts, the better. "I'll be bringing one of our technical experts. Actually, our only technical expert."

Sandy was disentangling his bike from the shrubs when he suddenly looked up and asked "Fran, how did your husband pass away?"

Fran pointed sadly to a tree whose branches hung perilously close to the roof. "It was just after that last big storm. A limb fell off of that tree right onto the roof! Carlson was always so good about keeping the place up...he had a heart attack. He might have survived it, but he... fell." She straightened her shoulders and shook her head slightly, as if shaking off the sad memory. "I'll show you. It's right around here."

Sandy let the bike fall back into the hedge and the three of us trooped around to the side of the house. "Isn't that your bedroom window?" asked Sandy, pointing to the window directly below the tree. She nodded. The stub of a limb still pointed right at the roof. "Did it do much damage to the roof?"

"Oh, I don't really know," replied Fran, waving her hand dismissively. "I never thought much about it after...afterwards, you know."

Sandy walked around, examining the roof intently, then said abruptly "Well, I guess that's everything." We bid Fran goodbye and made her promise to call if anything happened before the investigation. Sandy walked his bike to the street.

"Nice lady," he remarked.

"She sure is. I hope we can help her."

"Hmm, I think there's a hole in the roof. I'm willing to bet money she's never gone up there to look."

"We'll make it a point to check out the attic when we're there tomorrow night. We can fill Ernie in on all the details this afternoon. You wanna put your bike in the back and I'll give you a ride to Ernie's?" Terrified though he may be of ghosts, looking at evidence somehow doesn't seem to bother him.

"No, thanks. I'd rather ride. I'll probably get there before you do." He waved as he pedaled away.

# The Mission

*When I* pulled up in front of Ernie's apartment, I was surprised to see that Elaine's car was already there. Sandy, as promised, cycled up just ahead of me. We walked up the sidewalk together and Sandy rang the doorbell; loud, high-pitched yapping ensued.

The door opened and a tiny ball of white fluff bounded out the door, barking hysterically. "Shut up, Fang." Ernie scooped up the dog, which squirmed and struggled mightily for something so small. Elaine was already sitting at the dining room table, examining something on a computer screen. Ernie finally gave up the struggle with Fang and put him down. He bounced energetically around our feet.

It was then that I noticed the look of excitement on Ernie's face. For an instant, I wondered if maybe there was some hope for him after all. But Ernie's excitement had nothing to do with Elaine. He practically dragged us bodily into his dining room. "Look at this!"

Elaine was looking at the footage from the video camera we set up in the upstairs hallway. She was wearing a slinky ankle-length dress, but it didn't completely hide the leg she'd injured, which was wrapped in a bandage. "We had been investigating about 45 minutes when this happened," she said, gesturing to her bandaged leg. "So normally, we should have 45 minutes of video to examine."

"This is that new invention I told you about," said Ernie. "My program edits out every frame that is exactly the same as the previous frame."

"In other words, the ones not capturing any movements," said Sandy, upon whose shoes Fang was now gnawing contentedly.

"Right," he continued, "in fact, it edits out the vast majority of the tape. We can play back the entire evening, all 45 minutes of it, in about two minutes."

Elaine clicked the Start button and I watched us moving around in the hallway. The first few seconds consisted of Ernie telling the camera the date and location. Then Elaine and I appeared at the other end of the hall with our gadgets. No surprises so far. But the next frame showed something totally unexpected. A fuzzy white blob appeared, floating, at the top of the stairs. It hovered there for an instant. Then I watched, transfixed, as it streaked, like a flash of lightening, toward the room where we had found the box. It vanished and I saw myself and Elaine charge after it and into the wrong room by mistake. A frame later, Ernie emerged on the stairs and followed us into the same room. Instantly, Elaine emerged and disappeared down the stairs. I saw myself go into the next room, followed by Elaine, then followed by Ernie. Then I saw myself heading down the stairs to tell the client our investigation was over.

"How long did it take you to find it?" I asked.

"About fifteen seconds," he answered proudly. I suspect his excitement had rather more to do with the success of his program than with capturing the apparition. Who can blame him? I'm just glad he's on our side.

We played the footage over and over again. The apparition lasted about four seconds.

"What about the video camera that you set up downstairs?" I asked.

Ernie shrugged. "No video, only audio. We got the footsteps that you heard, although it could be just you two walking around upstairs. Nothing in any of the still photos, either."

"I'll take this footage over to my buddy Lamar in the Photography department next week to be sure it's not just some kind of photographic anomaly," said Sandy. "What about the night-vision cameras?"

"The tool works on those, too. The place was clean. We got nothing except a cat running across the back yard."

"This is really fabulous, Ernie," I said. I ran the video again, clicking through the part with the apparition one frame at a time. There were no features, just a translucent white mass. "Something tells me our client is going to be none too happy when we tell her about this. By the way, did you see a doctor this morning, Elaine?"

She showed me some foul-smelling ointment she was supposed to put on her leg. "They gave me a tetanus booster, but didn't seem too worried. My jeans were the evening's only serious casualty."

"Do you at least get out of work for a couple of days?" asked Sandy.

"I should be so lucky. They said I could go to work as long as I keep my foot propped up on something. I guess it's time to listen for EVPs," she added.

"Too bad Ernie hasn't invented a nifty compression tool for those," I sighed as I put on my headphones. Looking for EVPs—electronic voice phenomena—can be a tedious task. I find it an oddly disconcerting experience, reliving those few recent hours of my life.

I put my headphones on and fired up my trusty iPod. I had just turned it on when we went into the first room, after the ghostly apparition at the top of the stairs. I listened to myself deliver my usual spiel: we come in peace, we're your friends, if you'd like to communicate with us, speak into this little thing here. For several minutes, I listened to mostly silence punctuated by some chatter. Then I heard something. It was very clear, and very disturbing.

"What did you find?" Elaine was holding one headphone away from my ear.

"Just wait till you hear this!"

Now, you must realize that a clear and understandable disembodied voice is very rare. While we do capture EVPs relatively often, most of the time they are incredibly faint and it's almost always impossible to understand what they are saying. They are very rarely more than the faintest of whispers, and generally sound like laughter or wordless babbling. The sound I was listening to was not of this category.

I plugged the iPod in and uploaded the recording, then played it back on the computer so we could all hear. I heard Ernie ask, "*Is this your home?*"then very clearly a woman's voice—definitely not mine or Elaine's—distinctly said, "*Help me. Save it.*"

For a few seconds, we just looked at each other. The only sound was a soft growl from Fang.

Sandy finally broke the silence. "So, who's got goosebumps?" Mutely, we all raised our hands.

Ernie played the sound clip a few more times. It was a soft, melodious voice—the voice of a well-bred young lady. She spoke shyly, almost hesitantly. Hearing it repeatedly did little to diminish the creepiness factor, but something occurred to me. "It could be saying 'Help me. Save it.' or 'Help me save it.'"

"You're right!" Ernie exclaimed. "It might make a difference." The four of us were equally divided on the subject; Ernie and I were certain it said 'Help me save it,' but Elaine and Sandy were equally convinced it said "Help me. Save it."

A spirited debate broke out, but I interrupted. "I agree that the exact meaning might be significant to the case, but either way, it's clear that we're being asked to save something. Instead of arguing among ourselves, let's try to figure out what it is that needs saving."

"Isn't it obvious? The new homeowner is remodeling. The spirit is uncomfortable with the changes in her home and is entreating us to help her save her home," said Ernie impatiently.

It was a logical hypothesis. It's not uncommon for paranormal activity to start suddenly with a major remodeling. But this explanation didn't seem quite right in this case for some reason. "I think it has something to do with the box we found."

"What's in it that leads you to that conclusion?" he asked.

"Nothing yet," I had to admit. "but I've only started looking. Ernie, you look skeptical."

He was shaking his head. "I think finding the box was just a coincidence. I mean, the old house sat vacant for several years before the client bought it. Half the floorboards in that room were rotten. I think it has more to do with dry rot than any ghost."

Elaine chimed in. "That's true, but was it a coincidence that we just happened to find the one with something hidden beneath it? What do you think, Sandy?"

"It does seem like a few too many coincidences," he said, with a good-natured shrug of his broad shoulders. "Let's take inventory of what we have so far. Even though you had to cut the investigation short, you already have a full-bodied apparition, a clear and understandable EVP, and an old box that might or might not contain useful information. That's never happened before, has it?"

Even Ernie had to admit it had not. It doesn't even happen on TV. The more I thought about it, the more I was convinced that there was an intelligent entity trying to get our attention.

# Letters from Uncle George

*By the* time I got home it was late and I had barely enough energy left to brush my teeth and flop into bed. But the box, sitting patiently on my nightstand, seemed to beckon to me. Extracting another newspaper clipping, I promised myself I would only spend a few minutes.

This clipping was larger and the date had been cut away. It was brittle and crumbled slightly at the edges when I unfolded it. Upon inspection it turned out to be a review of a musical recital.

> Friday evening last, residents were treated to a most delightful performance by the students of the esteemed Indian Springs Society of Musical Science. The program included selections by Bach and Mozart, as well as a sampling of works by the controversial young composer, Brahms.
>
> Of special note was the performance of one Master Milton Fairfax, better known as Stuffy. His performance of Mozart's Piano Sonata in A major provides yet another example of the outstanding musical talent being nurtured by the Society of Musical Science.

I was trying to imagine Brahms as young and controversial when the phone rang, startling me. I didn't recognize the number of the caller and contemplated not answering it, but curiosity got the better of me.

"Hello, Margo?" The voice seemed vaguely familiar.

"Yes..."

"Margo, this is Neil. We used to work at the same company. I ran into you at the store this morning. I hope I'm not interrupting anything."

Neil from Accounting! I was flabbergasted.

"Of course not, Neil. I was just reading."

"Well, I was just wondering what you were doing for lunch tomorrow."

"Oh, I um...I haven't made any plans yet." Was he asking me out?

"Great! How about pizza?" Without waiting for me to respond, he said "How does Umberto's sound? Great. I'll meet you there at 12:30."

"Of course," I stammered. "Umberto's. That would be great."

"Okay, see you then!"

Well, how about that? I had a date with the cute guy from Accounting! Elaine would flip when I told her. Feeling a bit smug, I returned to my reading.

Although it was getting late, I was full of energy now and wasn't ready to put the box down just yet. The next item was a letter. The edges of the envelope were disintegrating, but the postmark, though faint, was still visible—April 14, 1870. It had been mailed from Deerfield. It was addressed to Miss Louisa Grayson and I recognized the address as Marsha's. The ink had faded to brown, but the handwriting was clear and surprisingly easy to read.

Deerfield, April 13

My dearest Louisa,

As delighted as I always am to receive your letters, I must admit that I read yours of the 9th with some degree of distress. One of my brother's greatest strengths has always been his impeccable ability to judge character. It has always been so, even when we were children. I greatly fear that this is not what you want to hear, but my first impulse is to urge you to accept your father's opinion regarding Mr. Stevens. From what little I have heard, he hardly seems a worthy rival to young Roland, who I understand has been your ardent admirer for some time now. If your father's opinion is that Stevens is not a gentleman, my suggestion is that it could only be in your best interest to heed his advice. I can commit to promising only that on my next opportunity to pass through Indian Springs, I will endeavor to find out more regarding your father's objections regarding this matter.

On a happier subject, Celeste tells me that your father is holding a gala dance to honor your birthday. Oh, how it saddens me to imagine the speed with which these years have flown! How difficult it is to remind myself that my darling niece is no longer a little girl, but a young woman of almost twenty! Would that I could be present at your party, but I fear that business obligations require me to travel at the time. Rest assured that I will nevertheless be there in spirit.

All my best, dearest Louisa.

Your loving uncle,

George Grayson.

Louisa. I wondered if she was the owner of the box and the person who had so carefully stashed it under the floorboard. It seemed a reasonable assumption. I rummaged around some more and found a playbill from a concert on May 23 1870, in which a Monsieur Devereaux performed a selection of Beethoven violin pieces, and an engagement announcement from the newspaper for Miss Clara Fairfax. I assumed this was the same Clara who'd written the note tipping her off to Roland's plans to ask her to the dance. I wondered also if Clara was any relation to the aforementioned Stuffy, the Music Society's Mozartian piano prodigy. There was another newspaper review, this one from an Independence Day concert in the town square. I was ready to call it quits for the night, but found another letter from Uncle George that I couldn't resist reading.

July 19, 1873

Dearest Louisa,

I read your words with great sadness, but without surprise, I must admit. Some time back, your father made me aware of his failing health and reminded me of a solemn promise I made to him and your dear mother twenty years ago. I entreat you to remain cheerful and optimistic for your father's sake.

I am relieved to hear that my brother has placed his trust in you regarding the whereabouts of the treasure that he values more highly than any other material object in his possession. I must insist you not trust anyone else with the information regarding its location and under no circumstances must you refer to it again. To even write about it carries the risk of your words being intercepted by the wrong sort of person. It is now your obligation—not just to your beloved father but to all civilized people everywhere—to see that it remains safe.

The letter went on for another half-page, but the rest of it barely registered. Here, suddenly, was a mystery, ghost or no ghost. Was there a treasure lurking under the rotten floorboards of Marsha Darnell's guest room? Or in the attic, perhaps? What could be so important that its loss would affect all civilized people? I was pretty sure the treasure wasn't in the box, because I would certainly have found it already.

I glanced at the clock and saw, with surprise, that it was after midnight. I closed the box reluctantly, but sleep eluded me. I couldn't wait to tell Elaine and the guys.

The next morning I was the first to arrive at the office, which doesn't happen often. Sandy almost always gets there first and makes coffee, for good reason. I do not have Sandy's talent for making good coffee, and Ernie, as a general rule, is allowed near the coffee pot only to pour.

The only sound in our little makeshift lab was the humming of the computers. I heard a noise and looked up to see Sandy standing in the doorway.

"You're here early," he remarked, dropping his backpack on a table.

"Couldn't sleep last night."

"Does it have anything to do with the voice?" He rooted around in a cabinet and produced a sack of coffee beans.

I nodded and was quiet for a moment while he flipped on the grinder. "Have you finished looking through the box yet? What's in it?"

"Mostly a bunch of old newspaper clippings and some letters. I still have about half of it to go."

The coffee pot began to hiss and gurgle and a tantalizing aroma filled the air. "I found something last night that may be important." He raised an eyebrow. "I'll tell you both about it when Ernie gets here."

We sipped our coffee together in silence for a few minutes until Ernie staggered in. He grunted at us by way of greeting and shuffled to the coffee pot, looking rather like he'd wandered in from the set of *Night of the Living Dead*. We waited while he spooned a small mountain of sugar into his coffee and perched on a tall stool. It's useless to talk to him until he has had at least half a cup, so for a while no one spoke.

"So are you awake yet?" I asked finally. He mumbled something in reply. "I guess that means 'yes'." Ernie watched through half-closed eyes as I fished the box out of my tote bag. His expression didn't change when I plunked it on the counter in from of him.

"I think it probably belonged to a girl named Louisa. I haven't looked at it all in detail yet, but I found several old newspaper clippings and a couple of letters from one George Grayson, Louisa's uncle. I thought you guys might be able to help me make sense of some of it. So far, we have a couple of wedding announcements, some letters, and this advertisement." Sandy looked closely at the ad for Henry Grayson, Importer of Fine Teas.

"This building is now the hardware store downtown. It's in the Historic District. Changes to the outside of the buildings there are prohibited by city ordinance." No wonder it looked so familiar.

"But why save something like this?" asked Ernie, starting to show signs of life.

"Why keep any of this stuff? I'm pretty sure Henry Grayson was Louisa's father. Who knows. But the letters from Louisa's uncle, George Grayson, are particularly interesting," I said.

"Why do you say that?" asked Sandy.

"Louisa's father seems to have become seriously ill..."

"That's not unusual. They had all these diseases and stuff," Ernie mumbled.

"That was profound," I said. "At least he's waking up."

"Sounds to me like he still has a way to go," said Sandy. Ernie made a face at him.

"Didn't your mother ever tell you your face would freeze like that?" I asked.

Sandy snickered. "In his case it would be an improvement. So what else did you find? You said you found something really interesting."

"As a matter of fact, I did. It's right here." I took Uncle George's letter out of its envelope and unfolded it carefully. "Listen to this: 'I am relieved to hear that my brother has placed his trust in you regarding the whereabouts of the *treasure* [pausing for dramatic effect] that he values more highly than any other material object in his possession.'"

"Treasure?" Ernie was awake now.

I nodded and continued, "It goes on to caution her never to mention it again, especially in writing, and says that 'It is now your obligation—not just to your beloved father but to all civilized people everywhere—to see to it that it remains safe.'"

Sandy scratched his head. "I can't imagine what it could be."

"It's probably a fortune in Confederate war bonds," answered Ernie. "Or stock certificates for a company that went out of business a hundred years ago."

I pondered these words of wisdom. He was probably right. "I agree. We shouldn't read too much into it—it's probably nothing."

"Still," he said, rummaging around in the box "suppose it is something. What if there's a box of Spanish doubloons stashed in the basement and the map is here in this box? Now why do you suppose anyone would want to save this?"

Ernie held up a scrap of paper, about the size of the palm of my hand. Although faded and yellowing, the paper was sturdy and thicker than ordinary writing paper. Printed on it was a wooly cartoon lamb with a bow around its neck. The lamb seemed to be perilously close to stepping on half of a faded but fluffy yellow chick. A piece of newspaper was stuck firmly to the back of the scrap of paper. When I picked at the newspaper with a fingernail, small particles of it flaked off, but the two pieces of paper remained firmly bonded.

"Give it to me and let me try something," said Ernie, gently taking it from me. He took the scrap to the counter and flipped on the electric kettle that we use to boil water for tea. He mulled over it while waiting for the water to heat up.

"What time are you supposed to be at Fran's tonight?" asked Sandy.

"Around seven. Shouldn't take long—the house isn't very big."

What do you suppose this is?" He held up the bill of sale from the music store in Vienna.

"I don't know. All I can figure is that it's something to do with music. I can't read it...it's too faded. My high school German isn't much help here."

Ernie returned with a triumphant look on his face, carefully holding two pieces of very fragile paper. The bit of newsprint was faint and just barely legible. It was an article about a newly completed church. The caption was the only part I could read: "All Saints Episcopal Church Moves to New Home". I showed it to Ernie, but he barely noticed.

"Look at this," he said, showing me the back of the paper with the lamb.

In a neat, flowing script was written "Look for it here."

# Fran's Furry Ghosts

*"Did you* hear that?" Ernie pointed a voice recorder toward the corner of the Fran's attic. A sliver of moonlight shone through a hole in the roof. Except for this tiny patch of silver light, the attic was pitch black.

"Yes. It's coming from over there." There was another soft thump. I pointed my flashlight in the direction of the noise, but the tiny beam was lost in the darkness.

When Ernie and I arrived at Fran's a couple of hours earlier, she had seemed positively giddy with excitement. I soon understood why. When the noises had started up again the previous evening, she had taped them. Wanting very much to be helpful, she had played the recording back for us. Which is why I was already pretty sure that the late Mr. Friedman was not the source of the noises in her attic. As I had explained to Ernie, we were in a bit of a tight spot. She wanted very much to be reassured it was her deceased husband.

This investigation wasn't turning out to be much fun. There was so much electromagnetic interference that our meters were useless. Whether it was from the power pole on the street corner right outside or just poorly insulated wiring was difficult to tell because the readings were so strong. EMF meters are an indispensable tool for paranormal investigation, but are utterly useless if the readings are off the chart everywhere you turn. I used to be skeptical of people's claims that exposure to EMF radiation made them feel sick, but I've since learned better. Normally I'm not overly sensitive to electromagnetic radiation, but tonight I was starting to feel dizzy. That it was hot enough in Fran's attic to bake a pizza didn't help.

I finally gave up on the EMF meters and opted instead for dowsing rods. I always take a pair of dowsing rods with me for just such a situation. They can be an effective tool for the dedicated ghost hunter, although they take some practice to master. I once carried on a whole conversation with an entity. By asking yes/no questions, we were able to determine that our ghostly friend was looking for her husband who had run off and left her with two young children. Tonight I was—not unexpectedly—getting no response at all.

The attic was only partially floored, typical for a house of its time, and unpleasantly hot and stuffy. Ernie followed close behind me as we crawled carefully along the floor joists. The fiberglass insulation between them was making me itch. In spite of the heat, I was heartily regretting my decision to wear shorts.

"And so you think it's something to do with this Stevens guy?"

"Huh? Oh yeah." I had already forgotten what we'd been talking about. "The uncle certainly didn't mince any words. Apparently the girl's father didn't want

Louisa getting involved with him."

"Maybe it's because she already had a boyfriend...
Ralph or whatever his name was."

"Roland. You know, there just *has* to be a connection
with that EVP we picked up," I said.

"I'm not convinced. By the way, I took that scrap of
paper, the one with the animal on it, to Lindsey. She's
an art history major."

"And?"

"She said she'd have to get back to me. Hey...I think I
found Fran's ghost."

Ernie was peering into a box of old clothes, in which
were snugly nestled three baby squirrels. I snapped a
couple of photos.

"What are we going to tell Fran?" asked Ernie.

"The same thing we tell every client...that we'll call her
in a few days."

To be on the safe side, I made one last request for any
entities that might be present to speak to us before I
turned the iPod off. We took down the video camera,
which had been taping away merrily in the corner, and
climbed down out of the attic, relieved to be out of
the heat. I put the rest of the equipment in the car
while Ernie went to the next door neighbor's to get
Fran.

We loaded the car as quickly as we could. I didn't want to tell her too much, though I was pretty certain that we wouldn't find anything paranormal here. It occurred to me that Fran might be the kind of person who doesn't take kindly to wild things inhabiting her home. What if she called an exterminator? Now, I'm no fan of squirrels. They are beastly, evil little rodents that dig up my flower beds and hog the bird feeder. But these were just babies. I decided not to tell her about them just then, making a mental note to talk to Sandy first thing the next morning. We left with a promise to be in touch, and with warm wishes from Fran to Sandy.

Back at my house, we put the stuff away quickly and without much conversation. Ernie was tired and didn't hang around.

When I finally crawled into bed, I was still itchy from the fiberglass insulation in spite of a long, hot shower. I longed to sleep, but the box beckoned from my nightstand. Promising myself I would only read a couple of things, I picked up where I left off the night before. A couple of letters were stuck together. I pried them apart carefully.

"Oh, no!" I said out loud. To my dismay, the letter was addressed to Mrs. Bradford Stevens. The postmark on the envelope was was October 6, 1873. It bore the same address as the other letters—Marsha's home.

My dear,

I have just returned from my second meeting
with the attorneys, acting in my capacity as the
executor of your father's will, and I'm afraid the
news I have is not good. The stipulations of the
will are quite clear and the lawyers assure me
that it is legally binding. I believe it was not
your father's intention to punish you for marry-
ing Bradford against his wishes. Rather, his
concern was to ensure that the fruits of his
life's labors did not end up in the hands of a
man he had reason to believe was a criminal.
Indeed, in our last conversation your father
confided that he was in the process of disentangling himself from his professional association with this man. He would have succeeded
had Providence not cruelly taken him from our
midst so soon. You will remain in your home, of
course, and your father has seen to it that you
will be provided with an adequate allowance.
But the codicil in question is dated only one
week before his death and specifically be-
queaths, in the event of your marriage to Bradford, all assets beyond the house and a modest
sum for your living expenses to the Indian
Springs Society of Musical Science. In the event
of your subsequent demise, this august organi-
zation will receive everything remaining from
your father's estate, which, I hasten to add, in-
cludes his interest in the tea enterprise. As you
well know, Mr. Fairfax, the director of the Music Society, was a lifelong friend of your father
and is fully aware of your father's misgivings
regarding Bradford. He is well respected and I

don't need to tell you that your husband will find it difficult, if not impossible, to conduct business in Indian Springs. His only viable option will be to sell his interest. That your father felt the necessity of resorting to these measures indicates the magnitude of his fears for your safety, and should be viewed, I believe, as protective rather than punitive in nature.

Without exception, the lawyers are in agreement that the will is legally sound, and that the likelihood of successfully challenging it is vanishingly small.

Perhaps it would be best if you did not speak of this just yet with Bradford. I will communicate this information to him. I intend to deliver the news in person, although I fear it will not be well received.

Dear child, I can only add my fervent hopes that his fears were unfounded, but nevertheless I trust you will remain vigilant and exercise due caution. I will notify you within a day or two of my visit, which I hope will take place within the fortnight, as I shall be leaving shortly thereafter for my annual (and sorely needed ) trip to the seaside. Until then I remain,

Your affectionate uncle

George

I thumbed through the remaining items in the box, but found only some letters of condolence and a few pressed and dried flowers.

Try as I might, I couldn't stop worrying about this unknown and unseen girl. Is this neurotic? Maybe so, but I was convinced that Louisa had been patiently waiting more than a century for my help.

# Clues

"*I still* say that if there were ever a treasure in the house, it's long gone," said Ernie, looking up from the file of plastic parts scattered about the table in front of him. "Still, it wouldn't hurt to look into it, I suppose—it's way more interesting than Fran's attic full of squirrels."

"So what else did Lindsey's professor say about the scrap of paper?"

Ernie was working intently on something that looked like a kid's water rifle with a small parabolic dish of clear plastic attached to the end. He tinkered with it for a moment before replying. "Not much. Just that it's wallpaper, it probably dates from sometime between the Civil War and the beginning of the twentieth century, and it's fairly typical for that era. She suggested we have the lab analyze it for traces of adhesive on the back. Depending on what the adhesive's made of we might be able to narrow it down."

"And the handwriting?"

"This style of script is called Spencerian. It doesn't tell us anything; it was the standard penmanship taught in American schools at that time. It was popular until the 1920s."

I compared the writing on the fragment with the writing on Uncle George's letters. It was obviously the writing of two different people.

"So you think it's some kind of clue?"

"'Look for it here'. Doesn't it sound like a clue to you?"

"Super. Now we have a clue. Too bad we don't know what the mystery is."

"Well, think about it. It would make sense in light of what the EVP said."

"'Save it,'" said Sandy.

"Exactly. The activity didn't start until they started knocking out walls. But there's more to it than just a ghostly concern for something hidden in the house. I think something happened to her," I said.

"Stevens?" asked Ernie.

"That would be my first guess."

"Look," interrupted Sandy, "we don't know that the voice you recorded has anything to do with Louisa, or the box or anything. Think of how many people have lived in that house over the years. Maybe it's related, maybe it's not. We do, however, have a specific reference to something valuable that might still be in the house somewhere."

"So let's analyze what we know so far," I said. "Someone did a pretty good job of hiding this box. It's reasonable to deduce it was the owner of the box—I still say the most likely candidate was Louisa. The box contains a motley collection of personal memorabilia. It doesn't seem likely that it was just a sort of scrapbook, because why would she go to the trouble to hide it? It would have taken some effort to work the nails holding the floorboard loose, but it's something you could do quietly and without it being noticed."

"Good observation. But what do we know so far?"

"Have you noticed there's a kind of theme going here?"

"Hm...music?"

"Right. There's this playbill, these newspaper reports of various musical events, this receipt from the music store..." Sandy took the receipt from me and studied it closely. "And, when the father dies, he leaves his worldly possessions to the Music Society."

"Well, maybe he was a music teacher..."

"No, we know he wasn't...remember the tea business. He could have been a composer in his spare time, or given lessons, or maybe he was just a music fan. Who knows? I'm not certain where Stevens fits into this picture exactly, except that once the father was dead he convinced Louisa to marry him. And it was the very thing that the father feared. Otherwise why would he add this codicil to his will?"

"So the question is, who is Stevens, and why did the

father dislike him so intently?"

"If I may intervene." Sandy hadn't said much, but had been listening intently. "It sounds like a trip downtown is in order. There should be some records on file that could help clarify some of this. We might be able to find Grayson's obituary. Obits can be a good source of personal information. In the meantime, I'm going to see what I can do with this bill of sale." He trotted off to the computer with the receipt from the music store in Vienna.

The county records building in Indian Springs is one of those architectural monstrosities from the 1970s. Some famous architect no doubt received a great deal of money to design a square box out of concrete and glass—your tax dollars at work. I deduced that trees must not have fit into the architect's idea of contemporary urban design as I looked around in vain for a shady parking spot. A couple of hours in the afternoon sun would turn the car into a pottery kiln on wheels.

Sandy's bike was chained securely to a nearby bike rack and he was waiting for me on the steps. He double-checked his notes as I followed him down the endless hallway of linoleum that seemed to glow a sickly green in the flickering florescent overhead lights.

"I hope this doesn't take long," I told him. "I'm

supposed to be somewhere at 12:30. Don't let me lose track of the time."

"Ah yes. Neil from Accounting." Was there anybody in Indian Springs who didn't know about my date with Neil by now? "Finding out who owned the property in 1873 shouldn't take long, although none of these records have been digitized. We'll have to look through them the old-fashioned way."

We found the property records room in an obscure corner of the building. Enormous leather-bound books lined the shelves. Sandy found one stamped 1859-1885 and we lugged it over to a tall table.

We thumbed through the handwritten entries and after several pages, found Marsha Darnell's address. The entry confirmed that the property was owned in 1873 by Henry Grayson.

"When did the father die?"

"August of 1873."

Sandy shuffled through a few more pages. I wondered what he was looking for.

"Here it is," he said triumphantly. "It shows here that the property owner as of 1874 was George Grayson. Uncle George, no doubt."

"That's strange. The letter says he left the property to Louisa in his will. I have a bad feeling about this."

"Me, too. Let's go to the library."

"The library? What's there?"

"The newspaper archives."

We trekked down the linoleum corridor from whence we came and out the door into the blinding sunlight. "By the way," said Sandy. "I managed to squeeze some information out of that old sales receipt—the one that you found in the box. I scanned it and ran it through some filters. There's a date on it. It's either 1804 or 1824. I was able to enhance it enough to figure out it's for something that starts with a "V"—either a violin or viola, I would guess. I know it was sold to a man, because it's made out to a "Herr", whose last name starts with a "P". But that's about all I could get from it."

"Pretty impressive! Are you sure about the date?"

"Fairly certain. It's faded, but when I show you the enhanced version you'll see, it's fairly clear. It's far older than anything else in the box, by decades."

The Indian Springs Public Library is just across the street from the county offices. An imposing Gothic Revival fantasy, it makes the county records building seem even uglier by comparison. We crossed the street and climbed an ornate wooden staircase to the third floor, where we wound our way through the rows of books until we came to a bank of odd-looking machines.

A bored-looking young man with long, curly red hair sat behind a desk. He was wearing a black T-shirt upon which was emblazoned "The Oxymorons" in big blocky letters. He looked more like a musician than a librarian. As we approached, he looked up hopefully and smiled.

"We want to look through the newspapers from the 1870's," said Sandy.

"No problem," answered the library guy happily. "You want the *Herald* or the *Courier-Journal?*"

"I didn't know we had a choice," I replied. "I only know about the *Herald*."

"Hard to believe isn't it, in a town this size? But in those days there were two newspapers."

Sandy shrugged. "Do you have copies of both of them that far back?"

"Absolutely. We have the *Courier-Journal* back to the 1840's and the other one farther than that, I think." The librarian pulled open a large file drawer and shuffled through them until he found an envelope. He pointed to a machine. "Use this machine. You can print from it."

He showed us where the films were and spent a few minutes with us explaining how to use the machine. He seemed reluctant to leave us. I glanced around; we were the only patrons except for an old man sound asleep in a chair. "You guys doing a research paper?" he asked cheerfully.

Sandy and I looked at each other. The guy seemed harmless enough and I don't like to lie to people, but we do need to keep a low profile. "We um, well, we're looking into the history of a house that we think might be haunted."

"Wow! That's so cool! I'm totally happy to help you. Let me know if there's anything I can do."

Luckily, at that moment a woman came in and approached the librarian's desk. The librarian nodded reluctantly and went to help her. We turned our attention to the readers.

"He doesn't really fit the librarian stereotype," I said.

"No, but he seems to know his stuff."

It seemed logical that both newspapers would publish the obituary, so I took the *Courier-Journal* and Sandy took the *Herald*. The microfiche reader is probably older than I am, but I managed to find the page with the obituary for Henry Grayson before it gave me too much of a headache. Henry Grayson fell ill in the summer of 1873 and was dead by early October.

### Indian Springs Loses a Prominent Citizen

Family and friends mourn the death of Henry Grayson, who departed this life September 29 at the age of 56 after a short illness. Survived by a daughter Louisa and brother George.

Mr. Grayson emigrated to this country as a young man from Scotland and found his fortune importing spices. The business soon expanded to included fine teas. Mr. Grayson's late wife was the former Miss Maria Bettina Prantl, a child musical prodigy in her native Vienna. Mr. Grayson was a founding member of the Indian Springs Society of Musical Science and will be greatly missed.

Funeral services will be held Thursday at All Saints Episcopal Church.

I showed it to Sandy. "At least we've solved the mystery of the receipt from the store in Vienna," he said thoughtfully.

"This is great. I wonder what else we can find here." Idly, I flipped through the rest of the newspaper. 1873 had been a slow news year for Indian Springs. A summer drought was killing unusually large numbers of livestock. Mr. D. J. Mararity purchased a fine new bicycle. A Mrs. Fishbein wished to thank the anonymous good Samaritan who returned her lost handbag.

But far more interesting than the news articles were the ads. A very fine lady's corset cost about five dollars. I was pondering the virtues of Dr. Campbell's Safe Arsenic Complexion Wafers (Guaranteed to add charm and clear the complexion!) when Sandy nudged me. He showed me a page from the *Herald*. Next to an ad for some stoves was another ad in bold type: "Now offering the finest black tea from Ceylon. For discriminating tastes. GRAYSON and STEVENS, 153 W. Broad Street."

"Stevens was Grayson's business partner!" I said. "Who would have guessed?"

"Well, Grayson had apparently had his suspicions about this guy—enough that he tried to keep him away from his daughter."

"So why keep him on as a business partner? Grayson started out in business for himself. If he was having seconds thoughts about it, seems to me like he would have dissolved the partnership."

"Yes, but think about it for a minute. Maybe that's exactly what happened. Imagine: Grayson begins to suspect his business partner is up to something. We don't know exactly what; but maybe he approaches Stevens with the idea of buying him out. Stevens panics and comes up with a scheme to marry his partner's daughter, understandably thinking that she will eventually inherit everything. We don't know if he knew about the treasure—let's hope he didn't. But Grayson won't hear of a marriage, so Stevens decides he has to get rid of his partner. That leaves him free to marry the daughter; he has no way of knowing about the stipulation in the old man's will. Now, if you wanted to get rid of somebody, you could slowly poison them with arsenic or something like it. It wasn't that hard to come by and Stevens would surely have had plenty of opportunity."

"Sandy, you're absolutely brilliant! Imagine Stevens' reaction when he found out he wouldn't be getting anything."

"I did, and I hope it's not what really happened."

# A Date with Neil

"*Was that* your stomach making that noise?"

I realized suddenly that I was hungry enough to eat a small farm animal. I couldn't read Sandy's watch because it was upside down to me. "What time is it?"

"Twelve-fifteen."

"I completely lost all track of time. Look, I need to go. I'm supposed to meet Neil in fifteen minutes!"

"Well, this is just starting to get interesting. I'll stay here and see what else I can find." Good old Sandy; what would we do without him?

Gathering up my stuff, I dashed out the door and across the street to my car. When I opened the door, a wave of heat hit me right in the face. Not only was I not going to have enough time to go home and get myself fixed up, I would arrive looking like I'd just jogged ten miles. I turned the air conditioner on full-blast and slapped on some lipstick. It was the best I would be able to do and get there in time.

Umberto's Pizza Emporium was situated in a nondescript strip mall not far from my house. It seemed like a good enough place as any for a get-acquainted first date. No shady places to park here either, I thought grumpily as I parked and straightened my hair in the rear-view mirror.

It was comfortably cool inside Umberto's, but once my eyes adjusted to the darkness I could see that Neil was not there yet. I told the hostess I was meeting someone and followed her to a table that—thankfully—had some breadsticks I could munch on.

Fifteen minutes later Neil still had not shown up and I was ready to eat the tablecloth. Just as I was contemplating making a discrete exit and popping into the sandwich shop next door, the door opened and Neil sauntered in. Both relieved and annoyed, I waved at him as he looked around and spotted me. I had time to scrutinize him as he approached the table.

He hadn't exactly taken pains with his appearance. His T-shirt was worn and ratty and his footwear consisted of faded flip-fops that slapped his feet as he walked. At least now I was glad I hadn't had time to go home and get dressed up.

Allow me to interject a little unasked-for fashion advice to the men in the audience. Showing up for a date, no matter how casual, in a T-shirt and flip-flops is not—I repeat not—the way to impress a girl. Let's be frank. Guys, you have ugly feet. Your hairy Hobbit toes should be kept decorously hidden from view at all times. Women, on the other hand, wear sandals in public and they look good on us for the simple reason that we get pedicures. Also, please remember that any article of clothing that never failed to impress your college fraternity brothers, such as your now torn and faded 'I'm with Stupid' T-shirt, is guaranteed to impart exactly the opposite sentiment in a date.

I stood up as Neil approached the table and we shook hands. "Sorry I'm late."

"That's okay. I haven't been here that long," I lied. "So, how've you been?"

We had just begun to chit-chat when the waitress appeared out of the gloom to take his drink order, brazenly checking him out. "Have you had time to look over the menu yet?"

"Oh sorry. Can you come back in a few minutes?"

I was practically drooling from hunger, the breadsticks having only made me hungrier. His appearance was not that of someone likely to leave a generous tip. No doubt we would have to wait an eternity before she came back.

Neil was still deciding what to order when the waitress finally came back with his drink. I ordered a small mushroom pizza. The waitress refilled my tea, then hovered patiently for Neil to decide. My mind drifted to the Graysons; I could hardly wait to tell Elaine and Ernie what we'd found out.

"You know, the lasagna sounds really good," he said at long last.

"There's about a twenty-minute wait," warned the

waitress. I was going to starve to death, right here at Umberto's. "Could we have some more breadsticks?" She threw a look at me over her shoulder as she disappeared back into the darkness.

"So," said Neil. "You said you were studying plants. Is that, like, full-time? Or do you also have a job?"

I debated whether I should tell him the honest truth or just sort of skirt the details a little bit. I needn't have worried. Before I could get a word out, Neil launched into a diatribe against our former employer. When at long last my pizza arrived, cold and with grease congealing on its surface, I thought perhaps there might be a lull in this "conversation." By the time I'd finished my pizza, he was still ranting—now about his ex-wives, and had barely touched his food. I didn't hear much of what he had to say. My mind had clicked off somewhere around the second divorce, and I was wondering about the business partnership of Grayson and Stevens when the waitress came back around to ask us if we needed anything else.

"Oh, no. Just the check, please." I practically jumped at her. Neil, not getting the hint, continued with the harangue against his first ex-wife. I abandoned all pretense at paying attention and was looking for an opening so I could make an excuse to duck out when my phone rang. Please let this be someone who desperately needs to see me immediately, I prayed silently.

Thoroughly overjoyed, I saw that it was Ernie. "Excuse me, please. Hi, what's up?"

"I had an idea that I thought I should run by you about the investigation. But I have to show it to you," he said mysteriously.

"Hm. It sounds big. I'd better come have a look. Right away." At least Neil had stopped talking and was at long last eating his lasagna. I couldn't tell if he was politely trying not to listen in on my end of the conversation or just off in his own little world, but he didn't appear to be paying the slightest bit of attention.

"Huh? Well, yes, but it's not really an emergency..."

"No, Ernie. I don't think this can wait. Can you get away from the lab? Anyway, there's something really *important* we need to discuss."

I silently willed him to understand. He didn't sound like he was getting it. "Okay," he said, sounding hesitant. "Meet me at the corner of Elm and Hillside. It's the northeast corner. You can't miss it."

"I can be there in about ten minutes."

"I don't think I can get there that soon..."

"OK, Ernie. See you in a few minutes." I hung up on him before he had a chance to protest. The check had arrived and Neil was staring at it as if it were a dead fish. "I'm really sorry, but I just have to go." Noticing that Neil seemed frozen in place, I finally said "Hey, why don't I get this?" I rummaged in my wallet and, to my relief, there was enough to pay the bill and tip without having to wait for change.

"Sorry to have to rush off like this…"

"Oh, don't worry. I'll pick up the tab next time."

"Sounds great," I yelled back over my shoulder as I bolted for the door, waving. He waved back, looking rather confused.

A wall of heat hit me when I opened the car door. "Ouch, ouch, ouch!" The steering wheel burned my fingers, but I would rather have blistered hands than wait for the air conditioning to kick in, in case Neil recovered from his stupor and followed me outside. In reality, the corner Ernie had spoken of was probably not even five minutes away, but I peeled out of the parking lot as if demonic entities were on my bumper.

I was only vaguely familiar with the area of town he mentioned, but I knew that Hillside Avenue was only a few blocks from Umberto's. As I drove farther along Hillside I began to see more signs of urban blight. I was beginning to worry that I'd somehow missed it when I glanced up to see the sign for Elm Street. This had to be a mistake. There was only one corner adorned with a man-made structure—a red brick church, abandoned from the looks of it. The other three corners were just empty lots, covered in weeds and discarded beer bottles. On one corner, a set of rather lonely-looking concrete steps led forlornly from the sidewalk to the remains of a foundation. I drove around the block. Sure enough, there was Ernie's Mini in front of the church.

We got out of our cars at the same time. Ernie walked over to me with an expression on his face that hinted at fears for my sanity.

"Don't worry. I haven't lost it. Not yet, anyway," I grumbled.

"Well, you sure sounded like it on the phone. What's going on?"

"Lunch date from hell," I grunted.

"Ah, yes. Neil, the Cute Guy from Accounting. Am I to deduce that it didn't go well?"

"You've no idea." He arched an eyebrow at me. "For starters, he was 20 minutes late. A couple more minutes and I would have started eating my shoes. When he finally did show up, he looked like he'd been cleaning out his garage." I tactfully didn't elaborate on the specifics of Neil's attire, as Ernie was wearing shorts and flip-flops himself. "Then I spent the entire time listening to him rant and rave about his two divorces. After half an hour I was ready to climb the walls. Thank you for calling when you did. You saved me," I added, with all sincerity.

"So, are you going out with him again?" He smirked.

I gave him a look that I hoped said more than more than mere words possibly could. "Just show me what you found that's so exciting."

"I think this is an important clue," he said, waving a piece of paper. I recognized it as the newspaper clipping once stuck to the back of the bit of wallpaper. I studied the photo in the clipping for a moment and compared it with the crumbling structure before me. The two were similar, but the church in the photo was much smaller and simpler of design. The front steps and entry door matched the photo, but the spire was noticeably taller and thinner. There were wings on each side that clearly weren't in the photo.

"They're not identical. In fact, there's a lot of difference between these two. Look at the spire, for example."

"So they've done some renovations over the years. I'm positive this is a clue. Why else would it be in the box?" he asked.

"Because it's where Louisa's father's funeral was held. This is probably where they went to Sunday services."

"And where did you uncover this little tidbit of knowledge?"

"At the library, in the old newspaper archives. Ernie, I really don't think it's a clue."

"Why then, was it stuck to the scrap of wallpaper?"

"My finely tuned psychic senses lead me to the conclusion that it might be because the wallpaper still had some glue on it."

He brushed my objections aside with a wave of his hand. "You'll see." I followed him around to the back of the church, glancing around nervously and trying not to trip over brambles. "Just look up there!" He pointed to a stained-glass window high above our heads. That it was intact was probably attributable to the fact that it was protected by chicken wire. A lamb holding a large banner appeared to be sleeping soundly at the feet of a lion.

"I'm sorry, Ernie," I said, rubbing my forehead. A monster headache was threatening to erupt, and I was having trouble following Ernie's train of thought. "I don't get it."

"Okay, Sherlock Holmes. I'll spell it out to you. We have a picture of a lamb, the back of which says 'Look for it here.' The piece of paper that was stuck to the clue is an article about a church—this church, where we have a stained glass window with a picture of a lamb. The wall under that window is probably two feet thick. It'd be the perfect place to stash something you wanted to be sure no one would find. Who the heck's gonna rob a church?"

I had to admit there was a certain logic to it, but something about it didn't feel right. Anyway, it hardly seemed worth all the effort. He was so pleased with himself I didn't have the heart to remind him that any treasure we found—be it Confederate war bonds or otherwise—wasn't ours.

"How would she have gotten access to the church anyway?"

"You have a point. But I still think it's significant and we should at least check it out."

"But Ernie, we don't even know what we're looking for."

"We won't know until we look," he answered stubbornly.

Defeated, I said finally, "OK, but I think we should include Elaine."

"You just want to gossip about your date with Neil from Accounting."

"Well, there is that. But she's part of this investigation. It's hardly fair not to include her," I said, dialing her number.

When she answered the phone, I could tell she was having another bad day. "Sorry, I really don't have time to talk. I haven't even had lunch yet."

"Want us to bring you something?"

She hesitated for a minute. She continued tapping on the computer keyboard while we were speaking. "Oh, thanks, but I think I'll just grab some chips from the machine."

"Didn't know you were on a health food kick. Hey, Ernie is here with me and we have plenty to tell you about the Darnell investigation. I just left Sandy at the library and we're hoping we could meet tonight at the lab."

She hesitated for a moment.

"I volunteer to come pick you up. I was thinking maybe we can get Chinese delivered."

"Oh, that would be so wonderful." I'm not wild about Chinese take-out, but it's Elaine's favorite and it sure sounded like she could use a pick-me-up.

"Okay, you talked me into it."

I told her we would show up around 6:30 and hung up. I called Sandy, but his phone was turned off. This was probably a good sign. If he was still at the library he must have found more information. I sent him a text message.

Ernie, in the meantime, had been trying every door and window within reach, but nothing would budge. He disappeared around the side of the building and I set off to look for him. Hanging around here was giving me the creeps. Just then he reappeared around the corner waving his smartphone triumphantly.

"I couldn't find a way in short of breaking a window. But I wrote down this phone number I found on the door. It's the 'number to call in case of an emergency'."

As I was telling Ernie about my conversation with Elaine, my phone rang. It was Sandy, sounding as excited as a kid on the last day of school. I told him about the plan for the evening. He was more than happy to go along. "I'll take care of the liquid refreshments," he said, and hung up.

"So Elaine's coming tonight, then?" I couldn't help but smile. Ernie is so cute when it comes to Elaine.

A crushing wave of fatigue hit me as soon as I climbed into my car. I couldn't wait to get home and relax for a little while.

# Louisa's Fate

*By evening,* I was starting to recover from my lunchtime trauma. Elaine and I were on our way to the Horticulture Pavilion in my car. "You know that receptionist downstairs?" asked Elaine. "The one that's only there a couple of mornings a week? Well, she went out with him. She said he couldn't pass a mirror without stopping to look at himself." For some reason, this struck me as especially funny. I laughed so hard my mascara started to run. Poor Neil. He didn't really deserve the abuse we were heaping on him *in absentia*, but it had been a stressful day for both of us and Elaine needed some comic relief. We were still chuckling when I parked in front of the Horticulture building next to Ernie's Austin. Sandy's ratty old bike was propped up near the front door.

"I hope they're not ticked off at us for being late," said Elaine.

"They'll live."

In fact, they were both already on their second beers.

"Sorry we're late," I said.

"No problem, I'm starving, that's all. What're we gonna have?" asked Ernie. We spent a few minutes perusing the take-out menu from Lim Yee's, the local Chinese hole-in-the-wall. The food there is the best in town, but strictly for take-out. Only the bravest of souls ever actually eat on the premises.

As Sandy phoned in our order, I pointed to the now-empty six-pack container on the counter. "I hope that's not all you brought to drink."

"No worries," replied Ernie as he cheerfully bounded over to the small fridge that usually contains only cream for coffee. He opened it proudly; a stranger could be excused for thinking we were hosting a neighborhood block party.

Elaine extracted a bottle of wine. "That ought to hold us for a while. Maybe we should get our ghost business out of the way before we drink too much," she said, pouring a glass for herself and me. "I haven't talked to you much this week. Did you finish looking at the box?"

"I did. The father suddenly became ill and died, leaving Louisa alone in the world. After her father died, Louisa married Stevens. Then she learned that her father had put some very strict stipulations in his will in case of that very eventuality," I said.

"Such as?"

"Such as, the will specifically states that if Louisa marries Stevens, Louisa inherits only the house and a small living allowance. Everything else goes to the Indian Springs Society of Musical Science. And if Louisa dies, the Music Society gets everything. He evidently wanted to make sure Stevens didn't get his hands on anything of his. Which is really odd, because we found something today to make us think that Stevens may have been the father's business partner. "

"He was," said Sandy. "I found out more about that today. Wait till you hear!"

Elaine scanned the printed obituary. "What else do we know?"

"Louisa and her father seem to be quite the music enthusiasts. Other than that, the only other thing I know that might have any bearing on the case is that she mentions hiding a treasure."

"Cool," said Elaine.

Sandy's phone rang and he disappeared into the janitor's closet, returning shortly with a short girl with spiky black hair. She was juggling a mountain of brown paper sacks. A wonderful aroma filled the room. "Thanks, Tracy. Let me help you with that," he said, bending down to take the sacks from her. Sandy was taller than Tracy by about a foot. She smiled gratefully up at him but he seemed oblivious.

Tracy glanced around, her gaze lingering for a second on the empties. "You're working late tonight."

"Just unwinding after a long day," I said.

It's usually Tracy who brings us our orders from Lim Yee's. She doesn't ask inconvenient questions and takes

care to make sure we get our order before anyone else.
That she is as hopelessly infatuated with Sandy as
Ernie is with Elaine probably has something to do
with it. "Well, gotta run. They're really slammed
tonight. Who gets the bad news?" Sandy barely
glanced at the bill—we always give her a good tip, and
were in an especially generous mood tonight. Perhaps
the liquid refreshments had something to do with it.

"Thanks, guys," said Tracy, waving at us over her
shoulder as she headed for the door. "Bye, Sandy." But
his attention was already on the sacks and he was busy
distributing little white boxes.

My broccoli with garlic sauce quickly brought me back
to the land of the living. The silly mood Elaine and I
came in with must have been contagious. Or perhaps
it had something to do with the growing pile of empty
bottles. Either way, it was good for our collective
morale. After entertaining Sandy with a recap of my
date with Neil, Elaine had us all rolling on the floor
with her imitation of my former boss, the mustachioed
Noel. She'd had a confrontation with him today and I
could only offer my sympathies.

Eventually the conversation returned to the reason
why we were here this evening. Sandy had spent all
afternoon at the library and was patiently waiting to
tell us what he found out. "Actually, I didn't have to
work that hard. Not long after you left," he said with a
nod in my direction, "I found this." He handed me an

article he had printed from the *Courier-Journal*. "You're not gonna like this," he added.

### Sensational Murder - Local Businessman Sought

Local police say the body of Mrs. Bradford Stevens was discovered Wednesday in her home by Mr. George Grayson, the victim's uncle. The coroner's office has issued a verdict of homicide, but is not releasing any further information at this time. Police are seeking any information about the whereabouts of the victim's husband. A household servant in the employ of Mrs. Stevens, Miss Felicity Mavens, is also missing.

Well, okay. I can't say I was really all that surprised, given what I'd read in Louisa's letters. But the details hit me hard. It was almost like hearing about a friend. I had to remind myself that it happened more than one hundred years ago

Sandy continued. "Here's what I've been able to piece together. Most of this comes from statements made to the press by the uncle. Louisa, evidently having been abused by her charming new husband, wrote to Uncle George, asking him to come take her away. Unfortunately, he was away from home and didn't get the message until he returned a week later. By then it was too late. He rushed to Louisa's house, whereupon he finds his niece murdered and the house ransacked. Stevens is nowhere to be found. The police suspected that the house maid, Felicity, was Stevens' accomplice, possibly also his lover. Uncle George suspected Felicity was reading Louisa's mail. I checked the headlines in both newspapers for the next couple of years. The offices of Grayson and Stevens had also been robbed of cash and some inventory and the account books had been burned. Stevens, whose real name was Claymore Prudhomme, was the prime suspect in this and several other incidents around the state." He handed us a few more news articles that he'd printed.

Ernie leafed through the articles. "So what finally happened?"

Sandy shrugged. "I couldn't find any mention that they were ever caught. The excitement eventually died down, and Indian Springs returned to its normal comatose self."

"None of the articles mentions anything about the treasure," I pointed out.

"It probably financed Stevens' escape," said Elaine. "You said something about a church."

I showed her the piece of wallpaper with the writing on the back and the clipping.

"Look at this." Ernie produced his camera and showed us a snapshot of the church and the stained-glass window.

Elaine examined the photo, then stared at Ernie. "To

be honest, Ernie," she said, "I think it's a stretch."

"So do I," I said.

Ernie frowned at us. "Well, I contacted the caretaker. He's willing to let us in. I told him we would meet him tomorrow at 6:00."

Elaine shrugged. "If I can leave work on time."

"I think I can squeeze it into my busy schedule," I said.

When I checked my phone after I got home, I noticed that I had missed a phone call. I didn't recognize the number, but whoever it was left a message. I dialed voice mail.

"Hi, Margo! This is Neil. Listen, I had a really great time. Call me, okay?"

Who was he kidding? *Delete*.

The phone rang in my hand at that very moment. It was Neil; I let it ring.

In a few seconds, a chime told me he'd left another message. Annoyed, I turned the damned thing off and went to bed.

# The Rescue

*When I* parked in front of the church the next evening, Ernie was standing on the steps with a rotund man wearing a greasy T-shirt and pants of some indeterminate color. From the looks of him, he had not spent much time recently in the company of Mr. Soap and Ms. Water.

"Rollie, I'd like you to meet my friend Margo. Margo, this is Rollie." Rollie somewhat reluctantly extended a beefy hand. I shook it with as much enthusiasm as I could muster.

Rollie fixed me with steely, bloodshot eyes. "I don't know what kind of folks want to go snoopin' around in some dead lady's business anyways."

With an air of great patience, Ernie said "Look, Rollie, it's like I told you on the phone. We just want to look around."

"Well, if you don't mind me saying, it ain't so smart to be hangin' around here after dark. Ain't no 'lectricity, anyways."

"Don't worry. We won't be long," I said, looking pointedly at Ernie. "We still have a couple of hours of daylight left. We'll be through long before dark."

Rollie snorted derisively. By the way he was scowling at Ernie, I got the impression he thought we'd be sitting ducks if one of the less reputable neighborhood inhabitants decided to pay us a visit. He was probably right.

He unlocked the door and ushered us inside. "Well, don't you go messin' nothin' up, y'hear? It may be a little past its prime, but this is still God's house. Lock that door behind you when you leave." Rollie lumbered down the steps, shaking his head.

"Strange character," said Ernie as we watched him climb into a rusty old Ford pickup.

"He is that. How much did you tell him, anyway?"

He shrugged. "I just told him we were investigating an unsolved crime. Well, it's true! I left out the part about Ms. Darnell's ghost, though. I didn't think he'd let us in if he thought we were a bunch of ghouls."

"I hope you brought a flashlight." He produced one from his backpack. Sunlight still streamed in through the windows, providing us with plenty of light in rainbow colors. But not for much longer, I reminded myself, glancing at the time. Not knowing where to start, I sat down on the stone floor. I was crawling around, looking for loose stones when I heard footsteps on the sidewalk outside. Someone was coming up the front steps. Ernie heard it, too, and froze.

Did I lock my car? I couldn't remember. I don't usually carry much cash, but my purse full of credit cards and keys was sitting in full view on a pew near the center aisle. Ernie, still clutching the flashlight, grabbed my arm. We crept, making as little noise as possible, to the pew where my purse was sitting.

"Stay down," he hissed. "And keep your wits about you. There's only one way out."

Slowly, the sliver of light around the door began to widen. Crouching, I made my way down the pew and snatched my purse. The door burst open and I stood up, heart pounding, ready to flee for my life—when Sandy strolled in.

"Anybody here?"

Ernie sat down heavily on the end of the pew, clutching his backpack to his chest. "You about gave me a heart attack."

"Well, excuse me, Mr. Holmes and Dr. Watson. But I found out something I think you need to know.

"You know they have these things called 'phones' now," I shot back, irritated to no end. "I almost wet my pants, I was so scared."

"Yeah, well, they work better when they're turned on."

Oops. I fished in my handbag for my phone and turned it on. "2 missed calls," it said. A little icon that is presumably supposed to look like a letter showed me that I also had voicemail messages.

"Sorry."

He made a face at me and turned to Ernie. "You're wasting your time," he said, waving a piece of paper in Ernie's face. Ernie took the paper and his face fell when he read it.

With a pained expression, Sandy summarized the news clipping for me. "The original structure burned to the ground in 1905. There was nothing left but a section of this front wall here. If your Confederate war bonds were ever here, they went up in flames more than a hundred years ago."

Had we been listening instead of squabbling, we might have heard another car pull up and park in front. I was still staring stupidly at the newspaper article when the door flew open and an enormous form filled the entire door frame. It was a burly cop—and he looked none too happy. For a minute, the four of us just stared at each other. I stood there clutching my purse and the newspaper article to my chest. How were we going to explain why we were here? From the way the cop was looking at us, I was pretty sure that telling him the real story was only going to get us into more trouble.

Ernie finally regained his composure. "I can explain everything, officer."

The cop shone his flashlight on Ernie's backpack, which was full of an array of mysterious tools and electronic devices. That the tools included a chisel and a spade had not escaped the cop's notice. "You can explain everything when we get down to the station."

Squinting at the cop's badge, Ernie chirped with alarm, "Station? Oh no, Officer...um, Kruszinsky. You see, we have permission to be here."

"Permission?" Unfortunately, one really irritating thing about Ernie is that he can come across as an insufferable egghead. Even more unfortunately, the cop seemed to have taken an instant dislike to him.

I tried to rescue us, but only succeeded in making things worse. "Yes, if you could just call Rollie, I'm sure he'll be more than happy to explain everything."

The cop glared at me. "Rollie. Yeah, right. Come on, you three. Move it."

Ernie protested as the cop led us down the steps and pushed us into the cop car. "No, really. I have the phone number right here. He let us in not half an hour ago."

"Put a lid on it. I said you could explain everything once we get to the station."

The three of us were jammed into the back of the squad car. Looking over my shoulder as we pulled away, I could see my station wagon and Sandy's rusty bike parked under the lone tree. I wasn't worried about my car, but what were the odds that Sandy's bike would still be there when he went back for it?

For once Ernie was at a loss for words and the silence in the cop car was broken only by the occasional disembodied squawk from the police radio. We turned the corner onto Main Street and the car screeched to a stop in front of the town municipal building.

The cop got out and irritably stomped around to my side of the car to open the door. I climbed out, awkwardly. The cop was herding the three of us up the sidewalk when I looked up and saw, to my absolute mortification, my former spousal equivalent walking down the steps of the municipal building directly toward us.

Oh, the horror! Imagine being arrested for trespassing, especially when you weren't really trespassing. Now imagine your ex strolling casually toward you, just as you're getting out of the squad car. Could it be any worse? Yes it could be. He was with a girl—bleached blonde, surgically enhanced (if you catch my drift), some years younger than myself. Whether it was the same girl I saw coming down the steps of the mansion the day I spotted Roger's car, I couldn't be sure. In a case of colossally bad timing, there was no way I was going to be able to avoid crossing his path.

Just at that moment, Roger tore his attention away from the bimbo long enough to look up and glance around. I knew this man quite well after having been with him so many years. This was not a man that missed much. He didn't show any sign of recognizing any of us, but I could tell from his smirk—and by the way he put his arm protectively around the floozy—that he had taken it all in. They leaned toward each other and he whispered something in her ear. As we climbed the front steps behind the cop, all I could hear was the two of them giggling like schoolchildren.

Our friendly representative of Indian Springs' finest shepherded the three of us up to a desk. The florid, gray-haired policeman sitting behind the desk looked up from a magazine and surveyed us with undisguised boredom. "What have you got here, Kruszinsky?"

"Trespassers," he replied stoutly.

"We can explain." "We had authorization." "Rollie let us in." All three of were talking at once. The cop behind the desk held up his hand and we were silent.

"All right! That's enough. Will one of you please explain?"

Ernie cleared his throat. "I talked to Rollie, the caretaker and he's the one who let us in. We were, um...doing some research."

"Research?"

"That's right. Research." He fished out a scrap of paper out of his pocket and plunked it on the desk. "Here's Rollie's number. If you'll just call him, he can explain everything."

The cop behind the desk motioned to a row of empty

plastic chairs. We slunk over and sat down obediently as he reached for his phone. I held my breath and silently willed Rollie to answer the phone. But after a few seconds I could see that the cop was speaking quietly to somebody on the other end, although I couldn't hear anything he said. After a very brief conversation, the cop put the phone down and glanced over at us. I saw him beckon to Kruszinsky. The two soon seemed to be having an argument, albeit very quietly.

Ernie elbowed me in the ribs. "Stop snooping."

An eternity seemed to pass, then Rollie stormed in. He didn't appear any too happy. With barely a glance in our direction, he clumped over to the cop at the desk. This time I heard snippets of conversation.

"They'll need a ride." This was the desk cop. Rollie muttered something in reply that sounded like "amateur detectives".

"Sorry, Rollie. Rookie cops. You know how it is."

"It's okay, Bill. Come on, you three," said Rollie jabbing a stubby finger toward us.

We scurried after him, heartily relieved. I suppressed an urge to turn around and stick my tongue out at Officer Kruszinsky.

As soon as we got outside, I glanced around discretely, but thankfully saw no sign of my former beloved and his nubile young companion. The rusty old Ford was parked next to the curb. Sandy's bicycle was in the bed.

"My bike!"

"No point in taking chances. Might not have been there when you got back," replied Rollie gruffly.

"Oh, of course. Please excuse me. I'm Sandy, by the way." He stuck out his hand, smiling broadly. They shook, and I'm pretty sure Rollie has a new friend for life.

"Well, there's no point in taking me back to the church, so I'll just take my bike and leave you guys here," said Sandy.

Rollie eyed Ernie with obvious disdain. "Ain't room for three up front. You'll have to ride in the back."

Ernie grinned. "No problem. It'll be fun." He bounced into the back and helped Sandy unload his bike. We waved at Sandy as he pedaled off cheerfully in the direction of Throckmorton.

Ernie, obviously having the time of his life, settled happily into a corner of the truck bed while I climbed awkwardly into the front next to Rollie. After a couple of tries, the old truck roared noisily to life. Finally Rollie spoke, keeping his eyes on the road. "Is one of them your fella?"

"Oh, no. We work together, that's all. Ernie and I have

been friends since high school." I don't know what prompted me to say what I said next. "My ex boyfriend and I were together ten years, but we broke up a few months ago. He saw us being hauled into the police station."

"Did he now? You say anything to him?"

"No. He was with a girl. She looked like an overgrown Barbie doll."

Rollie snorted. I took this to be his version of a chuckle. Maybe his gruff manner was just a front. In any case, he seemed to be softening and I found myself actually liking the guy.

We were still a couple of blocks away from the church when my phone chimed from the depths of my purse. Elaine! We had forgotten all about her!

"Where are you?" She sounded alarmed.

"We're almost there. I'll explain when I get there," I said, and hung up.

We stopped at a red light. Rollie glanced over at me. "You sorry you broke up?"

"Oh no! Not at all. We just...we weren't right for each other any more." How could I explain that the man I once thought was the love of my life thought I had gone off the deep end?

"Well, don't you worry none, little lady. There's plenty

of fish in the sea."

"Yeah, I know. Thanks, Rollie."

The look on Elaine's face when Rollie's battered old truck pulled up and we got out was priceless. Ernie slapped his forehead. "Elaine! We should have called you! I didn't even think about it."

Elaine was now gawking at Rollie. Ernie scurried over to him and shook his hand effusively.

"Thanks Rollie. You're a real lifesaver."

Rollie shook his head. "Don't mention it. It was just a little misunderstanding. You three be careful, now. It's about time you were headin' off. This ain't a good place to be hangin' around after dark."

He climbed back in his battered old wreck of a truck and we watched him in silence as he drove off.

"See?" said Ernie. "I told you he wasn't so bad."

"Wasn't so bad what?" asked Elaine. "Who is that? What have you two gotten yourselves into? And where's Sandy?"

"Oh, it's nothing," I replied. "We just got arrested, that's all."

"Arrested? Silly me, of all nights to work late. I missed all the excitement. So why aren't you in jail or something?"

The sound of glass shattering in the distance reminded us of Rollie's warning. We decided it was time to take his advice, so we climbed into our respective cars and reconvened at the Monk's Habit.

The Monk's Habit is a dark, cozy dive about halfway between my place and town. In a previous incarnation, the building was a church. The specialty is beer; the beer menu by itself is the size of the entire food menu at most restaurants. Farley, a jovial Irishman of indeterminate age, nodded at us from behind the bar as we came in. "Evening, folks."

We spotted a vacant booth under a decrepit stained glass window and piled in. The torturously uncomfortable booths are constructed from church pews. They add to the ambience, but after a half hour your butt is guaranteed to be sore. We huddled around the candle that provided the only light and studied the menu.

A waitress with multiple facial piercings and spiky white hair took our order and put cardboard coasters on the table. "Back in a minute with your drinks."

"So," said Elaine, "I can see that the two of you are decidedly in need of some liquid refreshment. Somebody want to tell me what happened?"

We filled her in on the evening's escapade. She was not amused. "Whatever possessed you?"

"It seemed like a good idea at the time," lamented Ernie.

Exasperated, she said, "Ernie, your hare-brained schemes are bad enough when it's just you and Margo. Must you drag poor Sandy into it?"

"That was my fault. He tried to call me but my phone was turned off."

"Well, for once I'm happy I had to work late."

A different waitress brought our drinks. She smiled flirtatiously at Ernie as she set the drinks down.

"That girl was flirting with you," I remarked.

"With me?"

"Well, it certainly wasn't with me."

He craned his neck to peer over the back of the pew behind me. "Not my type. Besides, she's too young," he said, frowning. "Cheers."

We clinked our glasses together. The beer was just what I needed and I soon felt chipper enough to mention the encounter with Roger.

"Well, what do you expect? You kicked him out," said Ernie.

"I knew you would take his side."

"I'm not taking his side. I'm just pointing out the obvious."

"Well anyway, that's not the point. The point is, he saw us being hauled into the police station. You know, he used to say that sooner or later I'd end up getting myself arrested."

"So you proved him right? So what? Anyway, are you sure he saw you?" asked Elaine.

"He saw me."

"What's bothering you more—that he was with a girl or that he saw you being taken to the police station?" asked Elaine.

I had to admit I didn't know.

"Then why worry about it?" Ernie asked. "At least you gave them something to talk about."

The situation suddenly struck me as being quite hilarious. I had a mental image of Roger boring his co-workers to death with this story—probably for at least the third time. I couldn't help but laugh. "You're right. Cheers!"

# A Blast from the Past

*A little* surprise was waiting for me when I got home. At Elaine's insistence, I recently joined one of those social networking sites. At first, I didn't see the point and I frankly thought it terribly teenaged. Then I started hearing from people I hadn't seen in years. The day's events had left me exhausted and in no mood to be sociable. But on a hunch I decided to check my page before crawling into bed.

Two people had asked to add me to their list of contacts. One of them, I noticed—not without some irritation—was Neil. I opened my inbox and read the message he sent.

"Margo, really enjoyed lunch today hope 2 go out again soon. Tried to call U. Sorry U had to rush off CALL ME 555-5623."

So much for spelling and punctuation. I am ashamed to admit that I clicked Delete with unnecessary enthusiasm. It's the coward's way out, I know. But I was in no mood to think about Neil. Besides, the second request and accompanying message was much more to my liking.

Margo,—hi!

I know we haven't seen each other in a long time. Could it really be 20 years? LOL! What

have you been up to? I heard from Gretchen
Fulweiler (remember her?) that you are still in
Indian Springs. I live in San Francisco now, but
will be in town this weekend. I'd really like to
see you! Please let me know if you will be
around!

Love, Tim

I knew him when he was still Timmy. The last time I'd
seen him was at my high school graduation. He was a
year behind me in school, but we had some classes
together. Timmy was short, a little on the pudgy side,
and a bit of a brainiac. He didn't do sports and had an
unfortunate tendency to say whatever was on his mind.
My best friend Roxy and I had to rescue him on more
than one occasion from the jocks and other assorted
bullies who were also in our class. They christened him
"Frodo" in reference to his abbreviated stature,
although he wasn't really that short, now that I think
about it. Timmy was the kid brother I never had. He
was such a sweet little guy. Looking back now on how
easily we'd lost touch, I felt a bit ashamed. I
remembered now that I'd heard he had gone to college
somewhere in California. (The aforementioned
Gretchen Fulweiler was Timmy's sister's best friend. If
I recalled correctly, Gretchen had been Ernie's date for
the senior prom. She had five kids now.)

I dashed off my reply before going to bed, telling him
I'd love to get together and forwarded my phone
number and address. It seemed harmless enough. I was

looking forward to seeing him again.

Not surprisingly, it took me a long time to fall asleep that night. It wasn't the day's adventures that were keeping me awake, but memories of my past.

That night, I had a terrifying dream. An unseen man was chasing me through the hardware store downtown. Try as I might, I couldn't find the door. Suddenly a woman appeared before me. Somehow I knew, as one does in dreams, that she was Louisa. She held out her hand to me, but just as I was about to reach her, a dark shadow swept over me and everything went dark.

I woke, my heart pounding, and pulled the covers over my head. This just hadn't been my day.

# Visiting Louisa

*I woke* up after a sleepless night with memories of the dark dream refusing to fade. "Margo," I said to myself, "you're taking this far too seriously." Or was I? Maybe I wasn't taking it seriously enough. My client was terrified. I was supposed to be helping her and so far all I'd managed to accomplish was to get myself arrested.

I decided to share my sunny outlook with Ernie.

He answered the phone with a grunt. "Do you know what time it is?"

"Sorry. I know it's early. I think it's time to finish up the Darnell investigation."

"How proud you must be."

"Look, the client is still waiting to know what we've found. We have some information now, I think we should pass it along to her."

"What? Is that why you called me at the crack of dawn? Margo, go back to sleep." (Note: The crack of dawn to Ernie is mid-morning to everybody else.)

"No wait!" I said. "Don't hang up. First I want to go to the cemetery where Louisa and her father are buried. It's the least we can do."

For a minute I heard only shuffling on the other end of

the phone. Finally he said "OK, I'm game. But give me time to wake up."

"I'll come by and pick you up in an hour."

Indian Springs' only cemetery was one of the few bits of history left in town. Well-tended and peaceful, the town's founders and most of its early residents rest here.

The curved paths in this section were paved but barely wide enough for a car. Not having any idea where to start, we parked along the road and started off on foot down the nearest path. We passed an old man lovingly tending a grave. He paid us no notice.

"Hey, guess who I heard from last night!"

I told him about the email. Ernie knew Timmy in high school and had once warned me that some day I would regret treating him like a pesky little brother.

"So are you gonna see him?"

"Well, of course I am."

Ernie laughed mischievously. "Do you remember the time we went to Europe with the Foreign Travel Club?"

Do I ever! In olden times, when Ernie and I were still in school, Indian Springs High School had a foreign travel program. Every spring, the best and brightest of Indian Springs High's language students were taken on a heavily chaperoned guided tour in Europe. Only the language students with the best grades got to participate. It also helped if your parents had a little bit of money. My parents didn't have much money, but my grades were high and my father was on the school board.

So our junior year, Ernie and I, and my best friend Roxy, waving goodbye to our parents with promises to behave ourselves, boarded a plane bound for Germany along with twenty or so of our fellow students. Timmy was one of them. We had solemnly promised his parents we would keep him out of trouble and proceeded to do no such thing.

"I seem to recall," he continued, "that you threw him bodily into a snowdrift that was over his head. I ended up having to rescue him. Do you still have that picture I took of the three of you covered in snow?"

"I think the photo album is somewhere in my closet."

"Then there was the night you took Timmy to the beer hall and didn't get back to the hotel until two hours after curfew, proudly lugging your stolen beer stein."

"Uh, well, yes. I rather treasure that mug. I went to a lot of trouble to get it."

In Munich, Roxy and I took Timmy to the Hofbräuhaus, even though we were all under legal drinking age, even in Germany. For reasons unknown to me now, I took a liking to the heavy ceramic mug in which the beer was served, so I stashed it in my enormous shoulder bag. It would seem that I am not the first person to have had this idea, as a couple of intimidating bouncers, dressed rather oddly in traditional Bavarian costumes, were making random checks of ladies' bags as they exited. They looked disconcertingly incongruous in their leather shorts, but I didn't think they would cut us much slack, so we decided to make a run for it using Timmy as a decoy. He looked so sweet and innocent—who would suspect him of being an accomplice to a petty theft? Already thoroughly inebriated after one beer, Timmy was turning an alarming shade of green. Doubtless sensing that a disaster was imminent, the Lederhosen-clad thugs were only too happy to rush us out the door, with Roxy and me clucking theatrically over Timmy. The ruse worked and the beer stein sits on my kitchen shelf to this day.

"You were lucky all three of you didn't get expelled from school."

"He forgave us. We stayed friends until I went away to college."

We continued walking, without any idea of where we were going. Paths snaked around statues and benches. We found something called a Garden of Remembrance. There were no gravestones here, only small brass plaques with names and dates. Peaceful, but infinitely creepy.

When, after an hour or so, we hadn't found a trace of Louisa I was ready to give up. Ernie wouldn't hear of it. Taking my arm, he propelled me down one last meandering path that we hadn't seen before. The graves in this part of the cemetery were mostly older and much more overgrown than the other sections we'd gone through. We found her there, in a quiet corner. Ernie carefully pulled back some ivy to reveal the headstone.

"Louisa Grayson Stevens 1850-1873." The only embellishment was a musical staff with some notes carved on it. She rested between her parents, as though even in death they protected her. It was a little bit unnerving to think that I was standing probably in the very spot where Louisa once stood, little knowing how soon she would rest here herself.

Suddenly I felt terribly sad. Louisa was counting on me, and I had failed her. I could almost feel her imploring me not to give up. Marsha Darnell was counting on us, too. She might not be the most likable client we've had, but she wasn't the worst by far. Underneath the tough exterior, she was frightened. It wouldn't be right to just show her some spooky evidence and then say "Now it's your problem."

"Ernie, we can't give up."

He was busily pulling up the ivy around the Graysons' graves. Without looking up, he asked "Well then, what are you going to do?"

"No idea. What would you think if I asked Marsha if we could do a follow-up investigation?"

He smiled. "That what I like to hear! Let's go for it."

"Super. I'll call Marsha first thing tomorrow and make arrangements. Do you have any idea how to get back to the car?"

I followed Ernie down a path. "I think it's this way."

"What makes you so sure? None of this looks familiar." He gave me a funny look but didn't answer. Ernie is notorious for being directionally challenged, but you'd have a hard time convincing him of it. I was getting tired and didn't particularly relish the idea of spending the rest of the afternoon wandering among the final resting places of Indian Springs' former citizens.

"You know," he said after a while, "we've been focusing mostly on the apparition we saw and the voice recording but we haven't really given this investigation much thought from the client's point of view." It was true. I suspected that all the indignant grousing about her property values was just to cover up the fact that she was terrified. I sometimes forget that other people aren't used to interacting with dead folks. "And," he continued, "we don't have any proof that the box has anything to do with Ms. Darnell's ghost."

"No, you could argue that it's nothing more than a strong hunch. But you're right, it could be a complete coincidence. However, we did capture a voice imploring us to save something, which, by the way, might or might not be the same entity as the apparition on the stairs. We don't know whether it's Louisa or not, but we know it wants something. Entities usually don't just hang around for the fun of it," I said.

"How do you know?"

"What?"

"How do you know they don't just hang around for fun? Maybe being a ghost is really boring." For this disturbingly logical observation I had no snappy comeback. "On the other hand," he continued, "if Louisa really did hide a treasure in the house, it's logical to assume she's still there because she's trying to protect it. And now she needs our help. It's never been an issue before, but now it is because of the construction in the house. And if the apparition is Louisa, and we can address her concern, we get two important things out of it. One, it should theoretically solve Ms. Darnell's problem by putting the unquiet spirit to rest. And two, it's exactly the kind of evidence that we're supposed to be documenting for our jobs.

"Speaking of which, I have to tell you about my latest invention. I've been working on a program to identify voices that don't belong to anyone on the investigating team. It uses the same standard voice recognition technology that's been around for years."

"Cool. I hope we find our way out of here some day so we can try it," I said. We were approaching an archway guarded by two angels with outstretched wings. It looked vaguely familiar. "Anyway, I'm starting to feel a little bad about not contacting Marsha sooner. Maybe we should just be honest with her and tell her we want to investigate her place again because it would be a good opportunity to test a new gadget." On the other side of the archway, I thought I saw in the distance a glint of sunlight on metal. I hoped it was a parked car. We followed the path as it curved through some trees. We passed a couple of family plots bounded by short iron fences. One of them bore the name "Mortimer" in wrought-iron letters. Its gate was secured by a rusty padlock and chain and waist-high weeds covered the plot, obscuring the stones. How thoroughly depressing.

We edged our way past the long-neglected Mortimers and found ourselves back on the road we had come in from. The car was only a few yards away. "That's a relief," Ernie remarked.

"Were you worried we wouldn't find our way out?"

He glanced back over his shoulder. "No, but it's so quiet in there. I was starting to get creeped out."

An email from Timmy was waiting for me when I got home. He suggested we meet for dinner the following evening at the Lawrence Hotel. I was secretly impressed—the Lawrence is without question the poshest hotel in town. If he stuck me with the bill the way Neil did, I'd have to take out a loan. I fired back a chatty response and realized suddenly, with some surprise, that I was really looking forward to seeing him. I began to feel nostalgic.

A few minutes later, my bedroom floor was littered with yearbooks, stuffed animals and posters of Adam Ant. I got distracted briefly by a small suitcase containing my dad's high school letter jacket (San Guillermo Central High, 1963) and a couple of beaded sweaters from the 1950s that must have belonged to my grandmother. They were miraculously free of moth holes. I tried one on; it was snug but wearable.

In a box with a pair of holey jeans that I could last get into during my college years, I found the photo album. Without opening it, I took it with me into the kitchen and made a cup of tea. When the tea was ready I took the album to the sofa and started paging through it, still wearing my grandmother's sweater. The photo I was looking for was near the front. The caption read "Me, Roxy and Frodo somewhere in Austria."

I studied the image of the fifteen-year old Timmy. He was about half a head shorter than me and mostly covered in snow. In spite of faintly exotic features, from an Asian grandmother, if I remembered correctly, he looked like a typical all-American kid. He looked directly into the camera from behind oversized glasses that made him look much younger than Roxy and me, although the difference in our ages was only one year. My arm was around him protectively, the mitten on my hand caked with snow. A dorky knit hat covered my hair completely, focusing full attention on my mouth full of metal braces. Roxy stood slightly off to the side and appeared to be yelling something. Behind us was snow and more snow. We all looked so happy. For a minute the past twenty years vanished and I was that teenage girl again. On an impulse, I carefully extricated the photo from the old-fashioned photo corners holding it in place and put it on my nightstand.

How long had I spent rummaging through old boxes? I glanced at the clock; it was long past my bedtime. I hung both sweaters in the closet but packed the jacket back in its box. A voice in my head tried to convince me that it was time to throw out the stuffed animals and posters, but I just couldn't do it. Except for the photo album, Adam Ant and the other reminders of my adolescence went back into the deepest recesses of my closet.

# La Fantasma

*I was* rooting around in the fridge the next morning, searching (in vain, as it turned out) for some cream to put in my coffee, when the phone rang. "Damn!" I hate talking to people before I've had my caffeine. I managed to dig the phone out of my purse and answer it before they hung up.

"Ms. Monroe, this is Marsha Darnell."

What a surprise. "Mar—Ms. Darnell, um, how are you?" I stuttered.

"It just couldn't be worse. I don't think I can spend another night in this house. It's been a week since you were here and I haven't heard anything from you. You're supposed to be helping me!"

"Ms. Darnell—Marsha—please, let's start at the beginning. Has something happened?"

She took a deep breath and sniffed dramatically. I couldn't tell if the tears were genuine or an act.

"I saw it again. It came right at me this time."

"What? The apparition? Was it the same one you saw before?"

"Yes, only this time she seemed...agitated. But that's only part of it. Some of the workmen quit yesterday.

The foreman said he'd never seen anything like it—they just ran from the house. According to the foreman they were terrified."

Well, now. This was an interesting turn of events. And the timing couldn't have been better. "I appreciate you calling me. I'd like to talk to the workers and try to find out what they saw. If I stop by your place this morning, is there any chance I could talk to them? I'd like to see where this happened."

"Yes, of course. I'll tell Ramirez to let you in. He's the foreman."

"Good. I'd also like to do a second investigation, as soon as possible. We have some new equipment we'd like to try. Is there any chance we can come in and set up tomorrow night?"

"Yes, of course. tomorrow night is fine." I wasn't sure she'd heard a word I'd said.

After we hung up, I checked my calendar—there was nothing on my schedule until tonight when I was supposed to meet Timmy at the Lawrence. It was early yet and the day seemed to stretch interminably before me. Was it possible I was nervous? I decided not. After all, I've known Timmy for more than twenty years. Okay, we hadn't seen each other since school, but how much could he have changed? Quite a lot, I decided. I didn't know whether the butterflies in my stomach were excitement or dread. I needed to find something to do for the next few hours. Not that there aren't plenty of chores to do around my house.

I glanced around. The plants were gasping for water, and there was still a gaping hole in the wall from a useless phone jack I removed weeks ago. Taking pity on the plants, I filled the water can and gave them all a drink. Having a house full of dead plants, I decided, gives the wrong impression. After all, I am supposed to be a horticulture student.

Watering the plants took all of five minutes. So reluctantly, I decided it was time I finally patched the hole in the wall. And while I was at it, I could go ahead and finish painting the bathroom hall. I started that little project three weeks ago and stopped in the middle of the wall when I ran out of paint. This ought to keep me plenty busy until time to meet Timmy, I decided.

I rummaged through the shelves in the garage and made a shopping list. I needed several things at the hardware store, including the extension cord that we sorely needed on our last job. List in hand, I jumped in the car and headed downtown.

Charlie beamed at me from behind the cash register when I walked in. He ought to; I spend enough money in his store.

"Help you find anything?"

"I need some more of this paint. A quart ought to do it

this time. I ran out mid-wall." I handed him a paint chip and followed him to the paint aisle.

He pulled up the formula on the computer and put the can in the mixing machine. Always happy to talk shop, Charlie was offering me some pointers on how to remove rust stains from porcelain when a customer entered the shop. With dismay, I recognized her—Ernie's Aunt Muriel. Not that I have anything against Aunt Muriel; she's fascinating. It's just that she was the last person I wanted to run into today.

Aunt Muriel has a unique talent. She can see auras. She claims she can tell everything about a person with one look. It's a bit unnerving, to say the least. She also sees angels, if you're one of those people who happen to have one or two. Supposedly I'm one of the lucky ones. My question, then, is, why do they never seem to do anything but get me into trouble? I just wasn't in the mood for a discussion about my aura today and tried, unsuccessfully, to slump behind a display of carpet samples. It was no use.

"Margo, darling!" she exclaimed, floating toward me, trailing a cloud of *Soir d'Amour*, her signature perfume. It smells oddly like burning plastic.

"Aunt Muriel, how nice to see you," I said, trying to sound more enthusiastic than I felt. The perfume was already giving me a headache.

She kissed me once on each cheek, in the French style.

This is how Aunt Muriel greets everyone, although as far as I know Paris, Texas is the closest she's ever been to France. "How are you, darling? Doing a bit of painting, I see."

"Yeah, that mint green wall in the hall was starting to remind me of a school lunch room." I showed her the new color, an elegant (I hoped) mauve.

"It's lovely, darling, and it goes so well with your aura." She studied me over the frames of her vintage rhinestone cat glasses. "Tell me, dear, how is that handsome man of yours?"

Slightly embarrassed, I said, "Oh, Aunt Muriel, Roger and I broke up several months ago. I'm surprised Ernie didn't tell you."

She waved a bejeweled hand impatiently. "Not him. The new one."

An image of Neil flashed through my head. I must have had a strange expression on my face, because Aunt Muriel said, "Not yet, I see. Well, not to worry, darling. It's just a matter of time."

"Thanks, Aunt Muriel. You made my day. Well, it looks like my paint is ready." With some relief, I followed Charlie to the cash register.

As I went to the door, I turned to wave good-bye to Muriel. She appeared to be deep in conversation with Charlie, but she saw me wave.

"Goodbye, dear. Give my love to Ernie."

"Will do," I said. Mulling Aunt Muriel's prophecy over in my head, I thought about Neil and shuddered. If there really were a passel of angels following me around, they must be having a hell of a laugh.

I had another stop to make before tackling my project. Ms. Darnell's house was only a few blocks from the hardware store. Several commercial trucks and vans were parked in front. I finally found a place to park halfway down the block. The foreman must have been expecting me; he was waiting on the front porch.

"Hi, I'm Margo Monroe."

He accepted my offered hand without warmth. "Ramirez. Ms. Darnell said to expect you." His manner wasn't exactly welcoming.

"I was just wondering if you could tell me more about the incident yesterday and show me where it happened."

Without comment, he opened the door and motioned me inside. I followed him up the stairs. "It was here. They saw it, two of my men. It came up the stairs and disappeared right into this room." He showed me into the room where we'd discovered the box. The floors were covered with drop cloths, and large sheets of plastic adorned the walls here and there. A couple of guys in coveralls were working diligently in one corner. They spoke to each other occasionally, but their conversation was strangely subdued and I couldn't understand what they were saying.

"Was it one of those men?"

He shook his head. "Those guys said they weren't coming back here, ever again. Now we're short two men, so we're gonna be late finishing up here."

"They quit? Both of them? Just like that? But did they at least tell you why?"

Ramirez looked me straight in the eye and said "It's the devil's business, Miss. They ran away, but me, I got no choice. I gotta come back. I got three kids at home. I know what they saw. I seen her before. It was *la fantasma.*"

# Chez Claude with Timmy

*A few* hours later, the walls freshly painted and patched, I glanced at the clock. It was time to get cleaned and spiffied up. Where does time fly when you're having so much fun?

The photograph of me with Timmy and Roxy caught my eye. For no particular reason, I took it into the bathroom and stuck it in the corner of the mirror. I compared the face in the photograph with the face in the bathroom mirror. Longish wavy hair with a tendency to frizz. A little shorter now but otherwise not much difference. (Maybe it's time to update my style.) The big round glasses, although the height of fashion at the time, gave me a slightly bug-like appearance. They had long since gone out of style—thank heavens. I like to think my wire frames are more flattering; if nothing else they're certainly more discrete. Anyway, tonight I would wear contacts. At least the braces were long gone, but I noticed lines around my eyes that definitely weren't there a few years ago. And the cherished jeans that I'd found in the box with the photo album seemed to have shrunk a size. Or two.

On the other hand, I was still in better shape than many of my classmates. Last fall I ran into the guy who was voted "Most Handsome" in the class ahead of me. I spent my entire junior year mooning over him, but he wouldn't have given me the time of day, had he even known I was alive. Fast forward twenty years, and Father Time had not been kind to Mr. Most Handsome. He was now bald as an egg and wearing a faded Lynyrd Skynyrd T-shirt one size too small to cover his spare tire. I remember saying a silent prayer of thanks to the cosmos that he had never noticed me.

I wondered about Timmy, my date for this evening. I looked at the cute little boy smiling back at me from the photo and tried to picture him fat and bald.

A closer look in the mirror told me that it was still going to take a thick layer of heavy-duty concealer to hide the bruise on my head. It was now a nasty greenish-yellow color, but at least the bump was gone. Not that it really mattered. The topic of what we do for a living was bound to come up some time during the night. I briefly considered making up some story to tell him, but decided against it. After all, I've known him for twenty years. If he thought I was crazy it wouldn't be because of my job. Anyway, I reminded myself, it didn't matter. He'd be here a few days, then he would go back to San Francisco. End of story.

The Lawrence Hotel is reported to be haunted by the spirit of a bride who was quite literally left standing at the altar. I wasn't altogether sure what to deduce from the fact that Timmy—excuse me, Tim—was staying there. A night there isn't cheap whether you encounter a ghost or not. Even when we were kids, being able to afford a night at the Lawrence was the sign that you'd hit the Big Time. Other than the fact that the jilted bride has been seen wandering the halls in her wedding dress, I couldn't tell you much about it. I'd never been inside. Polite but intimidating bouncers made certain that riff-raff like us stayed outside where we belonged. This weighed on my mind as I pondered what to wear.

I finally decided on a flirty black skirt and white silk blouse. I hoped it struck the right balance between "happy to see you" and confidently sexy. My phone rang as I was dashing out the door. It was Neil again. Would he never give up? With irritation, I threw the phone back in my bag and let it ring.

At the hotel, doormen were helping a middle-aged man in a suit retrieve his luggage from a Mercedes. A valet pulled up in a shiny black Maserati. He got out and left the Maserati running. It idled at the curb, purring like an enormous cat. I debated with myself about whether I should use the valet service. Although my car has a few dings, I keep it fairly clean and it still looks good, but I decided the Maserati was much too tough an act to follow. I found a spot in the lot across the street and walked up the sidewalk, hoping I looked like I did this every day of my life. The doorman politely held the door for me—I had passed the first test.

In the lobby, I glanced around in what I hope was a nonchalant manner. It was cool and dark in spite of the chandeliers that sparkled overhead. At the front desk, a couple of impossibly elegant girls checked guests in with cool efficiency. Everything was in neutral, old money good taste; nothing artsy-fartsy about this place.

I paused for a minute to let my eyes adjust to the subdued light, when before my wondering eyes appeared a tall, devastatingly gorgeous man with almond-shaped eyes and a frosting of gray in his black hair. I gaped at him like a supermarket fish, then threw my arms around him. "Timmy! Can it really be you?" This was, I rather suspect, the reaction he was hoping for.

"It's really me," he said, hugging me tightly. "Margo, you look marvelous."

I studied his face with a frankness that would be rude under other circumstances. There was a calm confidence in those liquid brown eyes I'd never seen before. And perhaps a hint of something else. Maybe I was imagining things. He was wearing a crisp white shirt with a tailored sport jacket. A wisp of colorful silk peeked out of the breast pocket.

"Let's go somewhere where we can talk," he said. "I was hoping you wouldn't mind if we eat at Chez Claude. According to all the reviews it's still the best place in town and we can walk from here." I tried to be nonchalant. Chez Claude was Indian Springs' only four-star restaurant. At this point, I knew this was definitely not going to be a repeat of the Neil Incident. I was on the verge of being completely swept off my feet and our date hadn't even started yet.

Tim casually draped an arm around my shoulder and we sauntered off in the direction of the fanciest restaurant in town.

I'd love to tell you whether Chez Claude was everything it's cracked up to be, but I don't have the first clue. I passed the entire evening in a daze. Call me a hopeless romantic.

As we waited for our dinners with unpronounceable names to arrive, we sipped a velvety pinot noir and got reacquainted.

"So," he said. "Tell me everything you've been up to for the last twenty years."

"It's hard to believe it's been that long!"

"I remember when you went away to college. I really missed you."

"Well, I missed you, too. I missed everybody, for a while anyway." This was a little white lie. For the first few years I so happy to be out of Indian Springs that I took every opportunity to avoid coming home. I was having the time of my life and seldom thought about my old classmates. "You know my dream was always to move to the big city—any big city."

"Yes," he replied, "I seem to remember you went as far

away as you could get. What was your major?"

I chuckled. "That's true. I guess it was kind of obvious. I studied computer science because I thought it would get me a good job. What I really wanted to study was art. After graduation I worked for a few years at a large software company which I'm sure you've heard of. But finally the stress started to get to me, which is why I ended up back in Indian Springs. I bought a small house near the neighborhood where I grew up and found a job that paid the bills with enough left over to enjoy myself. I reconnected with my old friends and gradually readjusted to small town life. That's my life since high school in a nutshell."

"Husband? Kids?"

I told him about Roger, leaving out my recent humiliating encounter.

The waiter approached and placed the bill unobtrusively to the side of Tim's plate. He whipped out a shiny gold credit card and placed it in the folder without looking at the bill.

"What about you?"

"I went to UCLA," said Tim, "and eventually ended up in San Francisco. It's home now. I spent a few years in the corporate rat race, then I started my own consulting firm.

"I got married just before graduation. It wasn't the

smartest move I ever made. The marriage lasted almost twelve years, but we've been divorced for a while now."

Surely this wasn't a pang of jealousy I felt. Anyway, he was divorced and therefore fair game, so what did I care? "Any kids?" I asked nonchalantly.

"No. We talked about it for a while, but Kendra was always too busy with her career. Eventually that's what did my marriage in. We just didn't have time for each other. So what are you doing these days?"

This is the part where it always gets tricky. "I went the corporate route, too. I designed software for a long time. But I had a rather sudden career change." He was studying me with interest. No point in being coy. I took a deep breath. "Now I'm a paranormal investigator."

"You mean you hunt ghosts?" I waited for him to laugh or make a joke. But he did neither. "That's absolutely fascinating. How'd you manage that?"

So I told him the whole story about Noel firing me and Ernie recommending me to the department. I told him a little bit about the Darnell investigation.

"That's so cool," he said. "You have the most interesting job of anybody I know. Including me." He signed the credit card slip with a flourish. "Come on, let's go see what's going on in town."

The night was mild, and we strolled aimlessly around the town square for a while before we finally found ourselves in a nightclub where a jazz trio was playing. I'm usually not crazy about live music on a date, for the simple reason that it's impossible to talk. Tonight, however, the music was perfect; sensuous and unobtrusive. We found a table in a cozy corner and ordered drinks.

"I bet you get asked a lot of really dumb questions in your line of work."

"That's an understatement," I laughed. "I guess the one that really gets me is 'Do you believe in ghosts?' You'd be surprised at how often I get that."

Tim laughed. "I guess you wouldn't be doing this for a living if you didn't."

"That's true. I think most people don't understand what the word 'paranormal' really means. There might be something paranormal going on, but that doesn't mean we can say for sure it's a ghost."

He looked confused. "It's not as complicated as I'm probably making it sound. The paranormal is all around us. It's only paranormal to us because we don't understand it. Imagine what would have seemed paranormal to a person living in, say, the nineteenth century that we take for granted. Air travel, radio, television, the Internet—the list is endless.

"Imagine Mozart encountering an iPod!"

"My point exactly."

"So do most of your investigations turn out to really be hauntings?"

"Oh no, of course not. Only a small percentage—about ten to twenty percent—turn out to be something we can't find a perfectly normal explanation for. But these are the ones that make the job interesting. But even if it does turn out to be a spirit, most of the time all we manage to do is record a faint voice or capture a moving shadow on film. Occasionally an object even moves by itself. But sometimes, if we're lucky, we encounter a full-bodied apparition. And when we do, I try to communicate with it; it's my job."

"I guess it beats writing software."

"Another understatement."

We listened to the music for a few minutes, sipping our drinks. "Do you remember the time Buster Snellins pushed me into the fountain?" asked Tim, innocently.

"Do I! I was never so furious!" Twenty years vanished in an instant—suddenly I was the teenage me again, and mad as hell.

In the central hallway of the high school was a shallow pool, the gift of the class of 1966. In the middle of the pool was a fountain consisting of a few water jets that squirted a feeble spray of water into the air. Our principal was smart enough to allow it to be turned on only on special occasions. The pool was about the size of a large bathtub but only a few inches deep. Once, while the entire student body was at a pep rally before a game against our arch-rivals, Deerfield High, someone dumped enough green dye in the fountain (Deerfield's school colors being green and white) to stain the tiles green more or less permanently. This particular special occasion happened to be Homecoming and the fountain was going full-blast. Roxy and I happened by just as Buster was dragging Timmy into the pool. Timmy put up a valiant fight and was about half in, half out and still clinging desperately to the side when we showed up. One shoe and an entire leg of his jeans was already soaked. I took one look and lost all control. Buster was perched precariously on the side and all it took was one mighty shove to send him flying backward. I would have gone in after him if Roxy hadn't physically held me back. Meanwhile, the crowd that had gathered was laughing uproariously. Buster, not being overburdened with excessive amounts of intelligence, at first thought they were laughing at Timmy. Once it finally registered in his few active brain cells that the crowd was laughing at him, not with him, he became irate, and vowed before what was now most of the student body to get even with me.

"To this day, I can hear Snellins yelling 'I'll get you back if it's the last thing I do!'" said Tim.

"Oh, he did. One nice, warm afternoon about a week later I went to my car after school and found a sack full of garbage in the back seat. From the smell of things, I deduced that it contained a considerable amount of steamy fresh doggy-doo—remember, he used to have that enormous Rottweiler? It had apparently been there, ripening odoriferously, all day. I had to drive around with the windows down for approximately the next month."

His eyes flashed angrily. "What a dickhead."

"Well, in a way, we got the last laugh. Remember when he was voted 'Most Likely to End up on Welfare'?"

Timmy laughed. "Like it was yesterday! Whatever finally happened to him?"

"He won a football scholarship at State, but flunked out spectacularly after one semester. The last I heard of him, he was driving a garbage truck for the City of Deerfield."

Timmy smiled, savoring this information. "You and Roxy took me home so I could change clothes. You know, you could've gotten yourselves in a lot of trouble." We weren't supposed to leave campus without permission. Once again, the three of us could have gotten ourselves expelled.

"Well, yes," I admitted, "but you didn't live far away and Roxy always drove like a maniac anyway. Still does, by the way."

"We were still ten minutes late for class. I was certain that we would all be marched to the principal's office!" But we didn't. Instead, we got a standing ovation. Twenty years later, I could remember every detail, including the tears in our teacher's eyes—and Buster's empty seat.

Timmy's eyes met mine and lingered. "You were so kind to me."

Flustered, I finally said, "Well, you were always one of my favorite people." I meant it truly. I hoped he knew that.

He took my hand and kissed it. I thought I was going to melt—this man was scrumptious enough to eat.

When the evening came to an end, as all evenings must, we walked slowly back to my car. Mine was the only one left in the parking lot.

As we approached my car, I suddenly felt uncharacteristically bashful. Are there any rules anywhere for this kind of encounter? I mean, what's the proper way to end a date with an old school friend? I sensed that he was feeling the same way.

"Margo," he said, putting his hands on my shoulders, "I always liked you."

"Well, Timmy, I always liked you, too."

"No, not like that. Like this," and kissed me.

Rendered speechless once again, all I could do was kiss him back.

# My Dilemma

*Do I* need to tell you that I hardly slept a wink that night? I was so preoccupied on the way home that I actually drove past my street and had to circle the block.

A cop car was parked at the corner; our neighborhood crime watch, I assumed. I glanced at the clock; it was almost 3 a.m. and the bars were closed. He watched me drive past. I made a point of driving carefully, using my blinkers as I turned the corner. As I waited for my garage door to open, I glanced in my rearview mirror and saw him drive slowly past my driveway. We were probably the only two people in Indian Springs awake at this hour. With my luck it would turn out to be Kruszinsky.

Ten minutes later I was in my jammies, photo of the teenage me with Tim and Roxy in hand, sipping a cup of camomile tea. I had no delusions that the tea would help me sleep, however, as I played over the night's events in my mind. What had just happened here? Had I just gone head-over-heels crazy over someone that in my head and heart had occupied the post of honorary little brother for 20 years? I studied the picture of the little kid with the owlish glasses. Maturity had sharpened the contours of his face, and his eyes were no longer obscured by the glasses. But there was a confidence in the grownup Tim, a certain self-assuredness, that was new. I shivered. There was nothing brotherly in his kiss. I found myself hoping there was more where that came from.

Then I stopped myself. "You're playing with fire here," I said out loud. I put the photo on my nightstand and made a mental note to myself to put it back in its album tomorrow. Alarm bells were going off in my head. Timmy meant a lot to me, and had for a long time. True, it had been many years since I'd seen him, but that didn't mean I didn't care deeply for him. He'd only be here for a few more days. Did I really want to risk destroying an old friendship? I decided not. Then I changed my mind, then changed it back again, at least half a dozen times before I finally fell asleep.

At the crack of dawn I was wide awake. In spite of my nearly sleepless night, I was full of energy so I decided to get up and go to the lab.

Ernie greeted me with a smug expression. "So, how was it?"

All I could do was grin as Sandy smirked at me from behind the coffee pot. "If you're trying to be cool about it, you're failing miserably."

"Is it that obvious?"

Both guys burst into laughter. "Do you have anything of special interest to report?" asked Ernie, wiggling his eyebrows suggestively.

"None of your business. Actually, no. We had a very nice dinner and a lovely evening."

"Are you going to see him again?" asked Sandy.

"Honestly, you two sound like a couple of gossipy old women. I don't know. We didn't discuss it. Anyway, he lives half a continent away, so there's no point in getting all excited about it." They weren't buying it and I wasn't even doing a very good job of convincing myself. Cupid's arrow had shot me right in the ass. I was doomed and I knew it.

"We have business to discuss. We have a second investigation with Marsha Darnell tonight. There's been more activity." I told them about the workmen who refused to return.

"Did you tell her about the evidence from the first investigation?" asked Ernie, scratching his arm absent-mindedly.

"No, but I did tell her we have a new piece of equipment we want to test. So you'll get to play with your new toy. What's that rash on your arm?"

"Rash? It's nothing."

"Well, whatever it is, you better quit scratching it."

While I fixed myself a cup of coffee, Ernie turned to a computer. A particularly ancient and grubby contraption, it's actually our most powerful computer. We call it the Monster and use it when we need heavy-duty computing power. He punched the power button and we waited, seemingly forever, for it to boot up.

Sandy pulled a chair over for himself and me. "The only hard evidence we really have are the voice recording and this video," said Sandy.

"What did the photography guy say about the video?"

"He enhanced it and examined it frame-by-frame. It's not an insect or headlights. Says he even drove by the house—I hope the client didn't see him. But he still doesn't have an explanation. In the enhanced version you can just make out a human form."

I moved closer to the computer screen to get a better look. "I don't know, you guys. You kind of have to use your imagination to see a person here."

Sandy shrugged. "That's not unusual. Sometimes when people see a human form, it's more their imaginations at work than their eyes. But it really looks like a human figure to me."

"She's kind of short," remarked Ernie. I rolled my eyes at him.

"What about the EVP?" I asked.

Ernie pointed at the sound wave that squiggled across the computer screen. "In this part you can hear me." He marked off a section of the sound wave and clicked a button. I heard Ernie's voice ask from the computer *Is this your home*? "This is the section with the disembodied voice. We cleaned up the hiss and enhanced it." He sectioned off another chunk and clicked.

"*Help me save it.*"

I shivered, and not because of the air conditioning. "No imagination needed here. That has to be the most distinct EVP I've heard. Is everything ready to show to the client?"

"It's all on the good laptop." Ernie was referring to the laptop we use to show evidence to clients. We use this particular one because it still looks presentable. Most of our computers are pretty battered. Of course, none of them still have their original configurations either. Flipping open another laptop, he continued, "This is the new gadget we're trying out tonight. The way it works is not much different from the voice recorders we're using now. But this laptop is equipped with software with a voice recognition component that flags any unrecognized voice. And I've modified it to accept this extra-sensitive microphone that I'm going to attach to it."

"You know," I said, "Marsha is not going to be happy about our findings. That her home has a presence is the last thing she's going to want to hear. We'll have to think of some way to present this to her without her getting hysterical on us."

Sandy asked "You don't think she'll secretly be thrilled?"

Ernie and I shook our heads. "She's remodeling because she wants to sell it. She wants to make it into the showcase of the neighborhood," Ernie explained.

"Plenty of the clients we've had so far were happy to find they had a ghost. Or were disappointed that they didn't have one."

"That's true," Ernie said. "We could present it as a great marketing opportunity."

"I don't know, guys. She strikes me as the nervous type. She's there by herself, and if you're not used to dealing with this kind of stuff, it can be unnerving—at the very least—to know you're not alone in your own home."

Ernie drummed his fingers loudly while we pondered the possibilities. After a minute, he spoke. "Margo, I agree with something you said earlier. Maybe the best way to help the client get what she wants is to help Louisa get what she wants."

"Yes, if we can communicate with the entity, hopefully we can explain what we're trying to do. I predict that if we help Louisa by rescuing her treasure, she will leave Marsha alone. If that's who's really haunting her house."

"What if there's no relationship between the entity

you recorded and the box?" asked Sandy.

"That's a distinct possibility."

"Still," said Ernie, "this is the perfect opportunity. We show Marsha the evidence and explain that there's a good chance that the hauntings will stop once we've figured out what it is the entity really wants." He looked at Sandy, who was shuffling through his backpack in preparation for his next class. "Sandy, I don't suppose we could talk you into going with us tonight?"

"You are quite correct. You've got more than enough evidence to convince me that the place is haunted, and me and ghosts don't get along."

"There's absolutely nothing to be afraid of," I interjected.

Sandy looked pained. We'd had this discussion before. We would have to tie him up and drag him in chains to any place with paranormal activity. "I'll take your word for it."

Ernie was scratching again, this time his other arm. "You know, Ernie," I said, "if I didn't know better, I'd say you have poison ivy."

"That's crazy. Where would I have gotten into poison—oh."

He looked so comical I couldn't help laughing. "It was for a good cause." To Sandy I explained Ernie's valiant effort to tidy up the Graysons' graves.

"Maybe you'd better find something to put on that," he said. "Anyway, it will be time for lunch soon. Let's go into town." Scowling, Ernie agreed. A few minutes later they headed out the door together. Ernie was still scratching.

I was wondering what to do for lunch myself when, from the depths of my purse, my phone rang.

"Hey, do you have plans for lunch?" It was Elaine.

I knew she would call. I hadn't had a chance yet to tell her about my date. "I was just wondering what to do. Where do you want to go?"

I had a sudden craving for Mexican. "How about the Taco Loco?"

"Oh, good. I was hoping you'd say that. Where are you?"

"I'm at the lab. I'll meet you there in about 15 minutes."

We arrived at El Taco Loco at precisely the same time and parked next to each other. We were lucky. In another ten minutes the parking lot would be packed and the line waiting to get in snaking out the door.

We followed the hostess to a table in the corner, Elaine teetering precariously on impossibly high heels.

I glanced at the menu briefly, but I already knew what I wanted. The spinach enchiladas here are the best.

Elaine flipped through her menu. Without looking up, she said, "I get the distinct impression that someone is a very happy camper."

"I'm giving myself away. The guys said the same thing."

"You're positively glowing."

"We had a really nice time. It was probably the best date I've ever been on."

"Oh?" she asked, putting her menu down. As if by magic, the waitress appeared and we gave her our order. When she left, the conversation resumed.

"I don't know what I was expecting exactly, but ..." I looked around at the riot of sombreros and piñatas that passed for decor, and today it seemed like the loveliest place on earth. I suddenly wanted to talk to Roxy. Would Elaine understand what a complete and unexpected surprise this all was? "I was completely blown away. I mean, it never would have occurred to me to think of him as anything other than a friend."

Elaine smiled broadly at me. In spite of the fact that she avoided commitments like the plague, she always wanted to see other people happily connected. "What's so different about him?"

"Where do I start? He's about a foot taller than I remember him, for one thing. But it isn't that. He was always cute, but in a nerdy little kid sort of way. But now he's just...beautiful."

"What's wrong with that?"

"He lives in San Francisco." The waitress returned with our drinks and some chips and salsa. I grabbed an enormous chip and scooped up a greedy portion of salsa.

"It's not that far away," she pointed out.

"I'm not exactly swimming in extra cash these days."

"So what's next?"

"Who knows? We've only gone out once, but it was so romantic. Who would've thought?"

"I don't understand why you were so surprised." She poked the edge of a chip into the hot sauce and nibbled it daintily.

"You just have to understand," I said. "He was like a little brother to me. Roxy and I were very protective of him. One time, a bunch of the football players had been picking on him, so Roxy let the air out of all their tires. All of them. As in the whole team. Timmy was like a little kid. He was just so....sweet."

"Little boys grow up, you know. It was 20 years ago. What did you expect?" she asked.

"Well, when I tried to imagine how he would look twenty years older, I never imagined he would grow up so...nice."

"'Nice'? Define 'nice'."

"Sexy. Kind, attentive, polite. And good-looking. Jeez, is he ever good-looking."

Elaine drummed her carefully manicured fingers on the table impatiently. "If you'll forgive me for saying so, it sounds to me like you're letting your memories of the past get in the way here. How long is Tim in town?"

"Just for a long weekend."

"Will you see him again?"

"I don't know," I admitted. "We didn't discuss it."

The waitress arrived with our food. Conversation resumed after a few minutes. "I talked to Marsha Darnell," I said. "She's agreed to a second investigation. I also want to show her what we found during the investigation. Can you join us at 6:30?"

"Yes," she said, "but I'll have to meet you there. Might be a few minutes late."

"No problem. Anyway, Ernie has a new tool he wants to test out."

"So you see, Fran, nothing we found leads us to the conclusion that the noises you've been hearing were paranormal. We just didn't get the evidence. That's why we can't say for sure it was Carlson."

Fran looked utterly crestfallen, as I feared she might.

"I'm sorry," she said at last, "but I just can't believe you."

"Fran," said Sandy, gently patting her shoulder, "just because we didn't get the evidence we'd hoped for doesn't mean Carlson's not trying to contact you. It just means we didn't get what we were looking for this time. Entities don't necessarily appear on demand. What I *can* tell you, though, is that you have squirrels in your attic."

We were sitting at the table in a kitchen that looked like a spread in a decorating magazine. Every appliance, every surface gleamed. Before us was what was left of a tray of homemade cookies. They were heavenly, naturally. Exercising utmost self-discipline, I ate only two cookies. On the other hand, Sandy had devoured a half-dozen before we even got around to talking about the investigation. I'm pretty sure this is what Fran was hoping for. She beamed affectionately at him.

"You remind me so much of my late son, dear. Take another cookie, won't you?" Sandy didn't protest.

"That doesn't mean that you've seen the last of us, Fran," I hastened to add. "We firmly believe that there are unseen entities all around us all the time. It's just a matter of collecting the evidence to prove it. We'll be checking back with you, of course. And in the meantime, you have our phone number." I licked a cookie crumb off my finger and stood, picking up my handbag.

"Of course, dear. I understand. Would you like a cookie to take with you? Let me wrap one up for you."

"Oh, I suppose another one won't hurt." She looked so eager, I couldn't bear to refuse. Besides, I could always give it to Tim. She bustled over to the cabinet and extracted a roll of wax paper. Deftly bundling up the remaining cookies, she gave Sandy and me each a neatly wrapped bundle.

"Come back and see me any time you feel like it," she called after us as we walked down the sidewalk.

"We will," said Sandy, turning to wave at her. When we got in the car, he said, "She seems to have taken a liking to me. Maybe it's because I remind her of her dead son."

"Probably. I'm sure she gets lonely," I said.

"Yeah, I think she's a little lost without her husband. Maybe we should look into helping her get that roof fixed."

As we drove away, Fran was still standing in the doorway, a tiny figure, watching us sadly.

The phone rang as I was driving home that evening. Normally I don't like to talk on the phone while I'm driving, but I'd kept it handy just in case it rang. Not because I was specifically expecting, or even hoping to hear from anybody in particular, mind you. And much to my delight, it was Tim.

"Hi, Timmy." And because I couldn't think of anything clever to say, "How's your day going?"

"It would be going better if I could see you."

Oh, be still my beating heart! Deciding to throw caution to the winds, I responded, "Funny, I was just having a similar thought." After all, time was running out—he would only be here a couple more days. I explained about the investigation we had scheduled that night and suggested we try to get together the next night.

Sounding disappointed (or was it just my imagination?), he replied, "I have a meeting tomorrow night. It's kind of important."

"When are you leaving?"

"Day after tomorrow, bright and early."

"Oh." My happy mood was starting to dissipate. "Look, I really want to see you again before you leave. We could at least have lunch tomorrow."

"Tell you what. Let me see if I can do some rearranging. I'll call you back."

Dear me, but this was getting complicated. But I didn't have time to dwell on it. Marsha Darnell was expecting us in just a few hours, and I needed to keep my mind on the investigation. Lots of luck.

# The Investigation, Revisited

*I followed* Ernie up the stairs with yet another case full of gadgets. I could swear the cases got heavier with every investigation. At the top of the stairs I paused for a minute and tried to imagine my surroundings as they might have been when Louisa lived here. In fact, the place probably hadn't changed much since her time. The paneling and stair railing were still masterpieces of 19th century ostentation. I guessed they were original to the house.

The evening sun shone through the stained-glass window on the landing, lighting our faces and equipment with dazzling patterns. I hoped this wasn't one of the areas our client was planning to change. To modernize all this in-your-face Victoriana would border on the criminal, but I doubted that the dark, ornate woodwork fit with Ms. Darnell's modern decorating scheme.

Elaine was already upstairs unrolling the extension cords. "It's going much faster now that we know which parts of the floor to avoid," she said, plugging in a power strip. She helped me set up a small folding table and two portable chairs while Ernie unpacked the computer we use for the night-vision cameras and hooked up the monitor.

The wainscoting in this room was considerably less

ornate than in the hall, and badly damaged in some places. That workmen had been in this room recently was obvious. A solitary soda can stood discarded in a corner. Bits of plaster littered the floor near where a wall was being stripped down to the boards. Ernie, every now and then stopping to scratch his arms, tapped around on the computer while I unpacked the digital video cameras. "I think we should put this in the hall at the top of the stairs this time," I remarked, "but angled so we can also see into this room."

"That's a good idea. If our apparition appears, we can catch her from a different angle." Ernie had extracted a large plastic thing from his duffel bag.

"What on earth is that?" I asked.

He handed it to me. It was the listening device with the parabolic antenna I'd seen him working on in the lab. It was as light as a feather. Upon closer examination, I could see that a small device was taped securely to the outside.

"It looks like a toy," I said.

"That's basically what it is. It's supposed to be able to pick up the faintest sounds; I replaced the headphone connection with this wireless transmitter. Anything it picks up will be recorded on that laptop over there."

I marveled at Ernie's ingenuity as he propped the thing up carefully in the middle of the room. "Let me know if you need any help. I'm going to set this camera up." I hauled the camera and a tripod into the hall. There was just enough room for me and the tripod in a corner at the top of the landing. From this angle, the camera would capture anything near the top of the stairs and also anything in the doorways of both rooms we had worked in last time. I turned the camera on and recorded myself doing a test run: down the stairs, back up again, and into the room where Ernie and Elaine were working.

I checked the test tape; if the apparition followed the same path as last time, we would get some good footage of it.

"Hey, Margo, come in here for a second. You need to say something so that the VR software can learn your voice."

"'VR software'?"

"Yes, voice recognition," replied Ernie patiently. "I need you to go around to different parts of the room and speak a few sentences. That way we can control for acoustics."

Testing the floorboards cautiously, I moved to one corner. "Well, all right. Are you ready?" He nodded, and I suddenly felt silly. What should I say? "Um, testing one, two, three." Ernie scribbled something in a notebook.

"That's fine. Now try that one over there." He pointed to a far corner where Elaine was unpacking various gadgets.

I was creeping along, skirting the edge, when Elaine yelled, "Hey, look out. You're about to step on one of the new voice recorders." I looked down; my foot was inches away from an expensive new gadget. "Sorry," she said. "I was going to put it at the top of the stairs."

"I'll take it out there for you when I turn the camera on." I picked it up and stashed it in my pocket, promptly forgetting about it.

I found a comfy enough spot in the far corner near a section of damaged wainscoting. Several layers of old wallpaper had been peeled back in one spot, revealing a layer of crumbling plaster clinging precariously to the lath underneath. Something rattled around in the back of my head, trying to get my attention, but I couldn't quite identify it. I decided it was just nerves, and it had nothing to do with the fact that I hadn't heard back from Tim yet—I swear.

Ernie was waiting patiently for me to speak. I tried to think of some profound utterance. "What do you want me to say?"

"It doesn't matter," Ernie answered, sounding slightly irritated. "I just need a sentence or two."

Elaine chuckled. "Do you know any poems?"

"Are you ready?" asked Ernie.

I nodded. "There once was a man from Nantucket—"

Elaine giggled.

"That's enough. You two need to grow up," sniffed Ernie primly, frowning at us.

"Let's do one more. Try over there."

"If I'm not back in a few minutes, send out a search party." I eased my way across the room to the far corner.

"You should have left a trail of breadcrumbs for me," remarked Elaine.

"Okay, ready."

"Jack and Jill went up the hill to fetch a pail of water."

"That's fine."

I traced my footsteps carefully back to Ernie's table. Elaine joined us. "Now what happens?" she asked.

"Now we just drag each clip into this program..." He click the thumbnails with their miniature patterns of squiggly waves and dropped them into a window. "... and assign a name to the voice." He clicked a button labeled "Done". A small box appeared and he typed *Margo - Darnell house*. After a few seconds a chime sounded and a box appeared: *Margo - Darnell house successful*.

He turned his attention to Elaine. "Your turn."

She cleared her throat and struck her most

stateswoman-like pose. "'Fourscore and seven years ago, our fathers brought forth—'"

"Okay, that's enough."

I wandered out into the hall and made a last adjustment to the camera angle to pick up a little more of the interior of the room with the tricky floor.

"'The world will little note, nor long remember what we say here—'" I heard the sound of typing, then the chime.

The last light was fading from the stained-glass window. I turned on my flashlight and went back into the room with the others. "It's almost dark. I guess it's about time to turn the lights out and get started," I said.

"I still need to record my voice," said Ernie. "Who wants to take over here?"

Elaine said, "Here, I'll do it." Maybe it was just my imagination, but it seemed like Elaine was being a little more attentive to Ernie lately.

"You just click here when I start to say something and here to finish. You only need a few seconds." Elaine sat on the chair and waited as Ernie moved over to the first microphone. "Ready? This is Ernie at the Darnell house."

While Ernie went through the voice recognition routine, I looked for a place to sit. We were lucky the last time; our entity showed itself practically before we even got started. Unfortunately, this isn't how it usually happens. More often than not, ghost hunting is nothing more than sitting quietly in a dark room, waiting for something to happen, which it does not most of the time. It can be excruciatingly boring, so the least you can hope for is to find a place where you can get comfortable.

I ended up perched precariously on a workbench next to the wall that was being stripped of its wainscoting. The light was fading, but I could see that the section of damaged wainscoting was warped and buckling. Clearly, the wall had been damaged and repaired, but the repair work was badly done. I hadn't noticed it earlier, but when the light hit it just so, it was obvious. This is why it pays to hire a professional. I thought about the hole in the wall I just patched and imagined someone sitting in my house a hundred years from now having similar thoughts about my handiwork.

Anyway, Marsha was probably doing the right thing in redoing this old room. The paneling here lacked the overblown charm of the woodwork in the hall. Hopefully she had better decorating taste than the previous owner, whose choice of wallpaper was discouraging. The topmost layer had once been the height of fashion—a long, long time ago. When I picked at it, a flurry of little flakes crumbled and floated to the floor like snowflakes. While I waited for Ernie to finish setting up his new toy, I carefully picked up one of the larger wallpaper fragments and examined it. I could just make out what looked like it might have been something yellow. I tried to use my fingernail to scrape off a larger piece, but all I got was brittle dust that made me sneeze.

Then a thought occurred to me: Could the piece of wallpaper in the box have come from this room? I was mulling over this possibility when Ernie announced he was ready.

"Fine," I said. "Let's get the lights."

Ernie parked himself in front of the laptop to monitor the video cameras while Elaine and I, armed with an impressive assortment of devices, checked out the rest of the house.

For the next couple of hours, the EMF meters were discouragingly silent. I finally drifted back upstairs and sat down next to Ernie.

"You get anything?" he asked, without looking away from the laptop.

"Zilch. Not even so much as an EMF hit."

"Don't worry," he said absently. "The night is still young."

I pointed to a sound wave editor that I noticed was open on Ernie's computer. "Any luck with this?"

"Nothing yet."

"Well, how about if I try to liven things up a bit? I'll go over there and try to start a conversation."

I rummaged around in my bag of gadgets and grabbed a few things, then went in search of a comfortable spot in the middle of the room. I switched on a small book light and placed it on the floor before me. Its bulb was precariously loose; the gentlest of touches was enough to turn it on and off.

"Hello to anyone who's in here. My name is Margo and I'd like to talk to you. We're here with respect and just want to know a little more about you."

"Cool," said Ernie.

"What's cool?"

"When you talk I can see it on the computer. Keep talking."

"Louisa, if you're here, we want to help you. Don't be afraid. Bradford's not here and he's never coming back."

Suddenly Ernie interrupted. "Where was Elaine last time you saw her?"

"She was going to poke around in the attic."

"How long ago was that?"

"Less than five minutes ago. Why?"

"Come look at this."

Ernie's face glowed eerily in the dim light from the computer screen. Although it was the only light in the room, I could see he was excited about something. I scrambled to my feet and went to look over his shoulder.

"Look right here. This is the night-vision camera we set up in in the front hall."

The images on Ernie's screen were fuzzy and indistinct, but I could just make out what looked like a fuzzy blob near the stairs. "Could it be a trick of the light? Or Elaine's flashlight?"

"I've been watching it. I'm one hundred percent certain it wasn't there a few seconds ago."

As he spoke, an image appeared in another window on the screen. Although it was only a small pinpoint of light at first, after a few seconds we could see Elaine's face. The pinpoint of light was the hands-free LED she had hooked over one ear. We could only see half her face; it made her look a little bit Picassoesque.

"You see?" he said. "This is the camera we set up in the kitchen near the back door. That must be the door to the attic stairs right there. So Elaine at this very moment is in the kitchen."

We were silent for a few minutes as we watched Elaine make her way carefully through the dark house toward the stairs. By the time she got there, the blob in the front hall was gone.

As we watched her in silence, the room suddenly became cold. I shivered, but it had nothing to do with the sudden drop in temperature.

"Look," I whispered.

"I see it." On the computer screen, the zig-zag waveforms of sounds being recorded were flashing like little digital lightening bolts in the sound recorder window. Though we were silent they continued to move across the screen.

"Louisa, is that you?" I asked. On the screen, spiky waveform illustrated my words. A much smaller waveform appeared on the computer screen in response.

The wave patterns stopped. "Can you play it back? Maybe enhance it?" I whispered.

Ernie nodded. "Give me a second," he said, typing away.

"Anything interesting going on up here? Jeez, it's cold in here."

Ernie and I both jumped; we hadn't heard Elaine coming up the stairs.

"Come look at this," I said, pointing to the window on the laptop monitor. "Louisa, I'm holding a device in my hands that can help us hear what you're saying," We watched in silence as the lines flickered, then stopped.

Ernie clicked around on the computer. A status bar scrolled quickly across the screen, then a message popped up. *Is this Ernie?* it asked and I heard Ernie's voice say "*You get anything?*" He clicked Yes. Then another message, *Is this Margo?* followed by "*Zilch. Not even so much as a temperature anomaly.*" Again, he clicked Yes. Then a few seconds later, a different message appeared: *Unknown voice.* Ernie clicked Play as we gathered around to hear better.

"*He must not find it. Please hurry.*"

I've heard enough ghostly voices in my time, but this one sent cold chills down my spine.

"Looks like we have our orders for tonight," Elaine remarked. "Now if we only knew what we're looking for."

"It might be easier to find whatever it is we're looking for if we turn on the lights," I said. I flipped the switch. The single bare bulb dangling from the ceiling gave off a stingy light that faded to darkness before reaching the corners.

While Ernie fiddled with the computer, Elaine got down on hands and knees and began testing the floorboards. I joined her but for some reason, I was sure that this wasn't the right place to look. As I poked and tapped on the floor, I remembered the strange feeling I'd had earlier that I was missing something important.

I crawled back over to the place near the wall where I had sat earlier, testing the floorboards as I went. I found nothing more exciting than a few loose ones here and there. In fact, this part of the floor was in better shape than the center. Which was odd, considering the condition of the paneling. My eyes wandered to the flakes of wallpaper that I'd picked off earlier and that's when the alarm bells started going off in my head.

A quick survey of the room confirmed that this section above the flaking wallpaper was the only spot where the wainscoting was warped. A closer inspection revealed a piece that bulged out from the wall ever so slightly. I hunted around in my purse and found the small screwdriver that I carry for just such an emergency. The gap between the paneling and the wall was just wide enough for me to wedge the end of the screwdriver into it.

"Margo, what *are* you doing?" Elaine shrieked, as a section of wainscoting separated from the wall with a loud pop. Tiny bits of wallpaper fluttered in the air.

"Bring me your flashlight," I said, beckoning her over. She stared at me in disbelief.

"I'm over here minding my own business and I look up just in time to see you dismantling the client's house. Have you lost your mind?"

A minor detail that hadn't occurred to me. "Look," I

said, "she won't know whether it's us or the workmen. In two days, this whole wall won't even be here. I just want to take a look." Reluctantly, Elaine gave me her flashlight. Ernie came over and peered over my shoulder.

The top of the wainscoting was pulled away from the wall by the smallest of cracks, but it was enough to see that there was something behind it that didn't belong there. I guessed it was what had caused the wood to warp. It was the perfect hiding place for something very thin—you could only see the bump under the wood when the light hit it from a certain angle.

"I think we found Ernie's Confederate war bonds." I stuck the screwdriver in the gap and the paneling gave way with a brittle crack. Ernie stuck his face next to the wall and, closing one eye, looked in.

"Well, we'll never know because that space is too small for any of us to get a hand in."

"Nonsense," I said. "Just hold it for me like this."

I managed to get a fingertip far enough in to touch whatever it was.

"What if there's something gross in there? Like spiders, or mice or something?" asked Elaine.

"I've had all my shots. I can just touch it." Frustrated, I withdrew my hand, noting that it was now covered with scratches.

"Let me try," said Elaine. She carefully removed her rings and stashed them in a pocket. Ernie and I held the wainscoting away from the wall as she gingerly slid her hand behind the wood. Groaning, the wood pulled away a couple of millimeters more from the wall.

"I have it!" She extricated her hand, knuckles bleeding, and triumphantly held up a flat package, about the size of a magazine, wrapped in brown paper. Elaine held the package while we unwrapped it carefully. The remains of the twine that had once secured it crumbled to pieces. It wasn't particularly neatly wrapped, as though whoever hid it had been in a hurry. I caught myself holding my breath as I peeled several layers of paper back.

It took a minute for my brain to understand what my eyes were seeing. Written by hand, in a thoroughly illegible scrawl, it was a musical score. I paged through it. Whole sections were crossed out and reworked. It was decorated liberally with scribbled notes and the occasional stray drop of ink.

"After all that, it's just music!" sniffed Ernie with disappointment.

"How much you wanna bet this is the 'treasure'?" said Elaine, annoyed. "I can't believe I wrecked my manicure for that." She examined her nails ruefully.

"You think this is Louisa's dad's treasure?" asked Ernie.

"Well, it's obvious, isn't it? The old man lived and

breathed music. I mean, he left everything he owned to the Music Society." She rolled her eyes. "To him it probably was a treasure."

"But we don't even know what it is yet. How do you know it's not a treasure?" I asked.

Ernie raised an eyebrow. "I can tell you have an idea. What's up?"

"Oh, it's probably nothing. But look at it. What do you see?"

"A bunch of scribbles," he said with some disgust. "I don't read music."

"Well, I do. It's an orchestral piece. The writing is next to impossible to read, but I can decipher enough of it to see that it's in German. This is the part for the violin. And here's the part for the flute. But look here." I pointed to the date —1827—scrawled across the upper right corner. "If nothing else, it's almost 200 years old. Surely it has some kind of historical value. Some collector would probably pay big bucks for this at an auction."

"Before you two start picking out your luxury yachts, may I point something out? This manuscript doesn't belong to us."

Ernie looked at me and made a face. "I hate it when she's right."

"Let's pack up and I'll go talk to Marsha," I sighed. But

somehow I couldn't imagine Ms. Darnell getting excited about our find.

We spent the next few minutes rolling up cords and stashing the equipment away. I left Elaine and Ernie to finish up and went downstairs to find Marsha. The TV was off tonight; she was working at her computer.

"Working late, I see."

"Just trying to get caught up on emails. But I've had enough for tonight."

"You look exhausted. I just came to tell you we're wrapping up and to show you what we found." I unwrapped the package. "We found this in the wall you're tearing down."

"What is it? It looks like a bunch of old papers."

"We think it's a manuscript for music of some sort."

Marsha took the package and glanced through it, turning the pages with the tips of her fingers. The pages rustled loudly as she turned them. She stared at me dumbfounded, then said "So what are you going to do with them?"

"Well, technically, they belong to you."

"Me? Well, what would I do with them? It's just a bunch of old papers. Didn't you find something last time you were here?"

"Yes, the box we found last time was full of letters and

newspaper clippings. We suspect there's a connection between it and this music, although we can't be certain. We also don't know if either of them has anything to do with the activity here in the house."

Marsha shrugged. "You can do whatever you want with that stuff. I don't want it," she said, sounding as if she suspected I was a bit daft for even asking.

I decided not to push my luck, so I bid her good night and ran back upstairs. I got there just in time to help carry out the last couple of pieces of equipment.

"So what did she say?" asked Ernie.

"We're in luck. She couldn't be less interested."

"Cool. Now all we have to do is figure out what we've got here and whether it's anything worth getting excited about."

We must have set a new world's record that night for getting everything packed up and the cars loaded. I was about to get in my car when Ernie ran over. "Hey, wait a second. I'm missing a voice recorder," he said, waving the equipment checklist.

"Sorry, I totally forgot about this in all the excitement. It was in my pocket." I handed him the voice recorder that I'd almost stepped on earlier.

He frowned. "It's not working. Batteries must be dead."

"Well, considering everything that happened tonight, I'm not surprised. See you tomorrow." It's not all that uncommon for paranormal activity to drain the juice out of your gadgets. But that's not what was occupying my thoughts tonight. So preoccupied was I that I was almost home before I remembered to turn my phone on.

How could I have forgotten about Tim? He'd called but hadn't left a voicemail. Instead, he'd sent a text a few minutes later.

"Good news changed the meeting. R we on for dinner tomorrow?"

I glanced at the time; to call him back at this hour of the morning would be rude, I decided. So I sent him a chatty reply to his text message. Much to my surprise, the phone rang a few minutes later.

"Timmy! What are you doing up at this hour?"

"I couldn't sleep. Margo, I can't stop thinking about you."

I noticed with some annoyance that my hands had suddenly gone all cold and clammy. "Well, look, um..." Taking a quick inventory of my options, I decided to go for broke. "Timmy, I can't wait to see you again."

"Can I come over? Now?"

"Yes, Timmy," I said. "You can. I'd like that very much."

# What I Found

*It was* late before we got up the next morning. Really late.

I was on my way to the kitchen to make coffee when Timmy came out of the shower, his black hair wet and tousled, wearing only a towel around his waist. I suppressed the urge to rip it off of him and instead said demurely, "What time is your meeting?"

"Twelve thirty. I wish I didn't have to go." He smiled, a little sadly, it seemed.

"Well, we're having dinner, right?"

"Of course, but I'd rather spend the time with you."

Was I going to regret this later? "I feel the same way. Anyway, I need to do some work today."

"The score?"

"Yeah, I was going to see if I can find someone who can tell me something about it."

"Can I see it?"

We studied the score together for a few minutes. Timmy shook his head. "It looks like it was written during an earthquake. I can't make heads or tails of this writing."

"My theory is, the person who wrote this was either ill

or really old," I said. "I have an idea. Instead of going out tonight, let just have dinner here. We can get take-out, a pizza or something. I'd offer to cook for you, but I want you to still like me."

He laughed and hugged me. I again considered divesting him of the towel and suffering the consequences, but I could see the kitchen clock over his shoulder and decided against it—reluctantly.

He said "Did I mention that I'm a fairly decent cook? Why don't you let me do the cooking?"

We did a quick inventory of the kitchen cabinets and decided that we had everything we needed to make a pizza. He scribbled down a shopping list, then went into the bedroom to get dressed. I watched him, wondering what I'd gotten myself into. A devastatingly gorgeous and sexy man, who could also cook? Then I remembered the catch; he lived in San Francisco and would be leaving in two days.

"Hey Margo?" Timmy appeared in the doorway, now dressed, lugging a satchel full of papers. "Do you suppose, if it's not too late, I mean I don't know what the check-out time is but, ummm..."

"Would you like to stay here tonight?"

He smiled—a dazzling, wonderful smile. "I thought you'd never ask."

Margo, what have you found? I asked myself this question a half-dozen times while I poured over the score with a magnifying glass. I even hooked an electronic keyboard up to the computer and tried plunking out the parts for the various instruments on it, but succeeded in creating only noise. Some parts were almost legible, but after an hour of slogging through the spidery scrawl my eyes were burning.

I'd decided I was in over my head when a scribbled line adorned with a particularly bold ink blot caught my eye. Alarm bells went off in my head. Something about it seemed faintly familiar. I went to the computer and spent a few minutes surfing. It took me only a few minutes to find what I was looking for. As I printed it and jammed it into a folder along with the manuscript, my hands were shaking.

If my theory was correct, we had indeed found Henry Grayson's treasure, even if I still had no idea exactly what it was. I pondered the papers scattered across my dining room table. This was a job for someone who knew far more about this than I did. I was almost out the door when I realized I was still in my bathrobe. I threw on some clothes and five minutes later, I was backing out of my driveway.

Having decided this was something my boss needed to know about, I went to the lab to talk to Dr. Holmes. A few minutes later I found myself wandering the dark passages of Merrifield Hall, one of the oldest buildings on campus and home to the School of Music. Dr. Holmes had sent me in search of Dr. Weber, dean of the music school.

Disconnected fragments of melodies echoed randomly from somewhere down the hall, punctuated occasionally by raucous laughter. A guy emerged from one of the rooms. I knew him from somewhere, but no name came to mind. His red hair was long and curly and he was wearing a tattered and faded T-shirt bearing the image of Bullwinkle the Moose. To my chagrin, he appeared to know me.

"Hi," he said. "How're things at the haunted house?" No doubt sensing my utter cluelessness, he added, "I'm Seamus. I work at the library. "

Relieved, I offered my hand. "Hi, Seamus. I'm Margo. We, um, found some stuff that might turn out to be interesting, but I can't really talk about it. At least not yet."

"Really. What brings you here?" he asked, obviously curious now.

"I'm looking for Dr. Weber's office."

"Right this way." We turned down a hall and stopped in front of a wooden door with a frosted glass pane in it. Softly, Seamus tapped out a rhythm on the glass and a melodious voice answered, "Come in!"

I followed Seamus into Dr. Weber's office. "My friend

here is looking for you."

"You must be Margo," she said. "Ben called and said you were on your way over. Thank you so much, Seamus."

Seamus looked at me quizzically. "Well, okay, Margo. Guess I'll see you later." He tipped an imaginary hat to us and bowed quietly out the door.

Dr. Weber was a petite black woman with short, gray hair and a round, cherubic face behind vintage wire-rimmed glasses. She looked exactly like my idea of a college professor. She shook my hand warmly and motioned me to a rickety chair next to her desk.

"What have you got for me, Ms... Mason, did you say?"

"Monroe. But call me Margo." I placed the folder with the score on her desk. "This was found in the wall of a house in Lone Oak. I was hoping you could tell me more about it, or at least point me to someone who can. If I may, I was especially interested in this part here." I showed her the scrawl that had caught my eye earlier.

She glanced at it and looked up at me, startled. "You happened across this accidentally?"

"Yes, the wall is being demolished. I found it behind a piece of loose paneling." I hoped she wouldn't press for details. I didn't want to tell her any more than I had to.

Dr. Weber looked skeptical. "I see. And are you the

owner of the house?"

"No, but I'm...um, checking into the history of some things we found in the house. At the owner's request."

"And what was your purpose in coming to me with this?"

"Well, I was hoping you could tell me if there's any possibility that it might be, um—what I think it is," I stammered. This whole episode suddenly started to seem ridiculous. I felt like I certainly must be wasting this woman's time. "Could it be, I mean, in your opinion, is there any possibility...it might be authentic?"

"Do you know anything at all about when this might have been hidden inside the wall?" She eyed me sharply.

"I don't really know anything for certain, but we think it might have been some time in the 1870's."

Dr. Weber nibbled absently on a pencil. "To be honest with you, Margo, the chances against this being authentic must be astronomical. But even if it is a forgery, well...it's priceless. At least from a musical perspective. As far as monetary value goes, I wouldn't venture to guess. There's someone I'd like you to meet. Can you meet me here this afternoon?"

"Sure, what time?"

"I have a class at two...let's make it 3:15."

Which is how, that very afternoon, I found myself at the offices of the Indian Springs Society of Musical Science. Dr. Weber ushered me across campus to a musty old brick building tucked away in a forgotten corner of campus. We were now waiting patiently in a stuffy room paneled in dark oak. Stacks of books and sheet music covered every horizontal surface. A couple of music stands stood in one corner near an upright piano. On the piano bench was a shabby violin case. The door creaked open, stirring up a cloud of dust. In shuffled Dr. Weber followed by a stooped, white-hared gentleman who looked for all the world like he must have been around at the Music Society's inception.

"Margo," said Dr. Weber, "I'd like you to meet Dr. Kielstrup. Dr. Kielstrup, Miss Margo Monroe, one of Ben Holmes' students."

"Fräulein Monroe," he said, bending over my hand. I started to protest at the use of the word "Fräulein," but Dr. Weber caught my eye and shook her head ever so slightly.

"Margo, Dr. Kielstrup is the director of the Indian Springs Society of Musical Science."

"Pleased to meet you," I said. I hate that expression; it's so trite. But I couldn't think of anything else to say.

"Please ladies, take a seat." He motioned at some overstuffed armchairs near the piano. When we sat, little clouds of dust sparkled in the air. I rubbed my nose to try to keep from sneezing. "So. Fräulein Margo, Frau Doktor Weber tells me you are in need of some advice pertaining to a piece of music?" He spoke with a faint German accent.

"Well, yes, actually. I found something that I think might be important." I handed him the bundle and watched as he turned a couple of pages with a trembling hand. To my astonishment, a tear trickled down his cheek.

After what seemed like hours, he finally spoke, his voice a little unsteady. "Young lady, thank you for bringing this to me. I am most honored by your decision to consult the Society of Musical Science."

"Oh, I can't take credit for that," I said, not really wanting to admit that the idea never crossed my mind. "It was Dr. Weber's idea. I was actually a little bit surprised to find out that the Society is still in existence. I mean, I've lived here most of my life. Why is it that I never heard of it? Until recently, that is," I added, not wanting to hurt his feelings.

He arched a bushy white eyebrow. "Fräulein Monroe, surely you can understand the near impossibility of awakening in the younger generation any interest in anything akin to real music. *Ach*, this...this noise! This dreadful noise that the young people call music! It's impossible to escape it. I hear it everywhere I go." He sighed deeply. "It breaks my heart." He shook his head sadly.

"Dr. Kielstrup," said Dr. Weber gently, "what do you recommend we do next? Is there any way to find out if this manuscript is genuine?"

"My dear ladies, of course there is." He all but bounded from his chair, rubbing his hands together briskly. "Please, make yourselves comfortable. I'll be back in a flash," he said and tottered off down the hall. He returned a few minutes later clutching a piece of paper. "I have just the person for you. This is the person you need to talk to." He ran a hand over the manuscript and handed it back to me, almost reluctantly. "You will keep me informed, won't you?"

"Of course," I replied.

He walked us to the front door and waved goodbye, seeming suddenly twenty years younger.

❧

"Priceless?" Tim seemed suitably impressed.

"That seems to be the general consensus. It could be a forgery, of course, but an expert from the Beethoven Research Center is coming look at it."

He picked up a candle and gazed absently into the flame. This afternoon I'd been debating with myself about whether it would be just a bit too much to light some candles, when Tim returned from the store and presented me with a massive bouquet of flowers. Dilemma solved—candles were a must.

He put the candle down, his face thoughtful. "So the expert is coming here?" he asked.

I nodded. "Next week. We're meeting with him at the lab. A handwriting expert from one of the big auction houses is also flying out." Next week. I didn't want to think about it. By the time our experts got here, Tim would be home.

"Sounds serious. What do you think about all this?"

"I hate to get my hopes up. I mean, what are the chances that it's real? Anyway, I don't want to talk about work tonight."

"Me neither," said Tim, taking both my hands.

It was a Hollywood moment. I was dining by candlelight with a gorgeous, romantic man. He was everything I'd ever wanted in a man. It was like being in a dream. Then I remembered tomorrow, and the Hollywood moment was over. "What time do you have to leave in the morning?"

"Early. I need to be out of here by seven." He kissed my fingers. "Let's not talk about it. I just want to enjoy this evening."

Taking the bottle of wine into the living room, we curled up together on the couch. Gently, he pushed a strand of hair away from my face. We smooched for a little while. He kissed my neck; it sent little chills of delight up and down my spine. "Maybe we should get more comfortable," he whispered.

Then I remembered that this time tomorrow, I'd be sitting here on this same sofa, all alone. "Timmy, what are we doing?"

"Having a lovely evening," he answered, surprised.

"No, I mean are we getting ourselves into a situation we're going to regret?"

Abruptly, he sat up and ran both hands through his hair. "I have a confession to make."

Oh no, here it comes, I thought. I noticed his hands were trembling slightly. This was not good. My stomach suddenly turned into a block of ice. "Confession?"

"Oh, no," he said quickly. "It's not what I think you're thinking."

"Well, what is it? You're engaged? You only have six months to live?"

He chuckled and hugged me. "No, no. It's nothing like that. It's just that I wanted to tell you I've always loved you."

"Well, you know I always adored you."

He continued, "I know that, but not the way I adored you. To you, I was just a friend. I wanted so much to be more, but I knew I didn't have a chance with you. I tried to forget you. But in all those years, you were never far from my thoughts. What I'm trying to tell you is that I've never really loved anyone else."

You know that expression "You could have knocked me over with a feather"? Well, I understand what it means now. He was looking at me intently. The tears that had been threatening all evening finally made an appearance. I was powerless to stop them.

"You know, you're not helping matters," I sniffed.

"How so?" He seemed hurt.

"Look, these past few days have been the best of my life. But you live two thousand miles away, and you're leaving tomorrow."

"Don't remind me." He sat back on the couch and rubbed his eyes. After a few minutes, he turned to me and took my face in his hands. "Haven't you ever thought of leaving Indian Springs? I mean, it's such a ... a one-horse town. Wouldn't you rather be in a big city?"

"Like San Francisco, for example?" I asked.

"Well, now that you mention it..."

"I'll be honest. The thought crossed my mind once or twice in the last couple of days." His expression brightened. "Look," I said, "before either of us gets too excited, you have to understand that I love my work, and my work is here. Where else am I going to get paid to hunt ghosts?"

With a sigh, he pulled me to him. "I was heartbroken when you graduated. I moped around the house all summer long. I thought for sure soon as school started, I'd get over it. But I didn't. I never did." He lifted my hand to his lips and kissed it gently. "I dated a few girls, but I always ended up comparing them to you. Even after I went away to college."

"Why didn't you keep in touch?"

"I started letters, emails, picked up the phone and started dialing your number a hundred times, but I always lost my nerve." He smiled wryly. "It's, um, not exactly an accident that I'm here this week for these meetings."

"I didn't know, Timmy. I honestly would never have guessed."

He looked slightly uncomfortable. "I know that. But now my secret's out. You know, I even convinced myself I was in love with my ex-wife because she looks a little bit like you."

I didn't have anything to add to this and neither did he. We sat together without talking for a long time.

# A Temporary Goodbye

*Reluctantly, I* picked up Timmy's satchel and hoisted it onto my shoulder. He followed me out the door lugging a duffel bag.

The sun was barely up—I couldn't remember the last time I'd been up this early when I hadn't been out all night the night before. The morning was pleasant but warming up rapidly. It promised to be a muggy and oppressively hot day.

"Let me know when you've made it home safely."

"Will do."

We walked together to his rented car, parked in my driveway. The small patch of dew on the car's hood would be gone before long. Tim opened the door and I put the satchel on the passenger-side seat. He tossed his bag on the floor in front of it. Then he turned and caressed my face with his hands before kissing me tenderly.

I buried my face in his shoulder. "I wish you didn't have to go." I held him for a minute then stepped away.

"Me, too." Gently, he kissed my forehead. "Don't give up on me."

"I won't. But I miss you already."

We kissed one last time, then he got in the car. I watched him as he drove away, feeling as if a dark cloud had invaded my soul. I turned to drag my reluctant feet up the sidewalk. A squirrel eyed me warily from the flowerbed under the massive oak tree in my front yard.

"What you you staring at? Mind your own business. And stay out of my flowerbed!"

With an insolent flick of his bushy tail, he turned and scampered toward the tree. At the base of the tree, he stopped. Looking back over his shoulder, he scolded me before disappearing into the safety of the branches above my head.

The dark cloud followed me as I clomped back up the front porch steps and into the house, feeling like I was wearing weights on both feet. I didn't have anything important on my calendar for the day, but I couldn't bear the thought of going back to the bed.

I managed to maintain my composure until, glancing around the living room, I saw the empty wine bottle and two glasses on the table by the sofa. Making no effort to stop the tears, I curled up on the sofa and sobbed like a child until I finally drifted off to sleep.

A phone call from Elaine woke me out of a sound sleep a couple of hours later. "I think some retail therapy would be just the thing for you. Riley's is having a huge sale."

"I don't know, Elaine. There's absolutely nothing I need…"

"And your point is what? Get up, get dressed. I'll be there to pick you up in an hour." There's no point in arguing with Elaine; I knew from experience she would come over here and physically drag me to the department store if necessary. Without enthusiasm, I drug myself into the bathroom, which was spotless. There was no sign Timmy had ever been there. "At least he cleans up after himself," I mumbled grumpily to my reflection. But as I brushed my teeth, I realized I was ever-so-slightly disappointed not to at least have found a few whiskers in the sink.

The doorbell rang just as I was putting on my mascara. I let Elaine in and she bounded into the living room full of energy. "What have you got planned for this afternoon?" she asked.

"Nothing important. I thought about going by the lab for a while. Why?"

"You can go to the lab tomorrow. Let's go see a movie. Then we can have dinner in Throckmorton."

"Don't you have to go back to work?"

She flashed me a mischievous grin. "No. It seems I suddenly became ill and had to go home. I'm predicting a speedy recovery."

I shouldered my purse. "Then a little retail therapy

should do us both some good."

"Well?" she asked as soon as we got into the car.

I sighed. "I don't even know where to start. If you had told me even a few days ago that I'd suddenly fall head over heels in love with someone I knew in high school, I would have asked you what you'd been smoking."

"And has he told you how he feels?"

"He says he's always been in love with me."

Elaine clapped her hands like an excited child. "But Margo, that's wonderful!"

"You're forgetting he lives two thousand miles away."

I could almost see the gears turning in her head. I knew her well enough by now to know that Elaine, perpetual optimist that she is, would consider the distance between us a mere challenge.

"I'm dreading going home tonight," I admitted.

"But why?" asked Elaine, genuinely puzzled.

"Because everything reminds me of him. I couldn't even bring myself to make up the bed this morning."

She rolled her eyes theatrically. "Puh-leez! Why? Because he slept in it? Don't be so sentimental. You've known him since high school.

"True, and that's part of the problem. What if it doesn't work out?"

"Well, what if it doesn't?" she asked, sounding a trifle annoyed. "Are you going to get cold feet just because you knew him when you were kids? It's too late for that now—you've already ventured past the point of no return. It's not like you can go back to being just pals again."

"I guess you're right."

"What's gotten into you, Margo? He sounds like a dream."

"You know me. I don't have much faith in long-distance relationships. Remember Josh?"

"I didn't like Josh all that much. And if I recall correctly, neither did you. Anyway, it might not always be a long-distance relationship."

"Well, it isn't likely to be me that moves any time soon. I love my job. I live for my job."

"So? What about him?" she asked.

"He's in business for himself. Moving would mean starting over. Anyway, it's too soon to start thinking about that. We've only been out a couple of times."

"Have you heard from him since he left?"

"No, not yet," I admitted.

I was flipping listlessly through the clearance rack when a chime sounded from my purse. I dreaded looking at it. If it was from Timmy, knowing he was home would put me in a sour mood all over again. Of course, if it wasn't from Timmy, I'd be crushed. Either way I couldn't win.

Elaine appeared by my side carrying an armful of clothes. "Aren't you going to try anything on?" she asked, exasperated.

I held up a simple green silk dress. "What do you think about this?"

"It's perfect. Matches your eyes. Is that all?"

"But I don't have any place to wear any of these," I replied, starting to put the dress back.

She stopped me. "Just try it on."

I took my lone article into the dressing room and tried it on. Studying my reflection in the full-length mirror, I had to admit that the dress was fabulous.

"You're a knockout in that," said Elaine. She looked dazzling in the red velvet dress she had on. A sales tag dangled from one sleeve.

"Are you gonna get that? It looks wonderful on you," I said. Of course, everything looks wonderful on her. We went back into our respective cubicles.

"Hmmm, I don't know. I still have a couple more to try on," she said from the next cubicle. "Have you heard from Tim yet?" she asked.

"He just sent me a text. Guess I oughtta write back."

"That wouldn't be a bad idea. Honestly, I worry about you sometimes."

The afternoon passed by all too quickly. We spent way too much money and giggled like a couple of teenagers. I still wasn't looking forward to going into my empty house, but we'd put it off as long as possible.

"Thanks," I said. "I really needed this."

"Hey, what are friends for?"

I got out of the car and gathered up my shopping bags. She rolled her window down and called to me as I walked up the sidewalk. "Write back to Tim."

"I will."

"Now!"

"Okay, I will. Don't worry."

When I turned the key in the lock the sound seemed to echo through the entire house. The silence crashed around my ears like waves against the shore. I flipped the light on and dropped my purse on the sofa. In the kitchen our coffee cups sat next to the sink, just where we'd left them this morning. I was putting them in the dishwasher when the ice maker dumped a tray of ice with a noisy crash, causing me to jump. Suddenly I became acutely aware of the noise that the refrigerator made...how had I never noticed it before?

This is just silly, I said to myself. It was early yet; I decided to read for a while. I marched resolutely into the living room and looked around for my book, fluffing sofa cushions and tidying pillows in the process. However, the book was nowhere to be found, and after a few minutes I gave up the search went to the bedroom.

My book was right where I'd left it, untouched for the past few days beside the bed. Although a little rumpled, the bed had been made. I was pretty sure I hadn't made the bed this morning. Was it just this morning? It seemed like days ago. Suddenly, I felt a lump in my throat.

When I pulled back the covers, a piece of paper fluttered from my pillow. My hands shaking, I unfolded it and started to read.

> Margo, I just want you to know that the last few days have been a dream come true for me. I know we were only together a few days, but haven't we really been together all our lives? To me it seems like we have. I already miss you more than you will ever know. I know this is just the beginning for us. Please give me a chance. The distance between us is nothing if we genuinely love and care for each other, and I know in my heart that we do. As you read this, know that I'm thinking of you.

Love always,

T

I admit freely that I cried like a baby for the next half hour. When I had cried myself out, I staggered back into the kitchen. I dug my phone out of my purse and sat down on a bar stool. "Just got home its been a crazy day. Got your note miss you too LOTS. Will email tomorrow. Kisses"

As soon as I pressed the Send button I felt better. Eyes swollen, but feeling better than I had all day, I stopped in the bathroom to wash my face and went back to bed. When I finally fell asleep, I dreamed I was in high school again in German class with Timmy.

# Expert Advice

*One afternoon,* I was rummaging around in the kitchen cabinets when I came across the bag of dry cat food I'd bought at the store the day I ran into Neil. Had it been that long since I'd been to the park? I scooped some cat food into a plastic bag and put on my sneakers.

The ducks saw me coming from halfway down the block. In seconds there were a dozen or so clustered around me. They followed me to the bank of the creek that runs through the park. Several more ducks landed, quacking noisily, in the water and watched me patiently.

"Hey, guys. Long time, no see." I tossed a handful of dry cat food into the water. Ducks dashed around frantically, slurping up the morsels. Around me there was a mad dash for the water. A mother duck swam up leading a convoy of half-grown ducklings. I threw an extra handful to them.

"No need to be greedy," I said. "There's plenty for everyone." I tossed a handful to the ducks around me. They scrambled around my feet with surprising agility.

There's something therapeutic about communing with wildlife. I felt a stab of guilt when I tried to figure out how long it had been since I'd been here. So much had happened since then...could it have only been two weeks? I missed Timmy in spite of our daily video chats. That's not what was was on my mind today, though. Tomorrow's meeting with the Beethoven Research Center loomed large in my thoughts.

"Tomorrow's the big day," I said. The ducks watched me expectantly. "By this time tomorrow we'll know whether it's the real thing or not. Not that it really matters. " My feathered friends stared at me. "Here's the last of it." I emptied the bag onto the ground and walked back to the house. "Gotta go. It's time to call Tim."

"So now that you work with them professionally, what do you think ghosts really are?" asked Timmy from my TV screen.

"Well," I said to the slightly pixellated image, "I suppose the standard answer is that they're the spirits of dead people who, for whatever reason, decide to remain in the realm of the living."

"But you don't believe that?"

"It's not that I don't believe it, I just think it's not as simple as all that. I'll try to explain. To understand my theory of what is to us paranormal—beyond normal—you have to understand the physical dimensions. It also helps if you can imagine that there are other dimensions in our universe beyond the three we are capable of perceiving."

He rubbed his forehead. "Physics class was a long time ago."

"It's very simple," I explained. "Imagine a universe with only two dimensions. In such a universe there would be no concept of up or down. If you lived in this universe, you would only be able to move backwards, forwards, and sideways. Now imagine that a being from a three-dimensional universe visits your world. He—or it—would seem to have simply appeared out of thin air. You flat-worlders would only be able to see the point at which it touches the two-dimensional surface of you world. The rest of the visitor, the part that is up or down, is in a dimension that doesn't exist in your two-dimensional world."

"I thought there were four dimensions."

"There are. According to Einstein the fourth dimension is time."

"Hence spacetime."

"Precisely. So now try to imagine a new dimension—a fifth dimension."

"I don't know," he said, shaking his head. "I thought this stuff was only on Star Trek."

"Oh no, not at all! The idea of a fifth dimension has been around at least as far back as the 1920s. There's a scientific theory on the subject and everything. I once read a book by a scientist who used the fifth dimension to explain all kinds of paranormal phenomena, including UFOs. It gets even weirder when you get to the subatomic level. In one theory, there are eleven sub-atomic dimensions; in another there are 26. I am not making this up; look it up if you don't believe me."

He thought about this for a minute. "Well, I guess when you put it that way, an extra dimension or two would go a long way towards explaining all kinds of weirdness."

"Absolutely," I replied. "I think where we get it wrong is that we imagine spacetime to be all nice and flat and smooth. I think that's not right at all. In my theory, spacetime is all rumpled and wrinkly, like a wadded up piece of paper. It's so wrinkly that some parts of it overlap and intersect others. Remember, spacetime isn't just space—it's also time. Ernie calls this the Margo Monroe Crumpled Paper Theory. Do you see where I'm going with this?"

"Maybe...you think portions of our reality—the 'wrinkles' in the spacetime continuum—occasionally overlap with another reality?"

"Why not? It would explain residual hauntings—scenarios that seem to repeat themselves, where the entity doesn't even seem to be aware of our presence."

"But that's not what's happening at Ms. Darnell's. If the entity is trying to interact with you, she's obviously aware of your presence."

"Yes, I admit this is a bit tougher. But imagine that upon departure from this life, you leave your three-dimensional physical self behind, but the essence of who you are goes to one of these other dimensions. Call it heaven or nirvana or whatever you want, but the point is that the folks here in this life can only perceive you where your reality intersects theirs. You might be able to communicate with the loved ones you left behind, but only with considerable effort. After all, the three-dimensional visitor to Flatland had to expend some energy to make himself flat enough that the Flatlanders could see him. And he can only flatten himself out so far. I think ghosts are beings who exist on another plane and, for whatever reason, are willing to make the extra effort to appear in our world."

He analyzed this for a moment then asked, "Have you ever wondered, if perhaps we're the ones intruding on their spacetime continuum, not the other way around? Maybe they think we're the ghosts."

"That's absolutely brilliant! I never thought of it like that."

"My small contribution to the science of paranormal investigation," he said. "Are you nervous about the meeting tomorrow?"

"A little bit. It shouldn't really matter, I suppose."

"Why shouldn't it matter? It's important."

"Yes, but the focus of our investigation is supposed to be paranormal research. I don't want to get a reputation as publicity-seekers. Anyway, we're supposed to be keeping the whole thing quiet."

"Sorry, but if it turns out to be authentic you can forget about that. Anyway, maybe it will take something like this to establish paranormal research as a legitimate science. Margo, I really miss you. It's been a long week."

"It has for me, too. It's late. I guess I'd better go," I said reluctantly. "I'll let you know as soon as I find out anything."

He blew me a kiss, and we signed off.

"And you say that you found this behind some paneling in an old house?"

"That's right." I was getting tired of repeating this story, and Professor McCrae's raised eyebrows said clearly that he didn't believe a word of it. I sent Dr. Holmes an imploring glance, but his expression gave nothing away. There was an uncomfortable silence. "The homeowner asked me to look into some strange things that were happening at her house. It's my... hobby," I added.

Ernie shifted uncomfortably in his seat. Somewhere a clock ticked audibly.

A motley assortment of chairs had been hastily crammed into an office the size of a closet. We'd had to clear books and papers from every horizontal surface. The air conditioning, gasping feebly over our heads, was not equipped to cool a room—however tiny—with this many warm bodies in it.

"Before I begin, I'd like everyone's assurance that everything we're about to discuss will remain absolutely confidential. We are simply not ready for word of this to get out." Wedged uncomfortably between Dr. Weber and a shabby wooden filing cabinet, Professor McCrae, director of the Beethoven Research Center, was sweating profusely. On a stack of books piled haphazardly atop the filing cabinet was perched a large, rather luxurious fern. Professor McCrae hunched over in his chair, in a futile attempt to escape the fern, whose fronds caressed his shiny bald head every time the air conditioning came on. Dr. Weber smiled placidly, seemingly oblivious to her guest's discomfort. Holmes seemed equally relaxed, but Ernie was fidgeting like a kid in church. As for me, I could already predict I was going to need some ice-cold liquid refreshments when we finished here, and the heat wasn't entirely to blame.

Only the manuscript specialist, whose name I didn't catch, seemed unfazed. He had been introduced to us

as the leading authority on the handwriting of 18th-
and 19th-century German and Austrian composers.
Talk about specialization. A dapper man, fiftyish with
silver, carefully coiffed hair, he wouldn't have looked
out of place at Chez Claude. He studied me with grey
eyes that matched his expensive suit. "Miss Monroe,
it's my opinion that this is no forgery. Of course, to be
absolutely certain, we must perform certain tests on
the paper, the ink—to verify the age." He spoke with
the slightest trace of an accent that I couldn't quite
place. "But before we can do anything we must be
certain we have the consent of the rightful owner."

"I'm sorry," I said. "I'm not sure I understand…"

Professor McCrae leaned forward, eagerly it seemed to
me, although he might have just been trying to get
away from the fern. "Miss Monroe…"

I held up a hand. "Please, call me Margo."

"Margo," he continued, bowing slightly, "the Maestro
composed nine known symphonies in his lifetime. He
began jotting down some ideas for a tenth symphony a
couple of years before he died. That symphony was
never finished, or so it was thought until now." I never
heard Professor McCrae refer to Beethoven as
anything except "The Maestro." As he spoke, he
caressed the papers as though they were holy relics. To
him, I suppose, they were. "We have only a few
fragments and sketches from the Maestro's hand that
give us a rough idea of what he intended for his tenth

symphony.

"For example, this Presto and this Andante," he continued, leafing reverently through the score and pointing out some pages, "are already known to us from the Maestro's sketchbooks. We know from one of his first biographers that these pieces were intended to be part of the tenth symphony. Until now, a handful of sketches were all that we had.

"Another associate of the Maestro's, one Karl Holz, claimed that the Maestro played the entire symphony for him on the piano. He described, for example, an introduction in E flat major. As you can see, this introduction is in the key of E flat major." He showed me a page in the manuscript. I had to take his word for it; an expert on things musical I am not. Anyway, it looked more like ancient Egyptian hieroglyphics than any music I'd ever seen.

He turned the pages gingerly and pointed to a page that was nominally more legible, but seemed to be decorated liberally with corrections and notes. Large portions of it had been scratched out thickly and reworked. "This Allegro in C minor was also described by Holz, but until now its existence was only legend."

Ernie peered intently at the papers and frowned. "How can you be certain that Beethoven wrote this?" he asked. "This doesn't even look like the same handwriting."

At that moment, to my great embarrassment, my purse chirped loudly beside me. Someone had sent me a text message. Timmy, no doubt. Fortunately no one seemed to notice except Ernie, who caught my eye and smirked gleefully.

"That's a very good observation," said the manuscript guy. "Beethoven's health had been deteriorating for several years, which you can see reflected clearly in his handwriting. The handwriting on this introduction matches other known handwriting from this period. Now, this piece was probably written some time earlier than the introduction I showed you. You'll notice that the paper and ink are also different. Yet there is little doubt that this is Beethoven's hand. There were times during his final illness when he was strong enough to compose, and we know that he was working on his tenth symphony in the weeks before his death in March of 1827."

"But if Beethoven had completed—or almost completed—a new symphony while he was dying, why hasn't it come to light until now?" I asked.

Dr. McCrae shook his head sadly. "It's been almost 200 years. For much of what we know about the great man we must rely on the personal accounts of people like Schindler." He grimaced, as though the name left a bad taste.

"Schindler? I've heard of him," said Ernie. "Who was he?"

"Anton Schindler, an associate of the Maestro and one of his first biographers. His credibility has been all but destroyed in recent years. Who knows what such a man might have done to further his own interests?" Dr. MacRae fell silent and settled back into his chair, having forgotten the invasive fern in his indignation.

The manuscript guy spoke up. "If I may, we must take certain practical considerations into account. Beethoven manuscripts surface from time to time. In 2005 a working copy of the Grosse Fugue was discovered in Pennsylvania. It sold at auction for 1.95 million US dollars."

I stole a glance at Ernie. His face had gone pale. Next to him the normally unflappable Dr. Holmes looked stunned. "But the Grosse Fuge is a known work," said Holmes. "We're talking about the discovery of an entire unknown symphony."

"My point exactly. Nothing of this magnitude this has ever surfaced before. As a cultural artifact, it's beyond priceless. But we must nevertheless take proper precautions with so valuable a find."

"What do you mean?" asked Dr. Holmes.

"At this point we can only speculate how much an undiscovered mostly complete new Beethoven symphony might be worth. It would certainly run into the millions, probably the tens of millions. At the very least, it needs to be insured." Gently he added, "You understand now the need to ascertain beyond doubt the manuscript's legal owner."

They were all now looking at me. Never in a million years could I have predicted that a bunch of old papers hidden inside a wall might turn out to be worth a king's ransom. I stammered, "I showed the papers to the lady who owns the house. She said she didn't want them."

Dr. Holmes spoke up. "Was anybody else present?"

I shook my head. Ernie and Elaine had been upstairs when I talked to Marsha—I didn't have a witness.

"May I suggest," said the manuscript specialist, "that you speak to an attorney? Without delay."

After we took our leave of the Beethoven experts and Dr. Weber, Dr. Holmes made a couple of phone calls. Shortly thereafter we were on our way to Renaissance, one of Throckmorton's most expensive restaurants, in Dr. Holmes' Lexus.

The Lexus didn't fit my idea of a college professor's car; I'd always imagined him driving a vintage VW Beetle or beat up Toyota. As my boss steered us through the mid-day traffic, I checked my text messages discretely. "Any news? Miss U XX" from Tim, and "Where are you? What happened @ meeting?" from Elaine. I replied to Elaine's text: "Meeting w lawyer talk later." I would reply to Timmy when I had more time.

We pulled up and Dr. Holmes gave the car keys to a valet. The lawyer arrived just behind us. He was a well-dressed but rather pudgy middle-aged man. His sleek German sports car only emphasized his pudginess; I noticed that he had to struggle a bit to extricate himself from the driver's seat.

I got the impression he was a regular customer here—the hostess ushered us immediately to a prime table in a quiet corner. Our drinks appeared almost as soon as we ordered them. I sipped a glass of red wine demurely, and wondered what Tim was doing.

The lawyer listened to me intently as I explained once again how I'd come by a priceless undiscovered symphony from the very hand of Beethoven himself. At least this time I didn't have to be coy about what I was doing prying the paneling off of somebody's walls.

Wearily, he removed his glasses and rubbed his brow. "Ben, to say we're in a predicament with this would be something of an understatement. I don't like to think about the impact this would have on the reputation of the school if the homeowner decides to get nasty about this."

"Don't think I haven't thought about that," Holmes replied. "We have an obligation to go public with this. This isn't something we can keep quiet. It would border on the criminal!"

"If you say so. I'm not much of a fan of classical."

My boss shook his head. "That's beside the point. The historic and artistic implications of this are unprecedented."

"What's our next step?" asked Holmes.

The lawyer examined his wine glass closely for a moment, then focused intently at me. "You say she specifically said she didn't want the papers?"

"That's right. She sounded like she wondered why I was even asking."

"But no one else was present."

"No. How could we have guessed they were anything but a bunch of moldy old papers?"

"True enough. But money has a way of affecting people's memories. And I don't think this will be a paltry couple of million."

Dr. Holmes interrupted. "Of course, she has no proof that the papers were ever hers, either."

The lawyer thought about this for a second. "Ordinarily, I'd call that an astute observation, but my responsibility is to the University. A legal battle over the ownership of these papers could go on for years and do untold damage."

"So," I asked. "What do you propose we do?"

"Let's talk to her first and see how reasonable she's willing to be." He consulted his phone. "If I can arrange a meeting with her for tomorrow at this time, are you both available?"

"Of course," I said.

"I'll make time," said Dr. Holmes.

"I'll be in touch with you shortly," said Brundrett.

Our food arrived at that moment, delivered by a trio of waiters in starched white jackets. When they departed, the conversation turned to school matters. At first I tried politely to follow along, but my thoughts soon wandered. My companions didn't notice. While they were engrossed in discussions (notice I didn't say "gossip") about faculty and staff at the college, I sent Elaine a discrete text message: "Drinks later?" The reply came as the lawyer was paying the bill. Seconds after Dr. Holmes dropped me off at my car, I was on my way to the Monk's Habit.

I wheeled into the last parking space and made my way through the crowded patio to the bar inside. Elaine was already sitting at the bar, peering into a compact, putting on lipstick. I climbed onto the bar stool next to her near the end of the bar and gave my eyes a few seconds to adjust to the darkness. From behind the bar, our reflections stared back at us, obscured by bottles. Why is there a gigantic mirror in every bar in the known universe? Even in the gloom, I could see that this day was beginning to catch up with me. I frowned at my bedraggled reflection and dabbed on some lipstick while Elaine went in search of some menus.

"Well?" asked Elaine, handing me a menu.

"I don't even know where to start. Man, I'm just wiped out."

"What can I get you ladies?"

"Oh hi, Farley," I said. "I need a minute."

While I tried to choose from the overwhelming list of choices, Elaine said "I'll have my usual."

"A mojito. Sure thing. And you, Margo?"

Directly in front of me was the beer tap, a shiny contraption fitted with ostentatious brass handles. The brightly colored decorations on the handles caught my eye. I slapped the menu shut with a sigh. "Surprise me, Farley."

"Been one of those days, has it? Care to try a Belligerent Bastard Irish Cream Ale? It's the beer of the month," he added proudly.

"Why not? I feel adventurous."

"Back in a flash."

Elaine studied me curiously. "One of those days?"

"You don't know the half of it."

"Hmmm. So, how's the Timster?"

"Here you go, ladies." Farley sat our drinks in front of us with a wink, then disappeared behind the bank of beer spigots. My beer was still foaming, turning from opaque white to beer-colored from the bottom of the glass up. I watched it, mesmerized.

"Cheers," I said. "You're the only person I know who'd have the nerve to order a mojito in an Irish pub. Timmy's fine. We talked for a little while last night." I took a sip of my Belligerent Bastard. It was thick and slightly bitter, with a hint of something spicy. My kind of beer.

"What did people do before video chat? It could be worse. Imagine if you could only talk on the phone. Or had to write letters."

"You're right. Still, it's not quite like having him here."

"What about the score?"

"We met with the experts...and the lawyer."

She arched an eyebrow. "Lawyer? Sounds serious. Tell me about these experts."

"The head of the Beethoven Research Center and an expert on handwriting from one of the big auction houses. They think it's a never-before-heard Beethoven symphony."

Elaine sputtered and put her glass down, coughing. "Beethoven? Are they sure?"

"That's the issue. Before they can be absolutely certain, they have to do some tests. But they can't do anything without permission from the lawful owner—that's where the lawyer comes in."

"But Marsha told you she didn't want that stuff."

"You and I both know that, but she and I were the only ones in the room. What are the chances she won't change her mind when she finds out what it is? Who wouldn't? I sure would. The thing's probably worth more than the GNP of most small countries. The lawyer is reluctant to do anything that would bring negative publicity to the college. He says if it ended up in court it would be my word against hers. You and Ernie would end up having to testify, and you'd have to testify that we found it on Marsha's property."

A television above one corner of the bar was tuned to a soccer game. We sipped and watched the game for a few minutes. From time to time, a loud cheer erupted from a table in the corner behind us. Elaine flirted half-heartedly with a guy leaning against the bar next to her, but she was no competition for the game. Finally she gave up.

"How's Ernie?" she asked.

"He's fine," I replied, surprised. "Why do you ask?"

"No particular reason. It's just that I haven't seen much of him lately. Did he go with you to talk to the experts?"

"Yes. I think he was a little bit rattled when he heard how much it might be worth."

"So he went with you to meet the lawyer?"

"No," I said, "now that you mention it, he didn't. He said he already had plans."

She finished her mojito with a loud slurp. She stirred the ice with a straw glumly and set the glass on the bar.

A rivalry seemed to have broken out between the guys at the table behind us and a small group clustered around the bar cheering on the other team. Somebody scored, and conversation was impossible for a few minutes.

Suddenly, Elaine sat up and put a hand on my arm, her eyes enormous. "You'll never guess who just walked in the door."

"Who?" I asked, turning to look behind me.

She grabbed me by the shoulders and turned me back around. "No, don't look! It's too obvious."

"Well, who is it then?"

"Neil. From Accounting. Look over your left shoulder, but be nonchalant. Pretend you're looking at that menu up there."

I turned to look up at a blackboard on the back wall, upon which was inscribed in chalk in rainbow colors the week's drink specials. Hiding as much as was possible behind my glass of beer, I glanced at the occupants of the table in question and almost snorted Belligerent Bastard out my nose. Luckily, Neil and his date were too busy mooning over each other to notice.

"Who is that?" asked Elaine.

"She works at Umberto's. She waited on us the day I met Neil for lunch there." I said, dabbing Belligerent Bastard daintily from my nose and mouth with a hankie.

She watched them discretely over my shoulder. "They should get a room," she said primly.

Farley materialized at the beer tap and shoved a glass under a spigot, pulling the handle with a flourish. "Can I get you anything else, ladies?"

"No thanks, Farley. Just the check," answered Elaine. "What else do we know about the manuscript?"

"Beethoven always carried a notebook around with him. That way he could jot down his ideas as they popped into his head. He made a series of sketches for an intended symphony, but died before he could finish it. At least that's what everybody thought. Evidently he somehow managed to get most of it down in writing before he died."

"How many symphonies did Beethoven write?" she asked.

"Nine that we know of. That's not very many. Some

composers wrote dozens—Haydn wrote more than a hundred! That's one reason why this is such a big deal. A lot of people consider Beethoven's Ninth Symphony to be one of the greatest musical masterpieces of all time."

Farley materialized with the check. "I'll get this," said Elaine, brandishing a credit card. "What makes them so certain it's a new symphony?"

I shook my head. "According to one of his friends, Beethoven actually had the whole symphony in his head. It was just a matter of writing it down. This same guy claimed Beethoven himself played the whole thing for him on the piano. His description and the existing sketches that we already knew about match what's in the manuscript exactly.

"Here's my theory. Beethoven trusted only a few people, but I suspect some of them were motivated more by visions of their fifteen minutes of fame than any genuine concern for the composer. You have to remember that by the time he died, he was quite a celebrity. Dozens of people visited him as he lay on his deathbed, and dozens more came to pay their respects after his death," I explained.

"So it would have been easy in all the confusion to make off with something like that."

"Precisely," I said. "It could have been anyone: one of the doctors, the housekeeper, a visitor—who knows?"

"Any theories on how it ended up with Louisa?"

"Well, it's only a theory, but Louisa's mother came from Vienna. That was in Grayson's obit. But that's all we know about her."

"So how are you going to handle Darnell?" she asked.

"I'm not. I'm going to let my boss do it."

"Well, good luck. C'mon. Let's go. You okay to drive?"

"I'm fine. How about you?"

"Aw, you know Farley. The drinks he makes for me never have much of a punch."

"Okay, be careful," I said to Elaine with a sigh. "See you in a couple of days."

She climbed in her car and waved in her rear-view mirror as she drove off. I jingled my car keys as I watched her, reluctant to go home and face my empty house. A car pulled into the parking lot, the headlights snapping me out of my reverie. The Monk's parking lot is tiny, so I got in and backed out to let them have my space.

# Things get Awkward

*It happened* exactly as I knew it would. We could tell the minute she walked into Dr. Holmes' office that Marsha was going to be a problem. Some people can smell money; she's one of them.

"Marsha," said Holmes cordially, "so pleased to meet you. I'd like you to meet Wayne Brundrett, the university's legal counsel."

At the mention of the "L" word, her posture stiffened perceptibly and she clenched her fists, as if preparing for a fight. She shook hands with the lawyer warily and took the seat Dr. Holmes offered without a word, perching awkwardly on the edge of her seat.

"What's this all about?" she asked, sounding unusually shrill.

Things went downhill from there.

"We'd like to talk to you about the papers Margo and her team found in your house during the investigation," purred Holmes in his most professorial voice.

"What about them?"

Brundrett cleared his throat and said in his best courtroom manner, "We believe them to be of significant cultural and, umm...monetary value. We called you here today because we want to resolve in advance any issues that might arise regarding the rightful ownership of the papers."

Her eyes narrowed and she shot me a steely glance. I could almost see the dollar signs in her eyes. "What's in those papers? They belong to me, you know."

Before I could sputter out an indignant protest, Brundrett held up a hand and said silkily, "Ah, that happens to be the very issue we wanted to talk to you about. You see, there seems to be some confusion about that. Ms. Monroe is under the impression that you were not the least bit interested in the papers she found. I believe you specifically said Margo could do whatever she wanted to with them."

"She's lying," said Marsha petulantly, pointedly refusing to look at me. "I never said she could have those papers. I said she could take them to look at them. She wasn't supposed to keep them." She tossed her bleached head defiantly.

I started to protest, but the lawyer caught my eye and shook his head. He shoved his hands in his pants pockets and strolled around the room for a minute without speaking. An image of Gregory Peck as Atticus Finch popped into my head. "Are you certain about that, Ms. Darnell? Because if you are, this is a very serious accusation. There would certainly be repercussions."

"What kind of repercussions?" she asked, now sounding nervous.

"Well, the manuscript's monetary value depends on us being able to verify its authenticity. And a legal battle over ownership—if it ends up in court—could drag on for years." He shrugged innocently. "It could run into some money."

"What's in those papers? I demand to know what you found in my house."

"Ms. Darnell, there's no point in being coy. We believe that these papers were penned by Ludwig van Beethoven. Any more than that, I'm not at liberty to say." He strolled casually over to the window and looked out for a second, long enough to let his words register, then turned back toward us, smiling benignly. "Perhaps it would be better not to discuss it any more detail until you have legal representation of your own. You know, lawyer-to-lawyer."

Marsha bolted out of her chair, her face flushed. "That's the best idea I've heard all day. I'll just do that." She stormed out of the room indignantly. The minute she was out of earshot—much to my surprise—Brundrett chuckled.

He beamed at me, looking, I thought, rather self-satisfied considering the circumstances. "Don't worry. They all do that," he said. "Sooner or later she'll realize that a lengthy legal battle will eat up most of her windfall. I can just about guarantee that she'll settle with us, especially once she's talked to a couple of attorneys. The reputable attorneys around here wouldn't touch this one with a ten foot pole, and the rest of them will bleed her dry. The best thing we can do now is to be cool and let her come to her senses."

Holmes stood up, smiling broadly, and shook his friend's hand. "What would we do without you, Wayne?"

"I'll keep you posted. Margo, always a pleasure." We shook hands and I followed Dr. Holmes out.

"He seems awfully certain of himself. I'm not sure about this," I remarked as we walked to our cars.

"Why do you say that?"

"I just think he doesn't know Marsha Darnell very well.

Holmes chuckled. "He just might surprise you. I know he comes across as small-town hick lawyer, but it's just an act. I've seen him wrangle a confession from a witness before they knew what hit them. Are you headed back to the lab?"

"Yeah, there are few things I need to discuss with Ernie."

Holmes smiled kindly. "OK. Then I may see you later. Don't worry about the case. Or the manuscript."

Ernie was huddled behind an enormous screen when I walked into the lab.

"So, how'd it go?"

"Oh, Ernie! You just won't believe this. She just flat-out lied." I flopped into the chair next to him, still fuming.

"I was afraid of something like that. What did she say?"

"That she never said I could have those papers. She claims she only let me take them to look at them."

Fury flashed in his eyes. "I thought she might cause problems, but I didn't expect her to stoop that low."

"It wasn't entirely unexpected. I think what really makes me angry is the insinuation—in front of my boss, no less—that I stole something from her. I tried to defend myself, but couldn't get a word in edgewise."

"You don't think Holmes believes her?"

"No, of course not. But it still makes me mad. Wouldn't it you?"

"Me? I'd be livid. Tell me about the lawyer. What's he like?"

"His name's Brundrett. He's a slick one. I think he believes me. When I first met with him for lunch the other day, I got the impression he was bit of a yokel. But according to Holmes, it's just part of his lawyer act. He thinks she'll offer to settle with us once she finds out how much it's likely to cost her."

"I hope he's right. There's a lot riding on this. Stop biting your nails! Look, there's no point worrying about it. Anyway, there's nothing to take your mind off of it like something excruciatingly boring. Like reviewing evidence, for example."

With a sigh, I admitted he might be right. On the screen in front of him was a series of photos. "What've you got there?"

"These are some images that my program flagged. See how they change from frame to frame?" He clicked through the frames. I recognized the view of the landing at the top of the stairs. The team and I appeared in quite a few of the frames while we were still setting up. But what caught my attention was several frames showing something fuzzy and grey, barely discernible, on the landing at the top of the stairs. Like the unexplained anomaly we'd caught in the first investigation, it seemed to move toward the room where we found the box and the papers before it vanished completely.

"Do we have a time stamp on that?" I asked.

He pulled up a screen with the file's information. "This field shows when it was recorded. Here is the time I ran it through my compression program."

"Nice. All the info right at our fingertips."

"That's the idea," he answered with a wink.

"Did we get any readings on the electronic temperature gauge that we set up out in the hall?"

"Let's look." He dug a small gadget out of one of the bags. We were quiet for a minute while he paged forward through the entries. "Margo, this is great!" He showed me the digital display on the palm-sized box. "Look," he said, punching a button. "These readings are two seconds apart. Here the temperature is 76 degrees. When we started it was 78 and went down to 76, where it stayed from the time we turned the lights out." He touched another button a few times. I watched the display with excitement as the figures dropped a couple of degrees with each click. "The lowest reading is 64. It took exactly six seconds for the temperature to drop 12 degrees."

"Well, if that isn't the greatest thing since sliced bread!" I exclaimed. "Do they have a timestamp?"

"No, sorry. But we still have the audio files. There's a timestamp on those."

Of course! We'd captured an EVP with Ernie's new voice recognition program: "He must not find it. Please hurry."

"I only ran the voice recognition on files from one of the recorders. Give me a minute to run it on the rest of them," Ernie said.

Watching Ernie sift through hours of audio files has limited entertainment value, so I looked around for something to do. I was winding up the cords to some gadgets when I thought I heard a soft rustling noise. I waited, trying to hear it again, but heard only the usual office noises. Just as I decided I had been imagining things, I heard it again.

I followed the sound to a seldom-used shelf near the sink in the kitchenette. Crouching, I found a box of some sort covered with a ragged towel. I pulled up one corner of the towel and peeked in. Imagine my surprise when I found a bright brown eye staring back at me. I jumped, startled. When I raised the towel again, the eye was still there.

"Margo, what are you doing?"

"I found something."

"Like what?"

"I don't know yet." I sat on the floor and lifted the towel enough to see inside the box, to discover it wasn't really a box at all but one of those transparent plastic cages for pet hamsters. Inside was a brown squirrel, eying me warily, and three babies.

"Oh, for crying out loud!" I extricated the makeshift squirrel habitat from its shelf and the towel and set it on the counter. Ernie took one look and burst out laughing. The squirrel, no doubt having decided she was in the custody of a couple of loonies, glared at us without moving a whisker.

Delighted, Ernie pulled up a chair. "Are these the ones we found in Fran's attic? Hello, Mama Squirrel. Don't be afraid." Mama Squirrel was not amused.

"It would stand to reason."

"So you didn't know about this?"

"Well, I admit I was worried about them. Fran seems so fastidious; I couldn't imagine her putting up with squirrels in the attic. This must be Sandy's doing."

At that moment Sandy burst through the door lugging a large shopping bag from Pet Planet. When he saw us hovering around his new friends, he looked a little sheepish. "She was gonna call Animal Control."

"Well, what are you going to do? You can't keep them here," said Ernie.

"Why not? They aren't hurting anybody. I can't take them home, my roommate's allergic. Anyway, it's only until the babies can fend for themselves, then I'm going to take them all down to the park. They only need a couple more weeks."

"You sure you're not planning on making pets out of them?" asked Ernie, eyeing the collection of plastic parts Sandy was taking out of the bag.

Sandy just smiled. "Might as well make a nice set-up for them while they're here. Anyway, this friend of mine liberated some lab mice and she's trying to find homes for them all. I might take one later."

Ernie went back to his computer, leaving Sandy and me to assemble the new rodent abode. We were busily debating the merits of various designs when Ernie called me over. He showed me the file from one of the voice recorders. "This is a really huge file. It's more than twice as big as any of the others. Any idea why?"

"Can't think of anything in particular. Have you listened yet?"

He shook his head. "Let's see what we've got here."

He clicked on the Play button. I heard Elaine say, *"Before you two start picking out your luxury yachts, may I point something out? This manuscript doesn't belong to us."* Then Ernie: *"I hate it when she's right."*

"That was when we found the manuscript. I thought we shut everything down about then," I said.

"This is from the device you had in your pocket, the one you forgot about."

"The one with the dead batteries?"

A light bulb went on over his head. "It must have been on and recording the whole time. That explains why the file is so big. Let's see what else is here."

He moved the indicator over and clicked Play again.

*"Working late, I see."*

*"Just trying to get caught up on emails. But I've had enough for tonight."*

We looked at each and whooped for joy. Judging from the commotion coming from the squirrel cage, our rodent guests were none too amused.

"What's up over there?" Sandy pulled up a chair next to me and plopped down. He watched over my shoulder as the indicator scrolled merrily across the screen.

*"We think it's a manuscript for music of some sort."*

*"So what are you going to do with them?"*

*"Well, technically, they belong to you."*

*"Me? Well, what would I do with them? It's just a bunch of old papers. Didn't you find something last time you were here?"*

*"Yes, the box we found last time was full of letters and newspaper clippings. We suspect there's a connection between it and this music, although we can't be certain. We also don't know if either of them has anything to do with the activity here in the house."*

*"You can do whatever you want with that stuff. I don't want it."*

I rubbed my hands together and chuckled. "Gentlemen, it looks like a meeting with Wayne Brundrett is in order."

# Bad News for Marsha

*The conference* room at the law firm of Brundrett
and McAlpin was comfortably furnished in an
elegantly bland, nondescript sort of way. Landscape
paintings in ornate frames adorned the walls, and the
small sofa and two chairs in one corner looked like
they'd never been sat on. We had been sitting for what
seemed like hours at the polished wooden conference
table. In the middle of the table, beads of
condensation dripped lazily down the sides of a
pitcher of ice water. Across from me, Ernie poured
some water into a glass and toyed absently with the
ring it left on the table. Dr. Holmes and Brundrett
were standing near a window speaking just a little too
softly to hear. Sandy, seated next to me, seemed
unbothered by the fact that Marsha and her attorney
were already 45 minutes late. Discretely I checked my
phone, only to be disappointed. No missed calls, no
messages. Having thus exhausted my entertainment
options, I had nothing to do but wait.

After a few more minutes Marsha made her grand
entrance, accompanied by a fortyish woman with thick
ankles in a severe dark suit and pearls. Marsha, not
surprisingly, looked as though she might have stopped
by on her way to a meeting with heads of state. She
smirked at Sandy, who had put on his best flowered
Hawaiian print shirt for the occasion. Unperturbed, he

returned her smirk.

In rushed a petite, grandmotherly woman in a pink floral print dress. "I'm so sorry, Mr. Brundrett," she said. "They said you were expecting them..."

Brundrett smiled kindly at his assistant and said "That's perfectly all right, Mrs. Sheridan. We were indeed expecting them. For quite some time." Mrs. Sheridan glared at the two women and hustled out of the room indignantly, closing the door behind her none too softly. "Ladies," he said graciously, "please have a seat. We were starting to get worried. Thought perhaps you'd gotten lost."

The woman in the suit and pearls, turning red in the face, slapped a legal pad on the table and started toward Brundrett. "Look, Wayne, before we begin, I just want to..."

Brundrett interrupted her. "Tina, perhaps introductions are in order before we begin. Please, take a seat. Everyone, this is Tina Hoffmeier. I'm assuming you're representing Ms. Darnell as her legal counsel?"

"That's right, and if you think..."

"What I think is immaterial here. This is Dr. Holmes; I believe you already know him. Tina Hoffmeier, this is Margo Monroe, Ernie Stapleton, and their associate, Mr., um..."

"Just call me Sandy."

Tina nodded curtly at each of us. Marsha again refused to make eye contact with me. She sat at the end of the table glaring at Brundrett.

"Ladies and gentlemen, if I might begin." Brundrett sat down and, with a dramatic gesture, opened a folder. "I have an offer here from someone who has heard about the find and is most interested in it. Provided, of course, that its authenticity can be verified. It says here," he continued with a nod toward the opposition, "that the interested party is willing to make a substantial offer to be split between the university and your client. I believe we should be able to come to some kind of agreement, considering the amount of money involved..."

"Nothing doing, Brundrett. Your people stole something valuable from my client and we want it back!"

"Ah, but you see, Tina, that's something of a point of contention, isn't it? My client claims your client relinquished all rights to the manuscript."

"You know as well as I do, Wayne, that they have no proof."

"Neither has your client any proof that anything was taken from her property."

Marsha had obviously not considered this line of

thinking. Her stony gaze shifted to Tina. "Just how much money is at stake here?" she asked.

"Oh, millions," said Brundrett breezily. "But of course, if we can't resolve the ownership issue, the deal is off. That leaves us both in a little bit of a bind, doesn't it, Ms. Darnell? Ladies, Mr. Stapleton here has something he wants you to hear."

Ernie gleefully retrieved his laptop from under the table and with exaggerated politeness pushed it toward the center of the table. "Remember, the whole purpose of us being there in the first place was to capture hard and fast evidence of the strange events going on at your place," he said, clicking a button.

*"Just trying to get caught up on emails. But I've had enough for tonight."*

"Ernie, pause it right there, if you would please," said Brundrett. "No doubt you recognize the voice, Ms. Darnell?"

"That's me," she said curtly, "but I have no recollection of this conversation."

"Then I'll refresh your memory. This conversation took place in your study the night the team found the manuscript. But please, let's listen to the rest of it."

Ernie was only too happy to resume playback. I watched their faces as they listened to the whole conversation I'd accidentally recorded.

*"You can do whatever you want to with that stuff. I don't want it."* At these words, Tina closed her eyes and inhaled sharply. Marsha looked desperate. I could almost see the dollar signs fade from her eyes.

With her eyes still closed, Tina said, "Okay Brundrett. What are your terms?"

"Oh, they're not my terms," he replied cheerily. "Our interested party is most generous. He's willing to pay you one-point-five million. In return, you relinquish all rights to the manuscript. The university gets ..."

"Did you say one-point-five million?" Marsha looked like she might suddenly need to make a mad dash to the ladies' room.

"That's right. The university also gets a sizable contribution—a generous sum that I'm not at liberty to disclose—and the manuscript becomes the property of the university." Positively beaming, Brundrett was obviously rather satisfied with himself. "Ms. Darnell, Tina, frankly you're not going to top this. My advice to you is to take the money and run."

Across the table from me, Ernie was staring, slack-jawed, at Brundrett. Even the normally unflappable Sandy looked stunned. I motioned to the two of them. We left Holmes, Marsha, and the lawyers squabbling among themselves and withdrew quietly to the little sitting room in the corner.

"He can't be serious," said Sandy.

"Sounded pretty serious to me. It's not fair." answered Ernie with a pout.

"Why not?" I asked. "It was on her property, and if it hadn't been for her and her ghost, we never would have found it in the first place."

"I hope there's something in it for us," said Sandy. "I could sure use a little cash right about now."

"You and me both, bro. What do you think, Margo? You think we'll get a little slice of this windfall?"

"Hmmm, that's a good question. He did say the university was going to get something."

"I just hope they don't forget us," said Ernie.

"I guess we'll know soon enough," I said, mentally scrolling through a list of ways to spend some unexpected lucre. A trip to San Francisco was somewhere near the top.

Dr. Holmes had noticed our absence from the conference table and casually strolled over. "I think Wayne can handle it from here on out. I'd like to have a little meeting. Can you be back at the lab, in say, twenty minutes?"

"Sure thing, boss. Come along, *garçons*."

We said our goodbyes to the others and they followed me out.

"We have to get back before he does," said Sandy as

the three of us climbed into my car.

"Why?" I asked Sandy's reflection in the rear-view mirror.

"The squirrels. I left the cage out on the counter."

"Oops. We'd better hurry." Such was not to be. Five blocks from Brundrett's office, we found ourselves in the midst of a traffic jam, a rare event in Indian Springs.

"Damn!" muttered Sandy from the back seat.

"Well, Sandy, if I may say so, maybe leaving the squirrels out wasn't such a good idea."

"Thanks, Mom. I was feeling kind of bad for them, always having to sit on that dark shelf."

"We found them in an attic. They like dark," Ernie reminded him.

The truck in front of me forced its way into the next lane. I took the opportunity to squeeze into his spot, and got off the main street. I know a back road to the lab.

We turned the corner and I decided to make up for a little lost time. This turned out to be the wrong thing to do. That I had just passed a flashing sign didn't enter my consciousness until Ernie said "You might want to slow down. This is a school zone."

Too late; just as he said that I saw the red and blue lights in the rear-view mirror.

"Damn. Just my luck." Indian Springs can get pretty nasty about school zones. There was no doubt in my mind that I was about to be slapped with a huge fine. I chastised myself as I fumbled in my wallet for my driver's license and tried to think of a way to sweet-talk myself out of a ticket.

The cop approached the car and I rolled down the window to hand him my license. Visions of the Golden Gate Bridge evaporated in a painful instant when I saw who it was—it was Officer Kruszinsky, and he looked much happier to see me than I was to see him. He took the driver's license that I poked through the window and leaned in the car to look around with a vicious smile. "Well, now. What have we here?" He studied each of us with an expression of disdain. "Seems to me I've seen all three of you somewhere before. Ms....Monroe?" he said, studying my license. "Are you aware that the speed limit in a school zone when the light is flashing is 20 miles per hour?"

"Yes, Officer." I thought about offering an explanation, but feared it would only get me in more trouble. So I kept quiet.

"Any idea how fast you were going?" His tone was positively gleeful.

I shook my head, trying to look sincere. I'd been going

almost 40.

"I clocked you at 39. Wait here please." He strolled casually back to his squad car.

"I think you might have just spent your bonus," said Ernie.

"Thanks, Ernie. You're not helping matters." My budget might stretch a little bit, but Indian Springs is legendary in these parts for its school zone speed traps.

"We'll be lucky if we don't get arrested again," groused Sandy. "Did you see the look on his face?"

The minutes ticked slowly by as we waited. I tried to watch him in the mirror without being too obvious.

"What's he doing, fer cryin' out loud?" asked Ernie finally. "It's been at least 15 minutes."

"Is that all? I would have sworn it was a lot longer than that." I eyed the mirror again. "He doesn't seem to be doing much of anything. Talking on the phone, maybe."

After a good long while, Kruszinsky sauntered slowly back to the car, a dark scowl on his face in place of the evil smile. He thrust my papers back at me through the window and glared at each of us." Against my better judgement, I'm letting you off with a warning this time." Stiffly, he turned around and stomped back to his car without another word.

I was putting my license in my wallet when he turned off the lights and drove away, tires chirping on the pavement as he pulled out. I'm not a particularly good judge of these things, but I'm pretty sure he was going a lot faster than 20 by the time he reached the stop sign at the end of the block.

"I wonder what that was all about," said Ernie.

"Yeah, did you notice how disappointed he looked? I got the distinct impression that he was just dying to give you a ticket," Sandy remarked. "Wonder why he didn't."

"Who knows? But I won't argue with it."

"Just watch yourself. He's probably still lurking somewhere," said Ernie.

I turned on my blinkers and pulled out carefully into the deserted street, making sure not to go any faster than 19 miles per hour. I was the very epitome of the model driver, staying at least 2 miles under the speed limit and signaling at every turn, but we saw no sign of our friend in blue.

Behind me, Sandy was biting his nails.

"Stop worrying," I said finally. "Even if Holmes does find the squirrels, he won't be mad at you."

"At least not for long," Ernie added.

At long last, we reached the campus and I deemed it safe to push the posted speed limits a little bit. I screeched to a stop in front of the Horticulture Pavilion. "Oh, hell!" cried Sandy. Holmes' car was already parked in front.

"Maybe he stopped by his office first," said Ernie. "You go, I'll distract him."

They piled out of the car and stormed up the steps. I turned into the nearest parking space, parked and ran after them.

Just ahead of me, Ernie dashed down the hall to the offices. Sandy ran for the lab and stopped cold in the doorway. I plowed into him; two seconds later Ernie plowed into me. Holmes was making a pot of coffee.

"Sorry, there was wreck on Logan Street," I said. "We, er, got stuck in traffic."

Sandy, eyeing the squirrel cage, tried to sneak around me discretely.

"It's okay, Sandy. I know about your...guests. It was all I could do to convince the cleaning lady not to quit yesterday."

Sandy froze in his tracks, then grinned disarmingly. "Sorry. It's only for a few more days."

"Just keep them out of sight on Mondays," said Holmes, his eyes twinkling. "So. I'm sure the question on everybody's mind is 'how much?'"

"Now that you mention it, that thought did cross our collective minds," I said.

"At the moment, I can only tell you that Ms. Darnell's million and a half is only a fraction of what the manuscript is worth. Half of that will probably go to legal fees." He chuckled softly to himself. "But there'll be enough to get more equipment with enough left over for generous bonuses and raises for the entire team. Including me, as well as your friend, the lady with the long hair..."

"Elaine."

"Yes, of course—Elaine. And myself. So you see? It works out for everybody. We'll be able to get Ernie all the equipment he's ever dreamed of, the program has enough funding for years to come, and the manuscript stays here."

"Wow, I'm impressed," I said.

"I'd like to thank all of you sincerely—for everything." Holmes shook hands all around and sauntered out of the lab, whistling a cheerful tune.

The minute the door closed, cheers erupted. The squirrels registered their displeasure.

Sandy rubbed his hands together briskly. "Maybe now I can get that new bike I've had my eye on."

"And it's about time," said Ernie. "I'm going to buy Fang one of those fancy collars with the rhinestones on it. How about you, Margo? What are you gonna get with your bonus?"

A dozen things flashed through my mind, but only one of them made me smile.

"I know what she wants," said Sandy. "A trip to San Francisco."

"What was your first clue?"

"Well, for starters, you've practically been glued to your phone since he appeared."

"Just trying to stay in touch with an old friend."

"I think you two are counting your chickens before they hatch," said Ernie testily. He plunked a coffee cup on the counter next to the coffee maker with a tad too much gusto and poured a cup.

"What's with you, Mr. Sunshine?" asked Sandy.

"Well what if the manuscript turns out to be a fake?"

"Then I'll put new tires on the old bike and Fang will have to make do with his boring old leather collar. Think positive, Ernie."

I listened to this exchange without comment, wondering what was bothering Ernie. He gets like that sometimes. And he had a good point, of course. But I wanted to be ready in case I did get to make that trip.

"Hey Margo, where're you going?"

"Gotta do some shopping. I'll see you guys later."

I was on my way to the dressing room with an armful of silk and chiffon when my nose caught the lingering scent of *Soir d'Amour*. Of all times for the dressing rooms to be full! There was nowhere to hide.

"Margo, darling!"

"Aunt Muriel, how nice to see you!"

"Getting ready for your big trip, I see. That's very smart of you. That young man of yours, he's quite a catch. You mark my words: he appreciates a woman who takes pride in her appearance. Unlike most of these young women today. Why, the things I see some of these girls wearing...." She shook her head sadly. "But I hear you've uncovered the most extraordinary find!"

"Well, yes. But we're trying to keep things quiet for now. How did you know about it? Did your um...angels tell you?"

"Oh heavens, no, dear. Inez Sheridan is my best friend."

"Ah, then you heard all about our little meeting this morning."

She chuckled. "Indeed I did. I'm very proud of you. And that clever nephew of mine." Her expression suddenly changed. "Maybe this will give him some confidence. I have my doubts about this new woman, you know. But that other one, she just doesn't know a good thing when she's got it."

"Muriel! Oh there you are, dear."

Mrs. Sheridan materialized from behind a rack of blouses, lugging a large shopping bag. "Oh, hello, Ms... Monroe, is it?"

"That's right. But I wish you'd call me Margo."

"Well, Margo. It was nice to see you again. We certainly had an exciting morning, didn't we? Come along, Muriel. I don't want to be late for my hair appointment."

"Goodbye, dear."

They strolled out past the clearance racks, exclaiming over this or that garment, reminding me very much of a pair of colorful, twittering birds.

A dressing room door opened and a large woman emerged, carrying a small mountain of clothes. "It's all yours," she said, heading for the cash register

I puzzled over Aunt Muriel's words as I tried on my finds. Who was this new woman she talked about? But then I got a text from Timmy, and soon forgot all about it.

# The Value of Music

*"Oh, thank you, kind sir!"* I muttered to the driver of
the car that was backing out of the parking space that
I wanted. Dr. Holmes had phoned me bright and early
this morning and asked me to come in "at my
convenience," which in reality means "get here ASAP."
I was still groggy, and the industrial-strength coffee I'd
chugged down might as well have been water. I'd been
up until the wee hours video chatting with Timmy and
was having trouble getting myself in gear;
consequently, I was running a little late.

Holmes and Ernie were already huddled around the
desk when I walked into Holmes' office. Ernie shot me
a look as I quietly took my seat in the empty chair
waiting for me. Dr. MacRae's face smiled at us placidly
from the computer screen on the desk. Next to him
was a young Asian woman wearing a white lab coat and
a serious expression. From a small inset image in the
corner of the screen, I could see Ernie and Dr. Holmes
as they appeared to Dr. MacRae on his computer.

"Marvelous. We can start now," said my boss. To the
computer he said "Margo has just joined us. I think it's
especially important that she hear this." I moved
closer to Ernie until my face appeared next to his in
the little inset image.

MacRae nodded in my general direction. "Good

morning, Margo."

"Morning. Sorry I'm late—got there as fast as I could."

"Not at all," he replied jovially. "We're just getting started. I'd like to introduce you all to Dr. Michelle Wei. Dr. Wei is our forensics specialist. She conducted the tests on the manuscript and I knew you all would be anxious to hear her results."

Both sides of the conference mumbled their greetings to their respective computers.

Dr. Wei glanced at her notes, then spoke, hesitantly at first. "Well, to begin, we did a simple ultraviolet light test which revealed the complete absence of modern synthetic materials. Now, that's not conclusive. A clever forger could theoretically create both paper and ink using historical formulas. So we also conducted a standard carbon age test. There is a certain amount of uncertainty in this method, of course, but it allows us to determine the age of organic matter with an error margin of about 30 years. The results of this test indicate a date of manufacture no later than 1835. The fibers in the paper are consistent with a Western European origin. We see no signs of retouching or alterations, although the ultraviolet light indicates the presence of a considerable amount of mold. Micro-spectrophotometry and thin-layer chromatography tests on the ink are consistent with the findings for the paper."

As Dr. Wei warmed to her subject, she seemed to be getting over her awkwardness at talking to a computer. "I found one particularly fascinating tidbit here. Several notes here and there are written in pencil." She held a page of the manuscript up to her camera with gloved hands. "Under intense magnification," she continued, "these pencil marks show natural graphite with an unusually high clay content. I didn't quite know what to make of this at first. The normal material for pencil lead at that time was graphite. So I did a little bit of research, and found out that at the beginning of the 1800s there was a shortage of natural graphite in Europe because of the Napoleonic wars. The clay was apparently used as a filler."

She smiled, warmly, for the first time. "I believe you already know about the handwriting analysis. So it appears that what you have here is the real thing. Congratulations."

Ernie clapped an arm around my shoulder. Dr. Holmes was chatting with Drs. MacRae and Wei. I didn't hear much of the rest of the conversation. Visions of the Golden Gate Bridge returned to my head as I reached for my phone.

I was texting away when suddenly I became aware that the room was unnaturally quiet. Next to me, Ernie was engaged in the same activity. We froze, thumbs in mid-air. We both looked up at the same time and the others burst out laughing.

"'Scuze us," said Ernie sheepishly.

"No worries. Just make sure your recipients know that this information is not for public knowledge yet."

❧

Ernie was already there when I got back to the lab. He was chatting on the phone when I walked in. For approximately the tenth time in the last hour, I checked my phone while Ernie bid whoever he was talking to a hasty adieu. Still no reply from Timmy.

"Where's Sandy?" I asked.

"He took the squirrels to the park."

Only then did I notice that the countertop was bereft of its plastic gerbil habitat. "No kidding? He didn't even give us a chance to say goodbye!"

"Yeah, I kinda miss 'em already. They were fun to have around. Say, has anybody told Elaine about this morning's meeting?"

"No," I answered, surprised. "You didn't call her?"

Before he could answer my phone chimed. I saw with relief that it was a reply from Timmy: "Thats wonderful congrats!! Will call you 2nite."

"Let me guess—it was from Tim."

Something in his tone didn't sound quite right. "How'd you guess?

"So are you going to visit him?"

"I hope so. What's up with you?"

"Nothing."

"Well, what then?"

"You really like him, don't you?"

"I really like him. But we haven't been around each other in 20 years. Anything could happen."

"Yeah, but you like him."

"We've established that. Ernie, if I didn't know better, I'd swear you were jealous."

"I'm not jealous," he said defensively. "Okay, I'm a little bit jealous. Everybody seems to have somebody special. I feel a little bit left out."

"Ernie, you'll meet somebody. The right girl just hasn't come along yet."

"Margo, you're forgetting I know everyone in this town already. And now you have a Special Somebody and I can barely get the time of day from the only girl that rattles my cage."

"You're forgetting he lives a zillion miles away, which is why I'm trying not to get all excited about this. The odds are against us."

"You don't think you might move there?" he asked, sounding relieved.

~ *Sue Latham* ~

"What you're really asking is what I would do if I had to choose between Timmy and my job. It would be a tough decision. Look, all I can do is take this one day at a time and hope for the best. Timmy is an old friend and I love him regardless. But it's too soon to start worrying about 'what if'."

The door opened and in walked Holmes followed by Sandy. The empty hamster habitat was tucked under one arm and he looked like he'd just lost his last friend.

"So. Mission accomplished, I see," remarked Ernie. "How'd it go?"

"Okay I guess," answered Sandy glumly.

"You did the right thing, Sandy," said Holmes with a paternal pat on Sandy's shoulder. "I'm right proud of you all. And I have some news that I think all of you will want to hear." He patted a piece of paper tucked neatly into his shirt pocket. "How about if we talk about it over lunch? At Renaissance. It's on me, or rather, it's on our most generous sponsor. Oh, and please invite Elaine."

Sandy grinned, having evidently recovered from his recent trauma in record time. "Okay by me!"

"I'm up for it," I said, dialing Elaine's number.

"Ernie?"

Looking slightly embarrassed, Ernie answered, "Can't. I already have lunch plans. In fact, I need to get going."

Sandy caught my eye and raised an eyebrow.

Dr. Holmes looked disappointed. "Stop by my office this afternoon, then."

"Will do." Ernie grabbed his backpack and slunk awkwardly out of the room.

"There must be a sale on rhinestone dog collars somewhere," said Sandy, rubbing his chin.

"No doubt. It's not like him to miss a free meal," I said. "I'll call Elaine."

"To the great Beethoven." Dr. Weber raised her glass. "Cheers everyone. I thank you, and the Maestro thanks you."

We raised our glasses in return and clicked them together with a dainty tink. I watched a stream of tiny golden bubbles journey frantically to the top of my glass. Chamber music provided a soft backdrop to the soft buzz of conversation around me, punctuated by occasional genteel laughter from an elegant woman at the next table. Sandy was entertaining us with stories about his roommate; Dr. Weber seemed especially enchanted. What is it about Sandy that older women find so attractive? Everyone seemed to be having a grand time except Elaine. She seemed distracted. Perhaps she was, like me, simply overwhelmed by the contents of the envelope Holmes had handed her. I have no idea how much she got. My envelope held enough for a trip to San Francisco and then some. And that was just the bonus; we were all getting substantial raises, and I was already mentally reassessing my monthly budget. Perhaps such trips might not have to be a special occasion.

"Are you gonna finish that?" asked Sandy.

"Be my guest." Elaine pushed her barely-touched chocolate mousse toward him. He finished it in two bites just as a small army of busboys arrived and began clearing the table.

Shortly thereafter, champagne finished and check paid, we strolled out to our cars. I pulled Elaine aside. "Give me a ride back to my car. I'll see you all back at the office."

Leaving Sandy with the professors, I climbed into Elaine's BMW.

"You feel all right?"

"I'm fine," she said. "Why do you ask?"

"Well, for starters, I've never known you not to finish a chocolate mousse."

"Did Ernie say where he was going?"

So that was it! "No, he just said he already had plans."

"He should have been there. It was important."

"True, but it was kind of last-minute. You shouldn't be mad at him."

"I'm not mad at him," she said defensively. The light changed and we turned down a small side-street known for its trendy hang-outs.

About the middle of the block, I spotted Ernie's car parked along the curb. I started to say something, but changed my mind when I saw the look on Elaine's face. I followed her gaze to see Ernie coming out of Cafe Toulouse, one of the chicest see-and-be-seen spots in Throckmorton. He was with Tracy, the girl who delivered our take-out from Lim Yee's. He didn't notice us—his attention was focused entirely on Tracy as they walked hand in hand to his car.

When we stopped at a light, she studied them in the rear-view mirror. "I don't believe it," she said.

"He's entitled to a social life."

"No! That's not what I meant. He's opening her door for her. I can't remember the last time a guy opened the car door for me."

"Well, Ernie's a nice guy."

She didn't reply to this astute observation and we drove the few remaining blocks in silence. She pulled up next to my car and stopped the car. "Thanks for the ride." She seemed thoroughly preoccupied as I climbed out. I wondered what was going through her head as she drove away. It was none of my business, of course. Anyway, I had my own issues to deal with, not the least of which was a certain someone many miles away that I needed to talk to.

A veritable rainforest of butterflies fluttered in my stomach as I clicked the Submit button. A little clock with spinning hands popped up, begging my patience. At long last, a confirmation number appeared, along with a reminder that my credit card had just been charged for the cost of one round-trip airfare to San Francisco.

Well, there's no turning back now, I said to myself.

The door opened and Ernie meandered in. "Is there any coffee?"

I motioned toward the kitchen. He concocted his usual cup of sugar with some coffee in it and perched on a stool in front of which was a table covered with unidentifiable electronic bits and pieces.

"So, did you do it?" asked Ernie.

"Yes, Mr. Nosy, I just booked my flight."

"You don't sound too happy."

"Yeah, I know. For some reason I'm feeling apprehensive about this trip."

"Why? What's there to worry about? You said the few

days you spent with Tim were the best days of your adult life."

"I know. But spending a few days together isn't like living with someone in their environment for a week. What if we get on each other's nerves?"

"That's pretty much guaranteed. Look, Margo, the issue is not whether you can put up with each other for a week. It's whether the magic is still there after the week of putting up with each other. Remember, 'The course of true love never did run smooth.' I think it was Oscar Wilde who said that."

"It was Shakespeare. But he was right." I sighed. "How's Tracy?"

The awkward silence answered my question. "You know about Tracy?"

"We saw you coming out of Cafe Toulouse. We weren't spying on you," I hastened to add. "We just happened to be driving down the street."

"Was Elaine with you?"

"As a matter of fact, she was. She was...surprised. So what happened with Tracy?"

"She's a nice girl."

"But?"

"Well, she's...you know, kind of young. Immature."

"Well, what do you expect? She's a college student, Ernie. She delivers fast food for a living. Get real."

"I know. She's really nice and all. We just don't have much to talk about. I think I'd be better off with someone more...sophisticated. You know, someone closer to my age."

"You mean someone like Elaine?"

"You know as well as I do she barely knows I exist."

"I wouldn't be so sure about that, old friend."

"What's that supposed to mean?"

"I'm just saying you shouldn't be so quick to dismiss her. You haven't exactly tried to sweep her off her feet, you know. I'll be back after lunch." I shut the computer down and went in search of my purse.

Ernie scowled and picked up a circuit board, which he seemed to be examining with great interest. When I left he was still staring at the circuit board, whistling softly to himself and smiling.

# A Different Kind of Visitation

*I gazed,* mesmerized, into tearful brown eyes. He returned my stare, unblinking.

"You'd do the same if you were me, wouldn't you?"

He looked away.

"Hey," I said. "It's not my fault."

With one last, soulful gaze in my direction, he studied me. Then he turned, slowly, and with a splash rolled off the pier into the murky waters of the Bay. I watched as he slipped silently beneath the pier.

"Was it something I said?" I called after him.

An arm slipped around my shoulders. "I see you've made a new friend," said Timmy, handing me a steaming hot latte.

"Well, I thought so, but…"

"Don't worry. He'll be back," he said as the sea lion swam away. My new pal seems to have started a fad, as several of his buddies promptly followed him.

We walked along in silence. I barely tasted my drink. I think Timmy took three sips of his. In less than an hour, we would have to leave for the airport. My flight home was that afternoon, and neither of us wanted to see this morning end.

The relationship had survived a week of the two of us in each other's company more or less 24/7. The biggest bone of contention so far had been over a stray cat named Franklin that had taken up residence in Timmy's building. His unbridled affection for the mangy, ill-tempered beast annoyed me to no end. That Franklin seemed to have taken an instant and equal dislike to me didn't help matters. But so far we hadn't discussed the most important issue: this relationship and where we were going with it.

Although it was still relatively early, the Embarcadero was already crowded. The throngs of tourists seemed to be thoroughly enjoying themselves in spite of the gathering clouds that promised an imminent downpour. As we passed a bench, a woman stood and gathered up two small children.

"Let's grab that spot," said Timmy.

A group of Japanese tourists stopped in front of us and listened intently to their tour guide. She made a joke and they laughed politely. One of them, a small, ancient man wearing sneakers and a skipper's cap, noticed us and approached, smiling. He pointed to his camera and mimed taking a picture of the group.

Timmy obliged politely, then gave the man his camera

back. The man smiled, bowing, and Timmy returned the bow. As he sat down again, a drop of rain splashed on my arm. The tourists scurried off after their tour guide.

"You're awfully quiet. Are you okay?" I asked.

"As well as can be expected. You know how I feel, Margo."

"Look, you know I feel the same way."

"Then say it." He turned to face me, taking both my hands.

"I've always adored you. You know that."

"But you don't love me." He let go of my hands and turned away, hurt.

"I didn't say that."

"Well, what then? To you I'm still the cute little boy that worshipped you in high school. We're not kids anymore and I'm not that little boy any more!"

"Timmy, look at me. You know perfectly well I don't think of you as a kid. And I do love you. There. I said it. Are you happy now?"

"But...?"

"But what?"

"I can tell there's a 'but...' in there somewhere."

I sighed. "This is our last hour together. Let's not spend it arguing. I love you; you know that. But we live a thousand miles apart…"

"Actually, it's closer to two thousand," he said gloomily. "Margo, what are we to each other?"

A valid question. "Well," I said, choosing my words carefully, "I'm just not sure if, given the circumstances, we have any right to demand exclusivity from each other."

"So what you're saying is, you want to see other people." The hurt look in his eyes was almost more than I could bear. "Is there someone in particular? There is, isn't there? It's Ernie, isn't it?"

"Is that what you think? Don't be silly! I've known him since we were teen—. Oh duh, sorry."

He gave me a dark look. "That Sandy guy, then."

"Timmy, get real!"

"You still have a thing for your ex?"

"I definitely do not still have a thing for my ex." Truthfully, I hadn't given Roger a thought since Tim came into my life. "I don't want to see anybody but you."

"But you're not willing to consider moving here."

"It's not a matter of being willing. You know I love it here. It's so alive. There's so much to do…if you don't mind a few tourists. But we're just now getting started with the department."

"Couldn't you start your own department here? Think of all the fires and earthquakes! This city has to be crawling with ghosts."

"Well, you do have a point. But there's no possible way I could even think of leaving now."

He sighed and shrugged his shoulders, apparently resigned. "Can't blame a guy for trying. So you never answered my question...what are we to each other?"

"Well, I guess...I guess I'm your girlfriend."

His face brightened. I got the first real smile of the day from him just as another drop of rain splashed on my arm. Wrapping an arm around me, he pulled me to him and we kissed. "We probably ought to make a run for it. It's about to pour."

I thought about little else on the flight home. What exactly was I so worried about anyway? I had plenty of time to ponder it—the downpour caused my flight to be delayed by almost an hour. Airborne at long last, the airplane creaked and groaned and made the occasional heart-stopping lurch. I sipped water from one of those stingy little plastic cups and stared out the window. The grey blanket of clouds around me matched my mood exactly.

What was my problem, anyway? Any female human in her right mind would be ecstatic to be in my shoes—a handsome man who says he's loved me forever wants to be my boyfriend. He's generous, kind, attentive; he even picks up after himself. He's a decent cook, has a job and most of his hair. The catch? We don't live in the same city.

So where is it written that you have to live with someone to have a happy, committed relationship? I asked myself. Is this not why Skype was invented? Of course, it's not the same as actually being together. Or having someone to go places with, and well, you know, all those other benefits that supposedly come with being in love. But—I reminded myself—we both make enough to afford to travel now.

How long could such a relationship last? Instinct told me that perhaps longer than a more conventional one. Visions of Roger, and his shaving stuff in my bathroom, and his tools in my garage, and his ratty old clothes in my closet (I could go on and on) filled my head.

I was still ruminating several hours later as I schlepped my suitcase around the parking lot of the San Guillermo airport trying to find my car.

# The Unheard Symphony

"*Margo, there's* absolutely nothing to be nervous about." Sandy looked very dapper, I must say, in his vintage tuxedo jacket, absence of neckwear notwithstanding.

"Easy for you to say. You don't have to say anything. I wasn't expecting this many people to show up, to be honest." The foyer of the Society of Musical Sciences building was fairly packed—much to my dismay. "Where's Ernie, anyway? He was supposed to be here half an hour ago."

"He texted and, um…, said he'd be a little bit late. He's bringing you a surprise by the way. Must have got stuck in traffic."

"Surprise? What kind of surprise?"

"You'll find out. I've said too much already. Don't worry, he'll be here."

"He'll miss Dr. Holmes' speech."

"He's heard it already."

"Maybe I shouldn't have told him I wanted to introduce the team."

Sandy smiled mysteriously. "Maybe. Of course, Ernie's not known for trying to keep a low profile."

Well-dressed people were standing around in clusters, balancing glasses of champagne and tiny plates of hors d'oeuvres. The room still smelled of fresh paint and it was starting to get stuffy.

"It's getting hot in here," said Sandy. "Let's go over here by the doors."

Outside, the first hint of fall was in the air. We positioned ourselves by a column near the front door, welcoming the refreshing wave of cool air that accompanied each new arrival. This is my favorite time of year, when we get the first break from the summer heat. My nerves were on edge, though, and at the moment I was just wishing this whole thing would hurry up and be over with. It wasn't just the ceremony. I'd been trying to get in touch with Tim all day. My text message from this morning remained unanswered. I'd finally broken down and called him. To my chagrin, his phone was turned off. I fished my phone out of my sequined bag for the tenth time—no messages from anybody.

To take my mind off my churning stomach, I did a bit of people-watching. A few college students roamed about—I noticed one girl who'd had her hair dyed shocking pink for the occasion—but most of the hair here was grey or non-existent. Across the room I spotted Seamus the librarian, who was decked out in jeans, high-top sneakers, and a colorful cartoon-character tie. He recognized me and waved. Earlier, I'd seen the manuscript guy deep in conversation with some professors I recognized, but he wasn't around now. Nor was there any sign as of yet of Ernie.

Sandy suddenly turned to me and put a hand on my shoulder. "You'll never guess who I just saw. Look behind me."

I peeked cautiously around Sandy's shoulder.

"Is that who I think it is?"

"Yes, it is—it's Roger." My ex was standing forlornly by himself in a corner. He was scanning the crowd and sipping a drink. He'd put on a few pounds since I last saw him; his slacks were just a little too tight.

"He looks lonely," remarked Sandy.

"Let's move on before he sees me." I gratefully accepted the arm Sandy offered me and we made our way slowly toward the dais. We stopped a couple of times to shake hands and chat with well-wishers.

Drs. Weber, Holmes and Kielstrup had been cornered by a woman I recognized as the local TV news reporter. All three professors seemed to be enjoying themselves immensely. Behind them a long table was covered with floral centerpieces and microphones. In a niche close by, a rectangular shape lurked conspicuously under a dark cloth.

Dr. Holmes caught my eye and motioned me over. With a courtly bow, Dr. Kielstrup excused himself from the reporter and shuffled around the table to the dais. He tapped gently on a crystal water glass with a spoon. A hush fell over the room. "Ladies and gentlemen, if I might have your attention please..."

Behind us, the door opened and Elaine scurried in. "Sorry I'm late," she mumbled.

"We'd better go," I whispered. "Have you seen Ernie?"

"Isn't he here?" she asked, surprised.

"Haven't seen hide nor hair of him." Where could he be?

We skirted the room, dodging the crowds and took our seats at the table. The hum of voices gradually died down.

"Ladies and gentlemen, fellow music lovers, to call this an honor would be the supreme understatement. It is indeed my privilege to welcome you all to share with me in the Indian Springs Society of Musical Science's finest hour..."

People were still filtering in. From my seat, I could see the doors open, but it was now so crowded I could see only the first few rows in front of me, which is how Ernie managed to surprise me completely when he slipped quietly into the chair next to me. I was too relieved to be annoyed with him.

Then I heard my name called and I stood up to—dare I say it?—thunderous applause. Cameras flashed around the room and for a moment stage fright threatened. Summoning up an old trick I learned in school, I took a deep breath and conjured up an image of these throngs of people standing before me in their underwear. That did the trick and I managed to introduce myself and my team without incident. More applause greeted me as I sat down. Ernie, grinning from ear to ear, I noticed, seemed especially pleased with my little speech.

After Dr. Holmes gave his little talk about the department and what we do, it was time for the unveiling. The cloth-draped shape was the manuscript, of course, in its new home: a state-of-the-art climate-controlled display case. Our names were even on the accompanying plaque. Yet something was just not right, and as Dr. Kielstrup swept the cover from the display case theatrically to yet more tumultuous applause and a blinding round of flashes, I just wanted to escape.

"Ernie," I yelled, tugging on his jacket, to get his attention over the din. "I need some fresh air!"

"Right now? But I have a surprise for you!"

"Well, can't it wait? I'm just going to step outside for a minute. I'll be right back," and turned and bumped squarely into Tim.

"Surprise!" he said.

He dropped his suitcase as soon as he crossed the threshold and we embraced without a word.

"I'm so happy to be here," he said finally. He pushed my hair out of my eyes. "And I'm sorry for keeping a secret from you. But when Ernie called and told me about the ceremony, I just had to be there."

Surprised, I said, "It was Ernie who called you? Is that why he was late?"

He nodded. "Actually, it was Ernie who orchestrated everything. But we were afraid you'd get nervous if you saw me, so I kept out of sight. When we were sitting stuck in traffic I almost gave in and called you. Were you nervous?"

"A little," I admitted. "And you were probably right. If I'd seen you I probably would have made a complete fool of myself. How long can you stay?"

"Only until Tuesday."

"Then let's not waste any time," I said, taking his hand and leading him to the bedroom.

The next evening found us at Ernie's, although I secretly would rather have spent the time alone with Tim. But it was Ernie to whom I owed the surprise visit from Tim, and he welcomed the opportunity to get reacquainted with Tim.

"Watch out for Fang," I said as we climbed the steps to Ernie's front door.

"Who's Fang?"

"You'll find out soon enough."

I rang the doorbell and our host opened the door with a theatrical bow. Fang, decked out handsomely for the occasion in his new rhinestone collar, tumbled out the door to greet us with his usual ear-splitting noise.

"Where's Elaine? I noticed her car out front already."

"She's tending the grill."

Taking pains not to step on the yapping fur ball bouncing around our feet, I led Tim through the house and introduced him to Elaine. Ernie had prepared a veritable barbecue feast. He must have gone to some trouble—and expense.

We stuffed ourselves, then migrated to the living room for dessert. As Ernie finished the last of the last slice of Elaine's culinary contribution, a chocolate cheesecake, Fang was lounging contentedly in Tim's lap, allowing his head to be scratched.

"Hey there, little fella," crooned Tim. The annoying beast gazed at him lovingly; I half expected him to purr.

"Who wants coffee?" asked Ernie. Tim started to respond but I elbowed him in the ribs.

Elaine jumped up and pushed Ernie back into his chair. "I'll make it."

"In that case," I said, "we'll drink some."

Ernie frowned. "My coffee's not that bad."

"Oh yes it is," said Elaine and I in unison.

"Don't take it personally, Ernie," said Elaine on her way to the kitchen. "You have many talents. Making drinkable coffee just doesn't happen to be one of them."

Ernie shrugged good-naturedly. "I admit it's a job best left to Sandy. But at least I'm not afraid of ghosts."

"Who's afraid of ghosts?" asked Tim.

We explained Sandy's aversion to the paranormal.

"A phantasmophobic ghost hunter?" he asked. Elaine returned from the kitchen carrying a tray laden with cups and assorted containers.

"Well, yes," I admitted, "but he's a top-notch researcher. He just doesn't go on investigations."

Tim thought about this for a minute. "I guess everyone's entitled to at least one phobia."

"Not me," crowed Ernie. "I'm not afraid of anything. Especially not ghosts. What's your phobia, Elaine?"

"Clowns," she answered. "They terrify me. I think it's because of an ugly doll I got one year for Christmas.

What about you, Margo?"

Everyone was looking at me. Reluctantly, I said, "Stairwells."

"There has to be a story behind this," said Tim.

"Why, yes, indeed, Timmy, there is. And we have Ernie to thank for it." Ernie squirmed in his chair and coughed loudly. Elaine rolled her eyes; the story I was about to tell was one she'd heard before. "You may recall that Ernie had quite a talent when we were teenagers for finding trouble for us to get into."

"Who, me?" responded Ernie sweetly.

I ignored his feigned innocence. "One time, Ernie decided we absolutely had to find a way onto the roof of the Northland Life Building."

"The Northland Life Building!" said Tim. "The one and only skyscraper in town, if you can call it that. There was supposed to be a great view from the roof."

"That's right. It was the Friday before Labor Day. We decided to start the three-day weekend off properly by sneaking in after everyone had gone home. Of course, the elevator took us only to the top floor."

Tim looked a little disappointed. "So there's no observation platform after all?"

"We still don't know," answered Ernie. "We looked everywhere, but all the doors were locked."

"But Ernie was determined to get to the roof no matter what," I said.

"Yes, I was sure we could get there by way of the emergency stairs. So all three of us went up the emergency stairs. We found the door to the roof—which, naturally, was locked tight. Finally admitting defeat, we went back down to the floor below that we'd just come from—only to find the door locked from the other side. We went down to the next floor; same thing, the door was locked from the other side. We tried the door on every floor, only to find every single one locked. It finally dawned on us that if the door on the ground floor was also locked we would be there for the next three days."

Bursting into laughter, Tim said, "You never told me about this. What was going through your mind?"

"We were wondering if we were going to have to resort to cannibalism. I could picture my parents anxiously steeling themselves for the worst possible news while the Indian Springs Search and Rescue department dragged the river for our bodies," I said. "By the time we got to the ground floor, we were terrified. Roxy needed to go to the bathroom so bad she was about to wet her pants and was almost in tears."

Ernie continued, "After roughly one geological age, we reached the ground floor. There it was—the last door. By this time Roxy was sobbing hysterically. We held our breath, I turned the doorknob—and the door popped open. There stood two security guards with tears of laughter streaming down their faces."

Imitating the burly security guard whose voice I will remember for the rest of my life, Ernie said, "'We been watchin' you three ever since you got off the elevator!' That's when we noticed there was a tiny security camera in the ceiling on every floor."

It's funny the way Ernie tells it, but the three of us found it somewhat less amusing at the time. Although we survived the incident unscathed, I to this day, don't take the stairs.

Fang, now sound asleep in my date's lap, began to snore loudly. "He must be trying to tell us something," said Tim as he carefully picked up the diminutive animal and moved him to the sofa. Fang opened one eye, regarded Tim mournfully, and promptly went back to sleep, resuming his snoring.

"You're probably right. Big day tomorrow, and I still have a few things to do," I said. "We'll help you clean up."

"No, no, don't worry about it," said Ernie hastily. "Spend some quality time together."

"Thanks, Ernie...for everything," said Tim, wrapping Ernie in a sincere man-hug. Ernie, I thought, looked rather proud of himself.

"My pleasure, bro," he said, returning the hug. "See you at the symphony tomorrow."

When we got in the car, Tim said, "You appear to be mulling over something of great importance."

"Me? Oh, it's nothing. I'm just surprised Elaine didn't leave when we did, that's all."

"Why? Isn't she his girlfriend?"

"No, Ernie has it bad for Elaine but she only likes him for a friend."

"Really? You could have fooled me. I got the impression they'd been together for a while."

"Only in Ernie's dreams."

"But I thought he said..." he shook his head.

"What?" I asked.

"Oh, nothing. Anyway, it's none of our business."

Both of us still had a few things to get before the concert that night, so we spent the next day doing some last-minute shopping. After a romantic early dinner, we went back to my house to get dressed.

I'd found an elegant blue velvet dress at Riley's. It had a row of rhinestones along the neck and the color complimented my hair. I was fussing with my hair, starting to feel butterflies in my stomach, when Tim peeked around the bathroom door. "Can I see?"

My first glimpse of him in a tuxedo almost took my breath away. "Oh Timmy, I..." I suddenly felt overwhelmed by it all. This was not the time to cry—the last thing I wanted was mascara running down my face. He kissed me and we cuddled for a moment. "Sorry," I said finally. "It's just that everything seems to have happened all at once. Thank you for being here. It just makes everything perfect."

"Thank you for letting me be part of it." He cupped my face in his hands. "You look absolutely stunning. Hey, our car is here. We'd better go."

♪

The premiere of Beethoven's newly discovered Tenth Symphony, naturally enough, was news around the world. The press converged upon Indian Springs from all corners of the globe. The demand for tickets far outstripped the concert hall's capacity, so an outdoor simulcast had been arranged, with the tickets for that promptly selling out. I was following these developments in the news, but was still unprepared for the sight of so many people packing the streets of our little town.

As we got closer to the Music Society, traffic slowed to a crawl. The limo inched through the crowds, finally pausing so a cop could move a barricade to let us turn down the main street. Cameras flashed and cheering crowds pressed against the barriers as we got out. Tim steered me possessively through the forest of microphones being shoved in our faces. Reporters called my name and shouted questions at me. I smiled serenely and waved, somehow managing to maintain my composure until we got inside.

"What a zoo!" I remarked to Tim. But there were more reporters to contend with in here. Ernie and Elaine were talking to the woman reporter I'd seen interviewing the professors at the dedication. Ernie spotted us and motioned us over.

With a grin, Tim said "I'll join you in a minute. I want to get us some champagne," and melted into the crowd.

The reporter and her crew moved us into position in front of some lights and a small crowd surrounded us. "Good evening, I'm here at the Indian Springs Concert Hall for the world premier of Beethoven's Tenth Symphony. With me tonight is the team of researchers that discovered the manuscript..."

I let Ernie answer most of the questions. He was in his element, and I suspected the anchor woman was flirting with him. While Ernie wowed the crowd with stories about his technical innovations, I scanned the room. I spotted a few famous faces, including a couple of pop stars, a well-known game-show host, and the occasional foreign dignitary in an exotic costume. I recognized one face in particular : it was the girl I'd seen Roger with. She was hanging for dear life onto a man old enough to be her father. He seemed vaguely familiar and eventually I placed him as the weather man on one of the local television stations. They looked utterly smitten with each other. Poor Roger. No wonder he looked so down when I saw him at the dedication.

At the drinks table, Tim was in an animated conversation with Sandy. They left the table together, both men with a drink in each hand. I wondered idly who Sandy's date might be, then saw him approach a short woman the top of whose head I could barely see. Following Tim through the crowd, he took her by the hand, smiling. As they worked their way toward us and I could see a her better, I realized Sandy's date was Tracy. I didn't have time to analyze this new development because the newswoman had turned the microphone on me.

"Margo, what impact do you think this discovery will have on your work in the future?"

"Well, Jessica, I don't honestly see this changing much for us over the long-term. Our mission is still the same; to learn as much as we can about the paranormal. This is an unusual case; most of them aren't as high-profile as this one." Luckily, I had an excuse to cut the interview short. "Now if you'll excuse us, we have some business to attend to before the concert starts."

"Thank you, Margo, it's been a pleasure." Microphone in hand, Jessica stepped back into the spotlight and we drifted away.

"Well, that went well, I thought," said Ernie. To my utter astonishment, he draped an arm casually around Elaine's shoulders. He grinned, looking right pleased with himself.

Tim handed me the flute of champagne. We toasted Louisa, Beethoven, and the anonymous philanthropist who had made the whole adventure possible, whoever he or she may be. More cameras flashed around us. I was beginning to feel like a goldfish. "Let's go, you guys. We don't have much time and there's something we need to check on before it starts."

In a cramped control room behind the stage that had been hastily thrown together just for tonight's performance, we found Seamus the librarian hunched over an array of control boards, pressing a pair of gigantic headphones tightly to his head. Ernie tapped him on the shoulder.

"Oh hi!" He pushed the headphones onto his neck. "I was just making a last check. Give me another five minutes and we're good to go."

"Thanks, Seamus," I said. "You don't know how much this means to us."

He gave us a thumbs up. "I should have a master ready in a few days."

A few patrons recognized us as we took our seats. There was a smattering of applause around the auditorium. The lights dimmed right on time and the orchestra took their places on stage. A voice boomed in the darkness.

"Ladies and gentlemen, the Indian Springs Society of Musical Sciences welcomes you to this world premier performance of the tenth and final symphony of none other than Ludwig van Beethoven. Photography and recording of any kind during tonight's performance are strictly forbidden and we'd like to remind you to take this moment to turn off your cell phones. Tonight's performance is being recorded."

The music was sublime, of course. Was it one of Beethoven's best works? Probably not, but I doubt if anybody cared. But I would be lying if I said I'd ever been to a concert I enjoyed more. Of course, having Tim at my side had something to do with it. Knowing that I was one of only a handful of people alive to have heard a Beethoven work for the first time was part of it as well, of course—and that I was partly responsible for bringing it about. But for me, the real satisfaction was in knowing I'd helped a troubled soul. I hoped that Louisa would finally be able to rest easily after all these years.

Marsha was surprisingly graciously when I asked if we could come back a third time. Along with the usual equipment, we brought along a state-of-the-art music system borrowed from Seamus. While Ernie set up the parabolic listening device in the center of the room as we had the last time, I recorded the base readings from the tri-field meter and temperature gauge into a log. As darkness descended, I pulled up a chair next to Ernie and set an EMF detector and the temperature gauge on the table in front of me. Ernie clapped a pair of enormous headphones on his head and nodded in my direction.

"Louisa, if you're here, I'd really like to talk to you." Almost immediately there was a noticeable drop in the room's temperature. With one eye on the computer screen and the other on the gauges, I continued. "Louisa, there's nothing to be afraid of. These devices we have are just to help us hear you better so we can communicate with you. They can't harm you. If you can hear me, can you move closer to this little device here?"

We waited patiently. The temperature gauge showed another small drop in temperature, but nothing else.

"Bradford's gone and you don't ever have to worry about him coming back here again. We just want to talk to you, because we have some good news to tell you. Your treasure is safe."

A light flickered on the EMF meter. "Louisa, we have something we want you to listen to."

I turned the music on and sat back to enjoy Beethoven's Tenth for the second time. I made a mental note to thank Seamus personally for his help at the first opportunity; thanks to his sound equipment it was easy to imagine I was still sitting in the concert hall with Tim by my side.

When the last chord faded away, I glanced at Ernie, who was gazing at the computer screen with a rapt expression on his face. I looked to see what he was looking at and saw a jagged zig-zag on the screen.

"Let me play this back for you," he said and put the headphones on my head.

He clicked a button and the pointer scrolled.

"*Thank you*," said Louisa.

# *Epilogue*

*After the* premiere of the symphony, the excitement died down and Indian Springs soon fell back into its usual stupor. Of course, things will never be the same for us in the lab. We were bombarded by requests for interviews (most of which we politely declined) and resumes from hopeful job seekers. It was clear that our work would be funded for a good long while; donations flooded in from sources anonymous and otherwise. I even got a few job offers, but none of them was in San Francisco. Not that I would have considered any of them, mind you.

The performance of the symphony wasn't exactly the end of the story. One morning a few weeks later, I was at the supermarket when I heard someone call my name. It was Marsha Darnell. To say I was a bit shocked when she came up to me and hugged me like I was her long-lost best friend would be an understatement. And the cause for her new-found cordiality? There'd been no activity in her house since the night we played the recording for Louisa. Louisa, it seems, has left the building. Marsha has had several offers on the house and is thinking of selling; I couldn't tell which of these new developments she was happiest about.

I'm happy to report that Ernie and Elaine are officially dating. Ernie's a happy camper these days; in fact, I've never seen him so happy. I may have noticed a new spring in Elaine's step as well. I wish I could say the same for Sandy. Not long after the premier, Tracy surprised everybody by suddenly getting back together with an ex-boyfriend and moving to Santa Fe. Luckily Sandy's broken heart didn't last long. He moped around the lab for a while, then returned to his old self.

Our faces are known around town now that we've given up on trying to keep the department a secret. We've been approached by a few nut cases, which I guess is inevitable, but for the most part people have been overwhelmingly supportive. I've been stopped on several occasions by residents and business owners who tell me how relieved they are to learn that they're not the only ones who have experienced strange happenings.

We've been working harder than ever, and now that we have some publicity we have a waiting list. A couple of our upcoming cases already promise to be unusual. Occasionally, I think of Louisa and wonder where she is now. I hope that, like me, she's reunited with someone she loves.

I talk to Tim almost every day. If there is a more wonderful invention than the online video chat I can't imagine what it might be. We're trying to decide on someplace cozy and romantic to spend the upcoming holidays, and I'm looking forward to a few days off. And I'll be thinking of all the troubled souls out there, who like Louisa, just need a little help. So remember, they're out there. They might be trying to get your attention this very minute. You just need to learn how to listen.

*The End*

# Author's Note

Beethoven, surely, must be one of the most fascinating characters history has to offer. Although he started going deaf before his 30th birthday, he is one of the greatest—arguably the greatest—composer of music who ever lived. Think about it for a minute: possibly the greatest musical genius of all time...and he was as deaf as a post.

The definitive cause of his deafness is not known. What is certain is that as a young man he was exposed to a toxic dose of lead. A sample of his hair, tested in the 1990s, contained forty-two times the normal level of lead. Lead is the gift that keeps on giving—it settles in your bones, then continues to release poison into the body. Despite the fact that it is a thoroughly nasty substance, there being no amount small enough to be regarded as safe, lead has been used for thousands of years in the manufacture of pewter, paint, and pottery glaze. It was even added to wine, and Beethoven was an enthusiastic oenophile. Lead poisoning could explain his chronic stomach ailments, his volatile temper, and the general crankiness that he was known for. It could also have caused his deafness.

I'm always interested to know what makes extraordinary people tick and am, therefore, an avid reader of biographies. One day I came across a mystery that captured my imagination, as mysteries

will do. According to a fellow named Thayer, one of
Beethoven's earliest biographers, the Maestro, some
years before his death, made extensive notes and
sketches for a symphony that would have been his
tenth. It turns out that quite a bit is known about this
unfinished symphony. Fragments and sketches are
known to exist; what we don't know is how much of it
he finally got around to completing before he died. In
the 1980s, a highly controversial hypothetical work
was recorded from these and other possibly unrelated
fragments. Thayer claims that Beethoven was working
on this symphony during his final illness, when, for a
brief time, he felt well enough to compose. This made
me wonder how much of the symphony he really did
complete and if so, what became of it. That such a
symphony might exist somewhere, just waiting to be
found, seemed plausible enough. Being blessed with an
overactive imagination, I soon conjured up a way to
get the manuscript into the hands of my intrepid alter-
ego.

Bettina and her father are purely fictional; however
Beethoven at one time really did employ a
housekeeper name Frau Sali. Anton Schindler, of
whom Frau Sali so disparagingly speaks, was also a real
person, although I don't think he was as bad as Frau
Sali makes him out to be. He was an associate of the
Maestro's, occasionally acting as personal secretary,
and he wrote one of the first biographies.
Unfortunately, he was also a shameless fraud who lost

no opportunity to profit from his association with the great man, and we now know that most of what he wrote was either forged or outright fabricated.

Indian Springs, along with the college in Throckmorton and its paranormal research department are entirely fictional. This is unfortunate. I know my readers will agree it's about time for some serious research into this most fascinating of subjects.

Alas, Belligerent Bastard Irish Cream Ale is also a figment of my imagination.

Thanks for reading, particularly those of you who've been so supportive. For the latest news about Margo and friends, and information about their next adventures, go to www.suelatham.net.

# About the Author

After living abroad for many years, Sue Latham returned to her native Dallas. She lives in a high-rise in Dallas with her parrot and enjoys ghost hunting and opera.